FISH NETS

FISH NETS

THE SECOND GUPPY ANTHOLOGY

EDITED BY
RAMONA DEFELICE LONG

INTRODUCTION BY KAYE GEORGE

WILDSIDE PRESS

FISH NETS

Published by Wildside Press LLC.
www.wildsidebooks.com

Contents

INTRODUCTION

BY KAYE GEORGE

The Guppies have done it again! In 2011, this Sisters in Crime chapter put out an anthology of crime stories, *Fish Tales: The Guppy Anthology*. It was published by Wildside Press and has enjoyed steady sales and good reviews all year long.

The Guppies are an online chapter made up of and devoted to unpublished writers, and created for mutual support. The name, Guppies, is a shortened version of "The Great Unpublished." It was a good attitude to take, calling themselves Great. The beginning Gups did such a good job that most of those originals are published authors now. Many of them stayed in the group to help out the newer members. The group grows every year and more and more of the members achieve their dream, a mystery book on a shelf or an e-reader, or on both. Or a story in an anthology or elsewhere.

The theme of this collection is Fish Nets. Every story herein contains a reference to a fish net. Some of the stories make it central and some peripheral, but it's there in all of them. Once again, the volume was ably edited by Ramona DeFelice Long, and the stories judged and chosen by fellow Guppies.

H.S. Stavropoulos's excellent "White Flip-Flop" starts the volume, setting our expectations high as ethereal images from the sands of a Greek beach shimmer through this tale of old wrongs—and a new one. Not to worry. The bar is set high, but keeps being met in each subsequent story.

In the historical "Netted" by KB Inglee, a daring young woman who wanted to be a pirate as a child helps solve a tangled mystery in eighteenth-century Delaware. Diane Vallere throws us into the fashion world of Versace...and Big Bird, in "Dress for Success." Warren Bull gives us a backwoods bible-thumper, an unusual character who picks and chooses Bible verses to suit himself.

Kara Cerise gets the Best First Line Prize in her "Reef Town": It was a dark and slimy night. It's all uphill from there, or maybe upstream. Judy Smith, with "The Girl in the Fishnet Stockings," takes us on a trip to a tough-talking speakeasy that feels like a fun visit to an old pulp story. In "Keeping Up Appearances" by Julie Tollefson, Nick's estranged wife disappears. But this emergency is not her usual drama queen stuff. This time their young daughter is missing too.

"The Hindi Houdini" by Gigi Pandian nets the reader and doesn't let go in this excellent locked room mystery. In Harriette Sackler's contribution, young Jamie has gone from a bad home situation into a worse place, the property of a member of the Devils biker gang. Eddie Bell, retired cop, avid fisherman, and author of the *Fish Nets* column, goes "Fishing for Justice" when he comes across a piece of his past.

Pamela's obsession is classifying everything as clean or dirty, in "Clean" by Steve Shrott. Killing someone is too dirty for her. Certainly, she didn't do it.

Gary Fish is in a scary situation when he runs into an "Inside Job" in this techno-thriller by Mysti Berry. This story gets the Best Use of the Fish Nets Theme Award with fish.net.

Michelle Markey Butler gives us "John Calvin Can Bite Me," a story of two bigoted people who were never meant for each other, clashing as books mysteriously disappear. There's a great cop duo in Teresa Hewitt Inge's "Fishing for Murder" that we should see more of in the future.

Captain Billie, the old net maker, is a poor, filthy creature, but because young Tracey likes his dog, Buck, in Katherine Russell's "In Seine," the girl manages to see her way through a tangle of fish nets. In "Lawn Ballerinas" by Beth Hinshaw, the new widow doesn't miss her abusive husband all that much. He loved fishing, but accidents happen to fishermen.

The net in Robin's Nest is for birds, but can have other uses, as we learn in Kate Fellowes' "Don't Take That Chance." When Abby's father dies in questionable circumstances, in Gloria Alden's "The Lure of the Rainbow," she nets the clue to the culprit, along with a rainbow trout. The book covers are being used in Elaine Will Sparber's "Cover Story," but not to cover books. The young runaway in E.B. Davis' "The Runaway" sees something horrifying and grows up fast, just in time for her birthday, on the boat she stows away in.

Julie starts forming a pilfering habit to get at a fishnet-wearing bimbo, but her plan goes awry in "Routine Changes" by Betsy Bitner. Fancy helps her policeman son get to the bottom of a surprising case in the nicely-put-together puzzler, "Fishy Business" by Jean Huffman. In "The Stonecutter" by Edith Maxwell, Eleanor falls for the exotic title character, but there's a problem. Edith weaves a gorgeous story soaked in the atmosphere of Portugal to end the volume.

These stories run from serious to funny to noir to cute to clever to scary. Now there is no longer "The" Guppy Anthology, there are two. Watch for the third.

THE WHITE FLIP-FLOP

BY H.S. STAVROPOULOS

August. The end of the season. Next week we'd return to Athens. Alone on my father's beach, I raked the sand. My job since I was ten. My children took my place over the years but now they are lawyers, doctors and teachers. I hope for grandchildren to do this one day. Or even nieces and nephews if only Zoi would marry. If a man existed to tame that one. At the end of the beach near the outcropping, I dropped my rake.

I inhaled the air off the Mediterranean. Stuck out my tongue like a snake to taste salt air. I pulled off my shirt. I slipped the chain from around my neck, then thought better of it and put it back on. I threw off my sandals, emptied my pockets, set my father's lighter gently on my shirt. I stripped down to my underpants. Hell, it had more coverage than a Speedo. I reached the edge of the beach and waded in.

Unlike the middle of summer when the sea turned warm and as easy to jump in as a bath. Today, cool water chased goose bumps up my legs. Like a man caressing a new lover, anticipating that exquisite moment when the woman would be mine, I entered slowly. And when I could wait no more I plunged in. Dove deep.

Through window glass clarity I watched tiny fish flee before me. When my lungs threatened to explode, I kicked for the surface and gulped air. I ran my tongue around my lips and tasted the salt. My eyes were too acclimated to sting from the salt. I floated on my back, watching white clouds drift across the sky, then swam further out, diving here and there, looking for the pirate reefs and sunken treasure ships of my childhood imaginings. But I kept away from the underwater ledge and its memories.

Closer to shore I set my feet down and wiggled my toes into the sandy bottom. I strove forward against the waves retreating into the sea and scanned the beach. I turned to the jut of land that sheltered our beach from wind and surging waves. At the end overlooking the sea, he stood. *Panayia!* As much a curse as a prayer. The hair on the back of my neck tingled, my heart began to beat faster and I was ten again.

"*Poios einai autos*, Baba?"

"Kosta, speak English. You must practice." My father spoke heavily accented but grammatically correct English, thanks to fighting alongside a stranded English student during the war. He waved his hands about even when he spoke English.

"Okay, who is that man?"

"A paying tourist. Now go fetch an umbrella."

"Please sir, where would you like to sit?" I indicated the lounge chairs arranged across the beach with one hand and almost clunked him on the head with the umbrella as it escaped my grasp. "Sorry." I grabbed it back into my arms, hoping my father had not seen.

The man laughed and ruffled my hair. "Where is the best spot?"

Encouraged by his smile I took him to a chair at the curve of the beach near the outcropping. One could see the entire stretch of beach here. Not too close to the water, yet not too far back. I punched the umbrella deep into the sand, praying it would hold the first time. When it did I turned and triumphantly bowed. I raised my head to find him looking at me. I felt his gaze enter my brain and run down my spine and into my being. His stance was taut. Muscles flexed like a cat before it pounced. I felt the fear churn in my guts and threaten to empty them right then.

"How is the sea around here for swimming?"

"Wonderful, if you stay within our cove." I pointed to the outcropping at his back "But if you swim to the end and try to go around it, the waves hit hard against the rocks and the water," I made a corkscrew motion with my finger, "can pull you in there and it is very deep." I didn't want to scare him away. "But here it's wonderful."

He smiled and flipped me a coin. I caught it and scurried off.

I ran straight to the *kafenio* my father and mother owned and operated overlooking the beach. "The best drink, Baba. And *meze*."

My father poured the amber liquid in a glass. As he was about to add ice, I said no. I took out our best tray, wiped it clean and laid the drink, the small plate with olives, pieces of roasted lamb, a slab of feta and a piece of warm sliced bread. My mother looked at me taking such care, then at my father and said, "Big spender?"

"No, Mama, this is on the house."

My mother crossed herself and my father's worry beads stopped their clack, clack, then continued, clack-clack-clack-clack. I walked fast as if the sound were bullets aimed at my back. We never discussed the Sight, but both knew how to tell when I worked under its sway.

That night I pulled out the coin from my pocket before bed to find that the man had tipped me a gold *lira*. Like the kind from the war. People still found bags of them where they landed from the Allied planes to seed the Resistance. My father had one from the English student who had fought the Germans. But the shining coin in my hand was not from a foreigner battling evil.

Now as I stood knee deep in the sea and watched the man, I thought about that coin at my home in Athens, safe. I hesitated then shrugged and walked out of the waves. What the gods decreed, no man can avoid. It is our *mira*. I returned to my clothes. Put on the shirt and buttoned it and tucked the chain around my neck inside. My pants still lay on the ground. He would know that I chose to be vulnerable for a reason. I should have put the pants on first but instinct kicked in rather than sense. I felt him rather than heard anything over the lap of the waves coming to shore. I bent and picked up my pants and hurried into them. Then I turned.

"It's a bit late but there is still sun enough. If you'd like an umbrella and something to eat and drink, I would be happy to get it for you." I stood eye to eye with him.

His face was the same. Age had been kind to him, the wrinkles, mere lines. Like those a child might make in the sand only to be washed away by the next wave. If I blinked my eyes, my father might just come down the path from our *kafenio* and I'd be ten years old again. His sandy blonde hair hid the white well. I ran a hand through my dark hair. My white hairs were like stripes on a zebra. Aren't the wicked supposed to wither under the burden of their guilt?

"Where is the best spot?"

I led him to the same spot as when I'd been a boy. Retrieved an umbrella and set it easily in the sand at his right near the rake I'd dropped before my swim. When I inherited the business, I purchased umbrellas with sharp metal points on the ends guaranteed to stand firm in the sand unlike the umbrellas that haunted my childhood, that usually flopped down to the ground or, worse still, right on top of a tourist to my shame and my father's disappointed look.

I left and walked up to the *kafenio*. Away from the view of the beach, I made a telephone call. Then I set up the best tray and returned with the amber liquid and *meze*.

I'd crossed that span of path to beach and back again a hundred thousand times in my life. Today, memories of my father filled my time. If this were my last walk down this path, I hoped my father would meet me at the end.

"Here you are." I placed our best tray near his cigarettes on the little table next to him.

"I remember your parents. How are they?"

His lack of pretense surprised me. I thought the game would play out differently. "My mother is well. My father's been dead for ten years."

"I'm sorry."

"Run down in the street. He bled out before someone could help him." I shivered. "I would have killed the man myself if he'd ever been found. To hell with the blood on my hands."

"It's only the blood of those who trusted you or the innocents that just got in the way that stains." He wiped one hand with the other then picked up his drink, saluting me with the glass. He sipped then smiled. "The best." I inclined my head in acknowledgment. He sipped again. "She is the only one whose face haunts me."

The goose bumps rose on my skin at his words as if I'd dipped back into the cool sea. That day rolled before my eyes like a film. The first time I saw painted toenails.

She strode across the beach. A wide brimmed hat hid her hair and large dark sunglasses, her eyes. Her strides were long. At each step her navy dress flowed and darted around her body as if alive. Sometimes covering her completely, sometimes revealing long tan legs. Whack!

"Hey." I rubbed the back of my neck where my father had just delivered a slap.

"Get an umbrella for the lady."

A moment later the umbrella was open and sheltering her from the sun. She smiled a wide open smile and showed big even teeth that only Americans had.

"Hello, would you like a drink? Something to eat?" I said to my reflection in her sunglasses. I looked wider and one side of my face was larger than the other. When she tilted her head to think, my image rotated dizzyingly, until my head almost touched the sand.

"Frappé."

I returned to find that she had shed the dress like an outer skin. Discarded carelessly on the back of the chair, it reached towards her with each breeze like a scorned lover. Her bikini was white and her skin was like the honey from my grandfather's hives. Smooth fluid amber. Her stomach made a round half dome above her bikini. I moved my eyes away reluctantly to the ground. White flip-flops lay next to her chair. My eyes betrayed me and sought the woman again. I forced them to her feet and noticed the painted pink toenails. This puzzled me about women. I set the iced shaken coffee down and watched a single bead of sweat trace a glistening line into the middle of her bikini top. I suddenly didn't feel right. First the man and now this woman. Maybe I was getting sick or had been in the sun too long. I trudged back to the *kafenio*, the sweat running down my back. My legs were heavy as if the sand were sucking me down. I asked for a glass of cold water while my father laughed and my mother flung him daggers with her eyes.

"Your memory of her is different, I think."

His words brought me back. The sound of the gentle lapping of the waves surrounded us. I looked at his face. It revealed nothing, as if carved from a single piece of marble, smoothed and polished into perfection.

"I remember her pink toes."

He smiled. "Ah. Her eyes haunt me."

"She wore the Jackie-O sunglasses most of the time I talked with her."

"Emerald green eyes, like the deep sea."

"A sacrifice for the gods?"

He tilted his head. "Perhaps Poseidon wanted her for a bride."

I laughed. The gods were known for their lust of mortal woman. "Or an all too human man wanted her dead."

"Or a jealous wife wanted her husband's mistress dead."

I crossed myself. "Never enrage a woman. Their wrath is limitless."

"Amen, brother." He became quiet. "How long have you known?"

I reached inside my shirt and pulled out the chain with its ring. "Since I found this."

I knew that ring was special when I touched it. The Sight hummed through my bones like an electric current. My father is, or should I say was, since he's been buried these past ten years, *Deos skoriston,* an honest man. My father would go over the sand with a pitch-fork wrapped in cheese cloth at the end of each day. He posted a sign *Lost Items* underneath our telephone number. He never kept what was not his.

When the sand combing became my job, I was almost always honest, I only kept the little cars the foreign kids would drop. The thought always made me sad that I was less like my father.

Then I found the ring I held out in my hand. I turned that day over and over in my mind like the beads of *komboloi* the men run through their fingers when they sit and drink their ouzos and play backgammon. I remember because the ring was not the only thing I found that day.

"You didn't turn it into the police."

"I knew we were dealing with things we didn't understand."

"That's a West Point graduation ring. Her lover was an American Naval officer. He loved her." He closed his eyes. "He was married and his father-in-law was a very powerful man." He stood up. "Had you turned it in, the ring would have implicated him."

Him? But, I'd *always* known it was his. The Sight had never failed me before.

The second day the man had come to our beach. Two bikini clad young tourists were playing paddle ball. They moved across the beach along the water. Their peals of laughter rang through the air. I watched them play. Their bodies glistened with the tanning oil they slathered on each other. Skinny foreign girls in bikinis when Greek girls still wore dresses and swam separately from men. *Would Greek girls look the same if they wore bikinis or were foreign girls different?* One of the girls hit the ball hard and it headed right for the man. I tried to shout a warning. He reached up and caught the ball. The ring flashed in the sun as he threw the ball back.

I blinked my eyes and the memory receded. He held a gun in that same hand.

I stepped closer to the umbrella, grateful for its pointed end. No other avenue of escape presented itself but I could use it as a weapon if I could bend my old body to snatch it up before he shot. Then I remembered. *What a fool I am.* The pointed ends of these umbrellas made them harder to pull out of the sand. *Would I die now, longing for the hated umbrellas of my youth?*

"I really did enjoy my time with you those years ago. I thought the ring lost and you too young to remember. I am sorry." He raised the gun to my chest level.

I watched for the muscle tension in his face right before he pulled the trigger. Instead his face drained of blood.

"It cannot be."

I turned to look, but kept the gun in the corner of my eye. A woman walked along the beach towards us. She had a flowing navy dress, a wide brimmed hat, dark glasses and white flip-flops. I knew if I could see her toes, they would be painted pink.

She reached us in quick long strides as if she floated across the sand.

The man stepped back. The back of his legs hit the chair edge. He fumbled to brace himself on the top of the chair with his free hand. A quick movement and a flash of navy. The man crumpled onto the sand. His one leg under him and the other out to the side. The metal tines of the abandoned pitchfork dug into his side.

Thirty years ago. During the last week of summer. The week before we would return to Athens. I raked the beach. But, the sea distracted me. The smell of the salt tickled my nose. I edged to the sea. I wanted to savor it, to fix it in my memory to hold over the long months that we lived in Athens. The waves lapped onto the shore creating a frothy edge. Each wave made a gentle slap, slap. I dug my toes into the warm wet sand. A breeze ruffled my hair. A wave hit my legs. At my feet the sea deposited a single white flip-flop. Its rhinestones and plastic flowers gleamed in the water. It hugged my ankle like a snake about to slither up my leg. I kicked it away.

The Sight took me. One does not throw a gift of the gods back in their face. I would regret it if I did not act. I dropped the rake and jumped into the water. I dove under and kicked hard. I broke the surface for air. My lungs protested the shallow breaths I took. My heart raced and my stomach tumbled, but I forced myself out and around the tip. The rocks that sat as hungry sentinels around the tip waited, churning the waves that would ensnare and pull one below. I dove down praying that my parents would see me again. A fishing net rested at the edge of the drop-off. I laced my fingers into the net, feeling something soft inside, and pulled. The net came apart. Something came at me. I screamed, swallowing water and kicked hard to reach the surface. In thirty years I have never forgotten. The dead eyes open and the surrounding skin sickly white.

"Gia ti mana mou," Zoi pulled the pitchfork out and then struck it deep into his flesh again. "For my mother."

"Zoi, enough."

I pulled her away, waved her to go. I picked up the gun from the sand and reached back and threw it far into the sea. Hoping the sea kept this secret.

I sat on his lounge chair and pulled out a cigarette from his pack. I lit it with my father's old flip lighter. It still had the marks on it from his accident. I took a long drag, filling my lungs, and blew it out slowly, savouring every sensation. How many years had I stopped? It felt like yesterday and my fingers itched to pull another out and smoke my way through the pack. Gods, like an addict, no matter the years in between my body still hungering for the taste and sensations of nicotine.

"I found her. There's a ledge before the drop." I took a drag and pointed to the spot near the cliff.

"But I saw a body being taken away."

I waved my cigarette hand. "The sea has many bodies. Poseidon demands his tributes. An old woman tangled in a fishing net. A young body thrown near an old one. I released them both." I crossed myself. "Now that crone's eyes I will never forget." I waved my hand again. "My parents got the American woman to our house. The local doctor owed my father a favour. Good man he was, he never betrayed her. Or us. When we left for Athens, she came with us. My parents said I was in shock at finding the body and they needed to get me away. No one was surprised that we left in the dead of night."

His fingers slipped holding his side between the tines of the pitchfork embedded deep in his gut. His shirt stained and seeping further. The sand beneath him turned red from pink.

"Z—Zoi," he coughed.

"Daughter. My mother says that's why she survived. A woman fighting for the life of her child. But if I hadn't found her when I did...." I waved my hand again. "The gods intervened. Perhaps Poseidon didn't want her after all."

He smiled though it didn't reach his eyes. "Where is she?"

"She died in childbirth. My parents raised Zoi like a daughter."

He coughed. Blood stained his hand to the wrist.

"You shouldn't have to suffer. I can make it end now."

He stared me in the eye. His power fading, it didn't go into my soul.

"I'd rather die by your hand than any other."

I crossed myself and didn't have the heart to tell him, that Zoi and perhaps her mother had really killed him.

"I've always known that you would be connected to my death." He coughed. "I just didn't know about Zoi."

"Women are like that, they show up when you least expect them. I'll be right back." I heaved myself up. Weary with the burden now on my shoulders. A burden placed there years ago by a fickle fate, *mira*. We Greeks pour our sweat and blood onto this rocky land fit only for goats, our mother *Ellas*. Our hard scrabble life nurtured *pathos*. We know tragedy with our mother's milk so we created drama to tell our sorrows. But we Greeks also created democracy, philosophy and science and fed the greatest creation, the Western World. I laughed. The same story recited to us as children as it was to our parents and our parents' parents. The greatness of the Greeks, their passion and their sea. This sea. My eyes hovered over it as a lover does his beloved. The sea would cleanse the sand and make my father's beach pure again.

I turned away and retraced the path to the *kafenio*. Zoi sat crying into my mother's shoulder. My mother looked at me then crossed herself. In the storage room in the back, I moved empty casks of beer and crates with empty bottles for return to the distillery. Hidden away where I had placed it with my father years ago, was an old box. I opened it. Inside lay an old fishing net, and a white flip-flop. I grabbed my grandfather's sickle that we used to cut away the weeds and a length of rope.

I pulled out the pitchfork and threw it aside. I stood over him with the sickle. "Tell me truthfully, you are her father. What you said earlier was about you."

"Don't tell Zoi. Please."

We looked into each other's eyes. He closed his then arched his head exposing his neck. A swift deep cut to the artery, just like the chickens when I was a boy in the yard of my grandfather's house. Quick and painless, my grandfather swore. I hoped that it was true today.

I placed the chain with the ring around his neck. I set the flip-flop on his chest, rolled his body in the net and wrapped the rope around, leaving an end loose.

I rolled his body into the sea. Then pushed it in front of me like the tugboats in the harbor. I kicked hard in the water. My arms occupied with maneuvering his body, my mind considered that now Poseidon's tribute was restored, the tally even. I rounded the tip of the preemptory. I let the swirling water suck his body down to the ledge. I dove in after. I found the stones that had weighted her body back then, now covered with algae and other sea life. I stuffed them in the net and tucked in the loose end. I crossed myself and said a prayer. Truth be told, more for my soul than his. Or perhaps more for Zoi. I pushed his body over the drop-off.

When I reached shore, the sun was setting. The deep burnt orange colour told of dust storms from Africa. Something glinted in the surf. The white flip-flop tossed in the waves. I crossed myself and hoped I never incurred a woman's wrath. Or that Poseidon required my body to balance his tallies.

NETTED

BY K B INGLEE

New Castle County, Delaware, July 1752

"What's that?" I asked, pointing to the tangled mass of string on the table.

"Good morning to you, too, Hannah Prospect."

I glanced at Silas Cobb and set the basket of fresh vegetables next to the string.

"You know that Phineas Beck was found dead in his fishing boat this morning?" he asked.

"Yes, it's all they were talking about at the market."

Constable Cobb lived with his mother in the house next to ours. He and I had been friends since childhood. Now as we were of marriageable age, he was courting a girl in New Castle and I found a young man from church interesting.

"This net was found in his boat. His wife says it isn't his. I'm thinking this fish net could tell us…what happened."

The pause led me to believe that Silas suspected it was no accident. "You think someone killed him?"

He nodded, as though unwilling to say the words.

"Tell me," I said as I moved the basket off the table and spread the net. "How does his wife know it isn't his?"

Silas pointed to a mend near the bottom of the net. "She says she does all his mending and that isn't her work."

The net was neatly done, each strand between the knots being the same length. The knots were even, each tied with the same tension. The mend, of a different cord, was poorly done, with uneven measurements and knots of different tensions.

I pointed to one of the knots and said, "See the way the cord passes over the knot from right to left? Most people tie their nets with the cross in the other direction. The knots in the mend, though poorly done, are tied correctly."

"That's not much help. I thought you might have something useful to tell me."

I was surprised how his words stung. He had somehow expected more of me than I had given, though he had asked me nothing. I would have said our relationship had not changed. If that were so, why was I so bothered? I had nothing to prove to this man.

I turned my attention back to the net. "Give me more details. Do you know what killed him? Why do you think he was murdered?"

"Beck was found in the bottom of his boat. Mrs. Beck said he went out early this morning to catch enough fish for the family dinner and a few extra to sell. His boat had drifted down river as far as the hook, so he must have stopped rowing less than an hour earlier. He was still warm. He had been hit with something long and thin that left a mark from temple to chin. There had been a lot of blood but the men who found him washed most of it away before they towed his boat to shore."

"Could he have been hit with an oar?" I asked.

"Perhaps."

"Why do you think he didn't just fall and hit his head on the gunwale?"

"Besides the net not being his, the mark on his head…well, it looked like it was made by something other than the side of a boat. Besides, even though they had cleaned up most of the blood, it was clear where it had been and there was no trace anywhere he might have hit his head, the sides or the seats. Like you say, an oar."

Cobb looked at me for some time before he spoke again. "We took the body to his wife. They are preparing it for burial now. Do you think you could go take a look at it and see what you think?"

Why was he asking me to do this? I was not a particular friend of the Beck family, though it would be my duty as a member of the congregation to do so. Much against my better judgment, I assented. It could have nothing to do with the slight smile that played at the corners of his mouth or his sparkling blue eyes.

It was a short walk from anywhere to anywhere in our village. Some seven hundred people huddled along the shore of the Delaware River not too many miles south of New Castle. No one was ever murdered here. Until now our biggest problem had been the issue of separation from the rest of Pennsylvania, to become our own colony of Delaware.

Our main income was from farming and fishing. The land here was too flat to allow for water power. A few windmills ran a mill or two, and reminded us that the colony had once been Dutch. In spite of our size, we had a tendency to stick with our own. The Becks were of the lower sort who scrabbled daily to feed their family and make a coin or two on the side. We Prospects and the Cobbs were of the better sort. My father served in the county government, and provided for our family by teaching and practicing law. Cobb had been constable for several years now, and his father had been mayor until his death last year.

* * * *

Mrs. Beck sat by the front window of her small home surrounded by her children and the neighbor women. They all seemed glad I had come.

Mrs. Beck stood and took my hand. "How kind of you to visit. We've laid Phineas out in the chamber. Except for the wound on his head, he looks to be sleeping peacefully."

"I hope he has indeed found that peace. May I pay my respects?"

"I'll take you in," said Mrs. Hooper, a woman I knew from church who turned out to be the next door neighbor. "You stay put, Maude."

The bed chamber was tiny and crammed with boxes and barrels. The bed was of good manufacture and was properly appointed. Mr. Beck lay on the bed washed and dressed in his finest night clothes. Ha'pennies rested on his closed eyes. The wound that Cobb had described to me was hidden by the cloth under his chin, tied at the top of his head to keep his mouth from falling open. His hands were crossed across his breast and the cuff of his night shirt had pulled back to reveal a bruise around his right wrist, as though someone had grabbed him and held on for dear life. His murderer, perhaps.

I left the bed chamber and shut the door behind me. "What will you do now, Mrs. Beck?" I asked.

"My oldest son still lives with us and makes a good living from our peach orchard half a mile from here. He sends dried peaches and the jam I make all the way to Wilmington. We will do well enough. Phineas was my dear friend." She paused to raise her handkerchief to catch a tear, but went on. "I will miss him, but I will not starve."

As she spoke, I glanced around the room. It was comfortable and inviting, though not lavish. The fire cheered and a tea kettle hung from the crane. No one offered me a cup of tea.

The mantle was decorated with a small bunch of flowers in a horn cup set on a doily of hand made netting. Closer look at the netting showed me that the knot was left handed like the net Cobb had left on his table. The net was even and the knots uniform but the backwards knots caused the net to twist a bit and resist lying flat. The result was a pleasing ruffle. Nice on the mantle but not so nice for fishing.

It occurred to me that I might find the net maker by walking along the waterfront at dusk when the men hung their nets to dry.

* * * *

I found Silas Cobb, as I expected, in the blacksmith shop. All the news of the town passed through that shop daily, and people who cared made it a point to show up.

"How is your mother, Silas?" I asked, more to get him away from the other men than to find an answer. I hoped she would be well soon, since I found shopping, even once a week, an onerous chore.

He stepped away from the others to talk to me. "What did you find at Beck's?" he asked.

"Mrs. Beck didn't make the mend in the net, but she has a doily on the mantle with the same backward knot. Why would someone leave their net in Beck's boat? We have only her word that it isn't his net."

He shrugged. "I have talked to everyone who had a boat out this morning and they all deny any involvement."

"Did you expect them to tell you they were the murderer? Who found him?"

"Ralph Hooper and William Tate. They were out on the river early, saw the boat in the distance and rowed up and towed it back here."

"That's odd. If the boat drifted down river I would expect someone from further south to have found it."

Silas stroked his chin, a mannerism that his father used when he was in deep thought. I remained silent until he spoke again.

"This whole affair is very odd."

I told him of my plan to look at the drying nets.

"Miss Hannah Prospect, would you walk with me along the shore later this afternoon? I would be very glad of your company." This sounded like he might be asking to court me until he added, "Then you can tell me how you know so much about knotting fishnets."

* * * *

Silas called at my door when the sun was several hand-breadths from the horizon, well before the time we had agreed to.

"I found out some things of interest this afternoon. Did you know Beck owned several acres of land west of here?" he asked.

"Yes, his son tends a peach orchard there. The family does well from it."

"How could a man like Beck afford to buy the land?"

"Perhaps he inherited it," I said.

"No, Beck's parents were poorer than most of the people here. Not much good at anything. He must have been a frugal man because he passed on the house which he owned free and clear, but not much else."

"Did you check into the land records?"

"Not yet. I haven't had time to ride to New Castle."

He stopped in the middle of the street and turned to face me. "The knots?"

I laughed. "My sister and I had the notion to run away to be pirates. We practiced knots so we would be acceptable. No pirates ever landed here to take us away."

"That was a good thing." His smile dazzled me.

"Yes. The reason I know how to do it and how not to do it is because I was so poor at it that I couldn't make any two knots look alike. I might have done the mend, but not the original net."

"Did you?" he asked. There was a current of seriousness below the teasing tone.

"No."

"I'm sorry, but I had to ask." Was he teasing me?

I nodded and started walking toward the river.

Nets were hung everywhere, some to dry, some to be repaired. It looked like everyone in the village had been out fishing today. Jacob Riss sat on an upturned wooden bucket working on a net. He threw the shuttle quickly and surely. His net was neat and even, the spaces between the knots larger than the net on the Cobb's table.

"Mr. Riss," I said, "Silas and I have been discussing fishing nets today. I see there are a great many here. Can you tell which net belongs to which fisherman by looking at it?"

"Sometimes." He set down his shuttle, unable to pass up the opportunity to be the expert and teach me something.

We inspected some two dozen nets hanging to dry.

"This belongs to the Tylers. See how the left side of each mesh is slightly longer than the right? Can always tell their nets. This next one is Smith's. Don't know where he gets his cord but it isn't like any other here."

"Looks like most everyone went out this morning," said Silas.

"Peaches will be ready to pick in a day or two, so everyone was out on the river this morning. Last chance until the harvest is in."

"I saw some fish being dried and plenty of smoke from the smoke houses," I said. "It must have been a good catch."

"Fair enough. Myself, I got no peach orchard, so I can go on fishing. You're looking for Beck's nets? Ain't here."

"They weren't in his boat this morning either."

The murderer took them, I thought, but didn't want to say out loud.

* * * *

I awoke the next morning with something tugging at the edges of my mind. I couldn't quite figure out what it was, but I knew it had something to do with Phineas Beck's murder. The image of the five women in the

Beck common room, all doing handwork seemed important, but for the life of me I couldn't say why.

I tried to remember who the women were. Mrs. Beck, of course, but she had been sitting with her hands in her lap. Mrs. Riss, Mrs. Hooper, Mrs. Tate, and two other women.

As I pondered Silas knocked on our door. "Want to ride with me to New Castle? I'm going up to check the deeds for the orchards around here."

"I would enjoy that, but there is something else I need to do today. I am going back to visit Mrs. Beck. Find me when you get back."

Silas tipped his hat to me and went to fetch his bay mare from the stable. Perhaps it was the unusual situation of the murder, but I found I did in fact want to ride with him to New Castle. It was a pleasant day, and the distraction of being at the hub of the county was appealing. Oh, well, I had my own work to do.

Gathering up a loaf of the bread my mother had baked the day before, some fresh butter, and a small crock of strawberries in brandy, I made my way back to the Becks.

Maude Beck sat as she had when I was last there, by the front window as if watching for her husband to come up from the river. Mrs. Hooper and Mrs. Tate were with her.

I handed my simple gift to Mrs. Tate and went to the mantle.

"Did you make this lovely doily, Mrs. Beck?"

Before she could answer, Mrs. Hooper spoke up. "No, I did. I was trying to teach Lucy how to tie a net and together we made enough to furnish the whole neighborhood with decoration."

"The twist that keeps it from lying flat gives it a lacier look. It is quite becoming."

"Ralph is always at me to tie his nets properly. I didn't grow up tying fishnets, like everyone else around here. There isn't all that much fishing in Townsend."

"No, I don't imagine. It's a bit land locked."

"Being left handed has been a hindrance in teaching needle work to Lucy," Mrs. Hooper went on as though she hadn't heard me, "but she is picking it up, in spite of my handicap."

The child herself looked up from her seat by the fire and said, "I will never be able to tie a net properly. I'd prefer to work in the peach orchard...." Her mother scowled at her and she added, "If we had one."

"I was never very good at knots," I admitted to the child. "Good thing my father didn't depend on me for his nets."

* * * *

It was dusk when Silas rode up to our door and asked my mother if I were in.

"What did you find out?" I asked without greeting.

Mother set out the tea things and left the room, but I had a feeling she was lurking behind the door to hear what we knew.

"Beck has worked the orchard for seven years but he doesn't own it. At least not yet. He has been leasing it with the prospect of buying it for the lease money at the end of ten years. His son takes over the lease from him. It is owned by a Middletown man named Anderson."

I looked at him over the rim of my cup to encourage him to go on.

"I couldn't find any will or probate inventory for Anderson. But it should be easy enough to find out by asking around."

"I have my suspicions. Let me tell you what I found out. Mrs. Hooper is the one who tied the net. Her daughter Lucy made the mend. Perhaps you can connect the peach orchard to the Hoopers. Mrs. Hooper is from Middletown, big peach center."

He paused for a long time, stroking his chin, and then at last said, "I think I will call on the Hoopers this evening."

I knew we would argue if I told him I was going with him, but I was going all the same. So I watched his front door until he stepped into the street. Then I ran to join him. "You can't come. This is town business."

I didn't answer, but I stayed by his side. At last he shrugged. "You will get yourself in trouble one day, young lady."

"This is the next best thing to being a pirate," I said.

Mr. and Mrs. Hooper were still seated over the evening meal when Lucy admitted us.

"Good evening," said Silas. "I have some questions to ask you about Phineas Beck's death."

Mrs. Hooper's eyes went wide. Mr. Hooper tried and failed to look calm.

"You and Tate found him. Is that right?" Silas spoke gently but Mr. Hooper tensed up at his words.

"Yeah," Hooper said, but added no more.

"He was dead when you found him?"

Hooper nodded.

"Where are your nets, Mr. Hooper?" Silas asked.

"In the shed where I keep all my equipment."

"Would you mind showing us?"

We went out the back door and up to a small building behind the house, next to the necessary. Hooper pulled out a mass of string much like the one I had seen on Silas' table. This one was tied in the more acceptable manner. A net waiting for mending showed the same left handed twist I had identified on the net in the boat and on the mantle above Beck's fireplace.

"Your net was found in Beck's boat. Can you explain that?" asked Silas.

"It's easy to mix up fishnets. They are all alike. Mebby he took mine that morning and I took his."

"That's a logical explanation," said Silas. I wanted to yell at him that it wasn't at all a logical explanation, but I held my tongue.

"Is your wife's father still living?" Silas went on.

"No, he died two years ago. What's that got to do with it?" I could tell by the way Mr. Hooper looked at Silas that he knew very well what it had to do with it.

"What was his name?"

Grudgingly Mr. Hooper said, "Jeremiah Anderson."

"You inherited the peach orchard that he leased to the Becks," I blurted out.

It was clear from the way his shoulders slumped that we had figured it out.

"Yeah, a piece of paper worth a few shillings a year. Beck was making a good income off my land. Beck wasn't about to give it back. There's years to go on the lease."

He closed his eyes, took a deep breath and finally he looked directly at me. "How did you know it was my net in his boat?"

"You may not be able tell one fishnet from another, but I can," I said.

Silas added the legal part. "You are under arrest for the murder of Phineas Beck."

* * * *

Once Mr. Hooper was safely locked away to be transported to New Castle first thing in the morning, Silas saw me to my door.

He took my hand and laid his lips gently on the back, then with a grin he said to me, "If you have decided not to run off and be a pirate, you would make a fine wife for head of the town constabulary."

DRESS FOR SUCCESS

BY DIANE VALLERE

It was the most outrageous shade of yellow I'd ever seen backstage. Yellow fur coat, yellow fishnet stockings. Yellow five-inch pumps that put his blonde hairstyle easily six inches over the heads of anybody else around. That's right, I said *him*. Big Bird was a man in drag.

Fashion week brings out all kinds, which worked to my benefit. I was here, undercover and under a tent at Bryant Park, on business. A certain designer had hired me to determine if there was anything to his assistant's suspicions that his collection had been knocked off—days before he debuted it down the runway.

The two people in front of me were too distracted by Big Bird to notice the woman at the check-in desk waving them forward. She leaned to the left and signaled for me to pass them.

"Name?" she asked.

"Katarina Jones," I answered, which, of course, is not my real name. My real name is silly and not particularly fashionable and tends to stick out in crowds where people are named Anna and Grace. Not only did I not want to stick out, I didn't want to be remembered for my silly and not particularly fashionable name, which also happens to be Polish. Two strikes.

"Here's your tag, Ms. Jones. Enjoy the show," she said mechanically.

I clipped the fake ID onto my carefully chosen vintage Versace dress and eased through the crowd. I have enough contacts to get into most fashion-related events in New York, but attending this one required the help of a stylist-slash-mentor, and one of the few people in the industry who knows my true identity. The terms: complete anonymity and all of the sordid backstage gossip, plus my word that, once inside, I'd blend. Clearly, Big Bird had never made that kind of agreement with anyone. I didn't even know where you bought a pair of yellow fishnets these days.

I took my seat. After double-checking that my cell phone was off I checked the time on my watch (really, it's a voice recorder, and I dictated a couple of observations while I waited), and touched up my lipstick (really, a lipstick. I haven't figured out what else to do with it). The air was warm, and a good portion of the crowd was fanning themselves with their invitations. I relaxed the cashmere wrap around my shoulders and sat back in the plastic chair. Big Bird was in the second row across from me, but closer to the end of the stage. I almost pitied the people behind him, trying as they were to get a better viewpoint around his wig. He must know someone, to get a seat like that. Someone with more relaxed standards than my friend.

The lights went down twenty minutes late and the show started shortly after that. I knew what I was looking for: Britt Ekhart, the hot new Swedish model who'd been popping up on runways from New York to Milan. My client had booked her six months ago. But what I also knew was that she was one of three models booked to work both his show and his suspected copycat, and that, on a covert mission where I posed as a student reporter from an out-of-state college, I found blonde hairs on both of their sample collections. The other two models were beyond suspicion: Diandra had shaved her head a year ago and had been rockin' the cue ball ever since, and Shandra was African American. Britt was the only person I had connected to the two designers in question, and it was my theory that she had somehow been the courier of my client's original concepts, straight to Thomas Quinn's design studio. As far as I could tell, she was the only thread that tied the two collections together.

* * * *

The show was a hit. Based on the applause, the audience liked what they saw. What I saw was a little different. I saw my client's collection being strutted down a runway in Bryant Park one day earlier than it was supposed to show. And when Britt Ekhart closed the show in a short, white coat of ostrich feathers that set off a strapless sequined rose-gold gown, I cringed. It was my client's *piece de resistance*, and it came alive against Britt's pale, Scandinavian skin. It was the most exquisite ensemble Quinn showed on the runway, and it wasn't even his. I adjusted my cocktail ring and snapped a few pictures with the pinhole camera hidden inside.

It was official. My client was toast. Or, he would be tomorrow, when every magazine with fashion coverage heralded the genius of Thomas Quinn while he showed a mirror image a day later. I had the proof I was hired to get.

When the models took a final spin around the runway, cameras exploded with pops of light. Despite the steady stream of lanky models, Britt stopped, stared directly at the crowd of paparazzi, and posed. She almost caused a runway traffic jam. Quinn, who ventured halfway down the runway after the models had returned to home base, didn't seem to mind her attention-seeking behavior. She linked her arm through his and kissed him on the cheek. The crowd erupted.

I scanned the audience. Six, maybe seven people weren't applauding. Big Bird was one of them. He flipped his blond locks behind his shoulder and stood, throwing his yellow fur coat over his yellow beaded shoulder (hitting one retail buyer in the process). When he turned to leave, recognition hit.

Big Bird was my client's assistant. Which meant, Britt wasn't the one selling off my client's collection.

His assistant was.

I snapped a couple more pictures with my oversized cocktail ring, now in the direction of the opportunistic trannie who had sold out his own boss for thirty pieces of silver. Adrenaline swept me like the spray of a self-tanner. It was my job to determine if my client's suspicions of thievery were legitimate, and now, thanks to a pinhole camera hidden in a chunk of blue agate, I could provide evidence that the answer was yes.

All in all, very *Rockford Files*. With better clothes.

My efforts to leave quickly were thwarted by slow movers and buzzing critics. I looked for another exit and spotted Big Bird ducking behind the chairs closest to the left side of the stage. A faint Exit sign glowed in the kind of orange-red neon that looked like an accessory to the fashion show. I followed.

I kept my head down and my wrap clenched around me. Leaving through an obscure exit might not draw attention to me, but being close to the designer, the models, and the general backstage hullaballoo was dangerous.

White parachute silk, mounted above the door, fluttered in the afternoon breeze. I ducked through the opening and found myself behind the tent. A hundred yards ahead was a deserted parking lot. A makeshift sign marked the entrance: *No Trespassing*. Two cars, a blue Explorer and a beige Volkswagen, marked opposite ends. Someone had written "wash me" on the window of the SUV.

A small, mobile flight of metal steps had been pushed up against the tent by the flimsy metal door, propped open with a concrete block. Cigarette smoke wafted through the air. I heard two male voices and recognized one as Thomas Quinn. I kicked off my blue and black leopard-printed, patent leather pumps and climbed onto a metal folding chair to get closer to the conversation. The occasional word floated to me: "Sorry. . . perfect timing. . . We sent a message. . . He's through."

I wanted to hear more but a dumpster separated the distance between us. Vintage Versace notwithstanding, I unzipped the borrowed dress and shoved it into one of the one-gallon Ziploc bags that I kept in my handbag in case of emergency. The dress went under the garbage receptacle, to be retrieved later. In my black foundations—strapless bra and Spanx Power Panties, I hoisted myself to the top of the dumpster and crawled across the top, getting closer to the voices.

"What's done is done. We just proved our point. There's no way he can touch us now," said Quinn. I crawled closer and aimed a voice recorder at the voices. "Tell the press I need a breath of fresh air. I'll be back in five."

This is when my job gets less than glamorous.

I have found, in my experience of jumping into dumpsters (which, sad to say, numbers more than once), that it is best not to spend a lot of time looking first. With upper body strength that was a by-product of my obsession with fitting into a sample size dress, I lowered myself into the interior, crouched in a corner, and stifled a scream.

As far as dumpsters went, this was almost a dream come true: yesterday's floral arrangements blanketed the bottom, along with confetti and empty champagne bottles. The problem wasn't the bouquet of day-old lilacs permeating the air, it was that I wasn't alone.

Big Bird's body lay awkwardly on a bed of pummeled petals and Perrier Jouet bottles. A growing stain of blood slowly discolored his yellow dress and coat. There was no question that he was dead.

* * * *

My mind raced. Who would have motive to kill Big Bird outside of a fashion show? The one person who knew he had stolen my client's designs. Quinn. The same Quinn who now stood inches from the dumpster. His cigarette smoke mingled with the discarded floral arrangements. I gagged from the stench of lilacs, blood, and nicotine and fought the urge to throw up.

"Quinn?" called a lilted female voice. "Are you coming back in soon?"

"Of course, Britt, my star," he said. Outside of my heartbeat thumping in my ears, I heard other noises: footsteps on the stairs, the concrete block sliding against the metal, the flimsy door slapping shut.

I unpinned the carefully styled coif that I'd arrived with and shook out my hair, then colored my lips with a dark burgundy shade, the opposite of the barely-there nude I'd touched up earlier. I jumped from the dumpster and felt around the ground for the Ziploc baggie with my dress. It wasn't there. I flipped my head upside down, regretting the loose hair, and looked underneath. The baggie had slid down the slope of mud under the dumpster and was out of reach. No time to retrieve it. So with the kind of confidence that must be adopted when wearing a black strapless bra and spandex support undergarments around fashion insiders, I pulled on my heels and ducked back into the tent, strutting behind the last of the attendees out the regular exits.

"There's a body in a dumpster outside of tent number five at Bryant Park," I said. I was huddled in a phone booth by Union Station, wearing a New York Jets sweatshirt I'd stolen from a street vendor two blocks from Bryant Park who had overcharged a sweet couple from Iowa on a pair of NYPD T-shirts last week. Once a month I updated my chart of working payphones, but this had long been my favorite thanks to the high foot traffic. I could always count on blending in.

My business lent itself to mingling in high profile circles, but on some days it had become best to fly under the radar. Those times, up to now, included spying, stealing, and sabotaging. I'm not particularly proud of the life I lead, but it seems I have a unique skill set that other people don't, and said skill set pays the rent. The fashion business might be known as glamorous to most people, but a seamy underbelly of greed and corruption exists, and it's my job to expose it—not to the authorities, who thought stolen designs were a ploy for publicity, but to the people who hired me, the true fashion insiders. Until today, I'd never encountered a dead body. Regardless of the confidentiality clause I signed, I felt compelled to notify the cops. With the fewest details I could spare, I told them who, what, where. I'd leave it up to them to find the body, determine the cause of death, connect the dots. My role as Good Samaritan was done.

My next call was to my client.

"You were right," I said. "Quinn copied your whole show. The rose gold dress was his finale."

"Bastard."

"Britt wore it well," I added. I toyed with the idea of telling him about Big Bird, but our agreement had said nothing about protocol in the event of murder, and the less I said about the body before the cops discovered it, the safer I was. In short, I needed the cops to get there, secure the scene, and conduct their investigation without having any possible way to connect me. I was innocent of murder but guilty of a lot of other things that started when I took the job.

"How soon can you deliver the proof?"

"I'll bring the photos to your studio tomorrow."

"Tonight would be better."

"Give me a couple of hours," I said. "Payment?"

"When you deliver the photos." He disconnected after we agreed upon a meeting spot in Central Park. I checked my watch. It was a tight schedule, but I could do it. I kept a darkroom at home for film development. Digital would have been easier, but harder to eliminate the evidence. I had just enough time to develop the photos, shower, change, and take a circuitous route to our meet. If only I didn't have unfinished business.

* * * *

I wiped the phone clean of prints and took a taxi to the airport. I paid the driver, walked to another airline and caught a second taxi home. I returned to my small studio apartment, two floors above a mediocre Chinese restaurant, and developed the film. The picture of Britt in the rose gold dress was close to perfect. Not only had I caught her in the ensemble, but in the background, Big Bird stared directly at me, a scowl on his face.

All eyes were on Britt, but his were on me.

He knew that I knew.

I developed the next four pictures that I'd taken in quick succession and blew up the detail shots. I zeroed in on Big Bird's next action, and the motivation behind it scared me.

He had sent a text message: *She Knows.*

I tried to imagine how the next several minutes had played out. Big Bird tells Quinn that I'm there. That I recognized him. That I am in a position to put the two of them together and blow the whistle on their stolen designs. Quinn puts two and two together, too, and realizes that there are two people, not one, who can compromise his newfound success. Big Bird and me. I didn't like the way things were adding up.

I thought about the potential scandal. A fashion designer gets the kind of reviews that can make or break him, and in the same twenty-four hours, is exposed as a thief? Quinn would be ruined. He had to have containment. He killed one of the only two people who could tell the world what he'd done, which meant the only one left was me.

I had to steer clear of anything involving Quinn, Big Bird, and Fashion week. I needed a low profile that took me out of the picture before Quinn could take me out of the picture first.

The vintage Versace in the Ziploc bag was going to be a problem.

* * * *

Black. Turtleneck, leggings, sneakers, gloves, hat. The color of night. I belted on a khaki trench coat and hopped on the subway. Two stops shy of Bryant Park I exited, took off the trench coat, and balled it up. After stuffing it in a plastic bag from Duane Reed, I buried it in a public trashcan outside of an adult video store, and took up a slow jog, keeping to the shadows as I approached tent number five.

A crowd of people stood by the dumpster, some in uniform, some not. Bursts of light from a flash pierced the darkness at uneven intervals.

Chances were, the crime scene techs had emptied not only the contents of the dumpster, but discovered the dress underneath. If anyone connected me to that dress, they'd link me to the murder. The need for anonymity had led me to "borrow" it in the first place, and now, replacing a vintage Versace was going to be damn near impossible.

I jogged past the crime scene, around the block, and back to the adult video store, where I fished my coat from trashcan, then headed to Central Park. Nothing else I could do.

* * * *

I sat alone on the park bench, surfing the web from my iPhone. Several credible fashion bloggers had updated their websites with a review of Quinn's show. They agreed with me; it was a breakthrough collection. The kind that caught the attention of senior editors, that generated orders from respectable retailers. Thomas Quinn's future, at least the near future, was set, thanks to what he stole from my client.

Conversely, my client would be ruined. He couldn't show a collection that mirrored Quinn's from today, and canceling at this late date would start rumors circulating, rumors that would be hard discount. Absolutely nothing good could come from this for him.

"You're early," said a hushed male voice from behind me.

"Couldn't be helped," I replied. My client circled the bench and sat next to me. I closed my Internet connection and punched a couple of keys on the iPhone, behavior common among twenty-somethings sitting in the park. "Did you bring the money?"

"Did you bring the photos?"

"Money first."

My client pulled a thick envelope from inside his brown leather bomber jacket. I took it, glanced inside and thumbed over a wad of bills, and pushed it deep into the right hand pocket of my trench. I extracted a flat mailing envelope from the other pocket and set it on the bench between us. He reached for it but I pulled it out of reach. "There's something you should know." I stared straight ahead, at the path, where a squirrel had stopped to pick up an acorn. "It wasn't Britt. It was your assistant."

"You know this for sure?"

"Beyond the shadow of a doubt." I tapped the mustard-colored envelope.

"That's too bad," he said.

There was something about the way his voice turned flat as he said the words that caused me to break cover and look directly at him. The lines of his face were hard, angular, tense. A rolled up copy of WWD sat on his lap and the barrel of a gun pointed at my left hip.

"Quinn didn't steal your designs, did he?" I asked, thinking out loud. "You stole from him. But why?"

"I needed what Quinn had. A fresh perspective."

"What about Britt? Wouldn't she know?"

"Britt's a wannabe actress who barely speaks English. Nobody's going to listen to her."

"Your assistant—he knew what you were doing. That's why he wore that crazy outfit—he thought no one would risk going after him in that getup. Too much attention. And when he saw me, he didn't notify you, he notified Quinn." I stopped talking, as pieces of the last twenty-four hours fell into place like a puzzle that completes itself. "But that means you were there, too. At the show."

"You're right, my little pussycat. I was there. Close enough to take my own pictures and send them to the police. Pictures that expose a young woman in a very attention-getting blue Versace dress that may or may not have been stolen from a hip resale shop in SoHo."

My hand rested on a stun gun deep inside the trench coat pocket. I estimated that it was about an inch from his knee. I shifted position on the bench and hit the button. The shock popped his eyes open and shook his body with convulsions. As quickly as I'd juiced him, I stopped. He slumped down on the bench, eyes half-closed. The newspaper slid off his lap, taking his gun with it.

My morals are loose, but even I couldn't leave a gun in the middle of Central Park at night. I picked it up with my hem and slid it into the plastic bag I'd used earlier to store my coat. Then I got the heck out of there.

* * * *

I traded taxi for taxi three times before arriving at a discreet payphone by the Hudson River. I called the cops anonymously, then hopped on the subway for home. It was after three AM. A vent of steam from the subway level filtered through a manhole cover, leaving a grey cloud next to a pair of stray cats who nosed through the trash behind the Chinese restaurant. Normally I would have stopped to pet them, but not tonight.

I bypassed the four deadbolts installed on my front door and locked them behind me. After tossing the photos on a second-hand table, I thumbed through the money in the envelope a second time. Not nearly enough, considering what I'd been through in the past twenty-four hours, but I was lucky. If my client thought for a second that I would walk away with that envelope, I was certain he would have shorted my fee.

I carried the money to the bathroom and knelt by the litter box, the surface unmarred by tracks. The no-frills plastic bin was nestled inside a second of the same size, stacked like they were in the store the day they'd been purchased. I pulled the top one out of the bottom and dealt small bundles of hundred dollar bills into the empty space, next to money I'd acquired from previous jobs. Credit cards told a story of what people do, where they've been. Sure, I had credit cards, in the names of each of my aliases. Katarina, Catherine, Cathy, Kat, and, on rare occasion, Claude. But none in the name I was born with. It was better that way.

I sat in the bathtub and let the hot shower water pelt me from above. When I'd first started freelancing in the fashion industry to spy on designers, identify knock-off rings, expose greed and corruption among investors, it had seemed like fun. Glamorous, dangerous fun.

And, I was good at it.

But this job had gone further than the others.

I locked the door behind me and went to my mentor's vacant apartment where I picked the lock and fell into troubled sleep on his very expensive bed.

* * * *

The next morning, sunlight announced the start of a new day. I turned on the news. *Murder Under The Big Tent*, said the headline. A newswoman in a nondescript beige suit stood in front of the camera, while my client's mug shot filled the screen. My anonymous tip had gotten the cops to the park in time to discover the stun-gunned designer, and I was no longer in danger. Only one matter of business remained. The vintage Versace.

I spent close to what I made from the job on a replacement dress from eBay. Just as I clicked BUY IT NOW, someone knocked on the door.

"Kitten Kowalski? It's the police."

Some days it doesn't pay to get dressed.

SNARED

BY WARREN BULL

Jesse Walters spat tobacco in the direction of the deputy sheriff's disappearing unit. The car's spinning tires kicked up dust and gravel as it sped away from his shack. Walters' German Shepherd barked and strained against its chain. He calmed the animal before addressing the trim but muscular young deputy dressed in spit-shined shoes and an immaculate uniform standing across from him.

"That fool don't know it but you just saved his life."

Deputy Ted Anderson looked the unshaved middle-aged man dressed in stained overalls up and down. He noted that Walters crossed his arms and stared back at him. Walters had a not unpleasant odor of wood smoke and dog. His jaw worked constantly on the plug of tobacco in his cheek. Anderson waited ten seconds before responding.

"How is that, sir?"

"In this state a man's home is his castle. If Deputy Johnson had busted his way through my door like he wanted to, he would have eaten a face full of buckshot. I set up a greeting for unwanted strangers when I left the house. It's legal too."

"You might not be guilty of murder," said Anderson, "but I bet a jury would go for a lesser charge if your trap killed a deputy. I'd be concerned that kids and dogs might wander in."

"Hmm, it would serve some sneaky kid right. There are too many punks hereabouts. They know better than to mess with me. The buckshot would go right over a dog's head. Anyway, you kept Big Jim alive. His people and mine have been going at it for generations. His temper's hotter than Tabasco sauce. He'd have gone ahead like a bulldozer if you hadn't sent him away."

"We didn't have a warrant and it didn't seem polite to go bustin' in," said Anderson. "The sheriff wanted us to ask for your cooperation. You and Johnson acted like two pit bulls about to go at it."

"You sent him off with his tail between his legs. He won't forget that you're younger than him and an out-of-towner."

"We have other people to talk with too," said Anderson. "The sheriff made me the lead in this case because of my experience with similar cases in the Military Police. I thought Deputy Johnson would be more effective with someone else. I hope you don't mind answering a few questions for me. You're not under arrest, Mr. Walters, and you have no obligation to answer."

"No, I don't mind at all," said Walters. "I'll answer your questions. Being the fine upstanding citizen that I am these days. I'm reformed. I always like to help the po-lice. Ask anything you want. Just tell me first. What miserable son of a bitch got himself killed? I know that. 'Cause that's when you law officers show up to question me. Every time some worthless piece of rancid dog meat takes a dirt nap, you think I maybe had something to do with it and come track me down again. So who was it?"

"It's not a secret. You'd hear soon enough, sir, from your neighbors. Glen Mason was the intended target of a car bomb."

"Intended target? That means he lived?" Walters' knees sagged. He took a step backward to regain his balance. "I guess God wanted to get his attention and tell him to change his evil ways. As many people as that asshole pissed off, you must have a list a mile long of people to interview. I'd be near the top of the list 'cause I know how to make a car bomb. I can tell you I didn't make that one. If I'd of did it, Mason would be a crispy critter by now. The Sheriff wouldn't have sent just two men out and you wouldn't have sent Big Jim away."

Walters pulled out a pocketknife, opened it and slid it carefully between one side of the door and the doorframe roughly chest high until he felt a tug and heard a click.

"Just a fishhook, an open-end eye bolt and twenty-pound fishing line is enough to set up a trap," said Walters.

"As long as one end of the line is tied to a shotgun trigger," said Anderson.

"Tell me, I'm curious," said Walters. "Why didn't Mason get blown to hell?"

"He stood right outside the car, and used a remote starter," said Anderson.

"Oh, I get it. He must have been blown backwards. The car frame would protect him from most of the blast. He'd be bruised, scraped up and lose his hearing for a while, but that's all. If he turns his ignition on before he gets in his car, sounds like he thinks somebody's out to get him. Since his car blew up, I'd have to say he was right. You can tell him for me to be careful. Real careful." Walters spat.

"Do you have any idea about who could have constructed the bomb, sir?" asked Anderson.

"Prettinear anybody," said Walters. "I could have. Making a car bomb isn't rocket science. Even dumb poor white trash like me can read and follow instructions. You can get directions from books."

"Anybody could have done it," agreed Anderson. "Who do you think would have been willing to kill him?

"Killing a man," said Walters. "Now we come down to what you're fishing for." He spat. "Are you a Bible reader?"

"Some, Mr. Walters," said Anderson. "Maybe not as much as I should."

"Take a seat," said Walters, pointing to a rocker and sitting down himself in another. "Tell me what happened when Jesus told his disciples to cast their fishing nets into the water, Mr. Lawman."

"They caught so many fish that the nets started to tear and sink the boat," said Anderson.

"That's right, boy and how many fish did they catch?"

"As I recall, a multitude," said the deputy. He started to rock.

"Right again," said Walters, leaning back in his rocker. "Now, some of those fish were the sort people like to eat. Other fish were the sort that like to eat people. You've seen my records. You know I have killed. Didn't bother me when I did it. Don't bother me now. I don't like people much. Besides, anybody I killed won't be missed. I have my rules. Since I been grown up, I never killed an animal except for food. Never killed a child or a lady."

"Killing seems a little strange for a Bible reader, Mr. Walters," said Anderson.

Walters smiled. "Maybe you should read the Bible more. Remember Matthew 10:34 when Jesus said, 'Do not think that I have come to bring peace to the earth; I have not come to bring peace, but a sword.' Every once in a while there's somebody who acts as the sword of God. I know that sounds loony, but I've studied on this. Was a time when I didn't believe in God. Being in prison with lots of time to kill, I set out to prove to myself there ain't no God. I read everything Biblical I could lay my hands on. There was some strange stuff too. Finally, I had to admit there was a God and I found out He had a purpose for a man like me. I know it sounds crazy, but I figured He sent me to prison to discover my reason for being alive. I am a sword of God like Joshua or Gideon was." He set his chair into motion.

"I don't get it," said Anderson, stopping his chair and raising his eyebrows. "Can you help me understand?"

"Who was the first murderer?"

"Cain," answered the deputy.

"Everybody knows that, Deputy. What is the mark of Cain? What did it signify?"

"It was a sign to others not to murder Cain."

"Very good." Walters nodded. "You'd be surprised how few people know that. But have you thought about it? You're right. God marked Cain so that nobody would murder him even though Cain had murdered his brother, Abel. It was a mark of protection. God said he would take sevenfold vengeance on anyone who killed Cain. Sevenfold. Think on it." He nodded at Anderson.

"Maybe it means God didn't want any more murders, not even of Cain," said Anderson.

"Or maybe it don't," said Walters. "Moses was one of God's favorites. He killed an Egyptian in cold blood. He saw an Egyptian waling on an Israelite, looked around to see was anybody watching him, killed the Egyptian and then hid the body. They don't talk about that much in Sunday school, do they? God still chose Moses to lead the Israelites out of bondage. God chose David over Saul. Saul was no slouch as a killer but David fairly swum in blood. They sang, 'Saul has killed his thousands and David his tens of thousands.' You see, God protects a few special killers and makes use of them for His purposes. I see you don't believe me, but it's true."

Walters patted his dog on its head. "It's like in Ecclesiastes: There's a time and a season for everything—'A time to kill, and a time to heal. A time to break down, and a time to build up.' When it's time to kill and time to break down, then it's my time. Other times belong to somebody else."

"I'm listening," said Anderson, leaning toward Walters.

"Maybe it started with my daddy. Nothing my daddy did ever bothered him none. He was one mean son of a bitch. I'm the same. Used to be in this country that we settled things with guns. Gunmen got respect. Hell, if my daddy and I had lived a hundred and fifty years ago, they would have written songs about us like they did about the James boys and the Younger brothers. There have always been desperadoes. There always will be. A poor man has to do what he can in a rich man's world. My daddy never took no shit from nobody. He was a legend hereabouts. You cops were after me before I was even born. My daddy would have killed me if I kissed up to John Law. I had to become an outlaw. What other choice did I have?"

Walters spat. Then he continued.

"Whatever else he was, my father was true believer. After he died I stopped believing for a while. 'Til God put me in prison so I could find the light for myself. My daddy taught me that the Bible is the word of God. When you have a question, you just open the Bible wherever the spirit moves you and point. If what you read don't make sense you keep going down the page until it does."

"Is that how you choose who to kill?" asked Anderson.

"I don't anymore," said Walters. "Back in the bad old days, before I reformed, should somebody come to me and ask me to kill somebody else, I would find out about who was asking and who they was asking about. Often enough it was one jackass talking about another one. If it made sense, I'd open the good book and check it out with God. If He said, 'No,' I wouldn't do it no matter how much money I was offered. Killing people pays right well, by the way. Not many men have the balls to sit down and figure out how to kill somebody they're not even mad at."

"You'd check it out with a Bible verse?

"Yes, I always keep a Bible handy. I have one right inside. Let me show you why I don't worry about you lawmen."

Walters entered his shack and returned with a well-thumbed Bible. Anderson stood and moved next to him.

"Last time I needed direction, I ended up in Ezekiel," said Walters. "It said... let me find it. Here it is, 'Their blood I will require at your hand.' It says that twice. Later on it says, 'You have feared the sword and I will bring the sword upon you.' That's clear enough for this mother's son. The whole Bible is the word of God. Whenever I read it, what I read is meant for me."

"Can I try that?" asked Anderson taking the book and, flipping pages. "What you find is meant for you. So what I find must be meant for me."

"Can't argue against that," said Walters.

"Deputy Johnson and I already talked to a couple of people who said they could identify the man they saw messing around under the hood of Mr. Mason's car," said Anderson.

Walters looked away. He stopped chewing and spat.

"How about these verses of mine, Mr. Walters?" asked Anderson pointing to a passage in the Bible.

"Ezekiel 8: 12 through 14?" asked Walters looking at the Bible in Anderson's hands. "I can read it for myself. Here it is. 'I will spread my net over him and he shall be caught in my snare; I will bring him to Babylon, land of the Chaldeans yet he will not see it; and he shall die there.'"

Anderson closed the Bible and spoke. "By the time he returns, Johnson will have a valid search warrant from Judge Matthews for your house, truck and property, Mr. Walters. Your 'greeting' makes it certain that nobody was able to sneak into your place and plant evidence against you. I wonder what we'll find in there. The sheriff asked the state bureau of investigation to send bomb experts. It's incredible what experts can do these days. You know they found the Oklahoma City bombers. They considered themselves Christians too."

Walters stared at the Bible. His hands began to shake. "Well I'll be damned."

REEF TOWN

BY KARA CERISE

It was a dark and slimy night. Overgrown hairy green algae covered the inside tank walls and blocked out ambient light; the darkness was only intermittently punctuated by flashing, broken moonlight LEDs. A malfunctioning electronic wave maker caused currents to surge and cease, creating dangerous eddies around stinging corals.

The inhabitants of Reef Town schooled together in fear. The hardy blue damsel and delicate orange anthias fish rode the angry, rollicking waves side by side. A rockmover wrasse fish swam up to join his surfing reef mates.

"Nice night for a murder, huh, Rocky?" a damsel quipped although his voice shook.

Rocky shuddered. It had been a scary week with a fish gone missing every few days then intensifying to one missing every day. It always happened at night and none of the reef people saw anything out of the ordinary. One day a tank mate was sucking algae off the glass and the next day he was gone—never to be seen again.

Suddenly a series of "snap, bang, snap" shots rang out. The damsel and anthias fish scattered and took cover behind rocks while Rocky dove head first into the sand.

After a few seconds he poked his head up cautiously and looked around.

A red pistol shrimp moved haltingly sideways on the sandy bottom with his antenna swaying. "Excuse me. I thought I felt something come after me and my hand gun went off." He clicked his large claw together to make loud snapping sounds.

A convict tang grumbled and wiggled his white and black striped body. "I'll say it again, S.H. Rimp, gun control should be mandatory, especially for you since you are semi-blind."

A clown fish chimed in, "I'm keeping my family safe any way I can until these disappearances are solved. How do I know that one of you isn't responsible?" Using a fin, she swept two of her fry into their anemone-home and swam in after them for the evening. The anemone's waving tentacles enveloped the clown family to keep them safe from any evil doer.

As the danger seemed to have passed, Rocky fully emerged from the sand and shook himself off. He looked up—directly into the eyes of a pretty female rockmover wrasse named Maria.

She stretched. "I guess you got a little scared by the bang of the pistol shrimp. I saw your bubble trail."

Embarrassed, Rocky spit out a piece of finely granulated coral that he had mouthed on his frantic dive. "Yeah, well, I went under just to be cautious. How about you?"

"I was safe with Flasher and stayed above sand," she said, tilting her head to the right toward a red and blue fish with his chest puffed up and top fins splayed.

Flasher alternately flexed his dorsal fins then his pectoral fins. "I'll escort you home, Maria. You'll be safer with me than with this dragon-finned small fry."

Rocky tried to flex a fin but it drooped and looked like he was waving.

"Bye, Rocky." The cute female waved back at him as she and Flasher swam off.

He shook his head and bared his two small protruding teeth. Flasher was nothing but a show-off and a bully.

Rocky looked around at the remaining inhabitants. The crabs and S.H. Rimp were in the process of tucking themselves in narrow crevices in the rocks while the schooling fish made for a dark corner in the back. Yes, there was something funky going down in Reef Town and Rocky hoped they would all be alive in the morning. He dove under the sand to wait out the night.

* * * *

The next morning Rocky surfaced, yawned and stretched his fins and tail. It had been a quiet night and he hadn't heard a thing. He was hungry and began to probe under nearby shells and rubble, looking for a tasty morsel.

A female damsel shot by. "Have you seen my mate? I've looked everywhere." Her blue color glistened in the daylight as she wrung her fins together. "You're so good at spotting things, could you look around... even in the Dark Zone?"

Rocky gulped, his fins getting sweaty. "I'll search Reef Town first then decide if I need to go into the Dark Zone." The Dark Zone was the isolated and untamed part of the tank where the overflow filter box slurped and burbled. It was a place where fish never dared to go or, despite parental warnings, juveniles would go on a dare and never return. He had sworn to never dangle a fin in there.

Rocky made a circuit of his home, flipping over small rocks with his nose and peering into crevices of live rocks encrusted with algae, orange sponges, small clams and worms. But he didn't find any part of the missing damsel.

He didn't expect to find anything since he had been over these rocks many times. Also, if a fish had died of natural causes he would have seen two large eyes peering in followed by a five fingered appendage holding a net. The net would descend into their world and scoop up the body and take it to the white whirlpool leading to the Big Reef in the sea. He suddenly realized that he hadn't seen the eyes, the net or even any new food since just before his tank mates started disappearing.

Mulling that thought, Rocky decided that he would swim to the top for an aerial view and to check on the water level. He hadn't said anything to his tank mates but over the last week he noticed that the water level was decreasing. Rocky pressed his body to the glass and measured the distance between the power head and the top of the water. It had gone down another fin length last night. At this rate they would run out of water in less than a month.

From his elevated vantage point Rocky could see all of Reef Town. He noticed a path of destruction through the field of stone-like antler corals, their white, pink and green fingers hanging at right angles off their stems. Something large had made a sweeping motion from the top of the tank through the coral forest and dragged itself along the sandy bottom. He dove to the bottom and swam low, following the trail to a valley surrounded by rocks. He saw two halves of a large open clam shell and a couple of crabs eating scraps left in the shell.

"Hey!" Rocky shouted at them, bubbles spewing from his mouth. He pointed a fin in their direction. "So you two are the reason our friends keep disappearing."

The two crabs looked at each other while one crab quickly moved a piece of clam behind his back with his large claw. The other snapped, "We didn't do it. The shell was upside down on the sand and open like this. We're just cleaning up the place." It came out muffled since he was chewing.

Maria, Flasher and the female damsel swam over.

"We heard the commotion. Did you find my mate?" the damsel asked.

"No," Rocky said, wiggling, feeling proud and excited that he could solve the mystery in front of pretty Maria. "But I found these two feeding on the remnants of a clam. They must be the perpetrators who have been eating the reef people."

The damsel flared, "Murderers!" She repeatedly and forcefully nosed into one crab then the other.

"Hey, lady, cut it out," the crab without food in his mouth shouted. "We're innocent. We only eat dead things, remember?"

The damsel rounded on Rocky who, sensing things could get ugly, was about to go underground. "You said they were the culprits!"

"Sorry," Rocky mumbled and looked down. "I forgot that scavenger crabs only eat the remains."

The damsel nosed into Rocky. "We've looked everywhere. What if my mate is still alive? You need to go to the Dark Zone. You can always dart underground if you need to hide."

Flasher chuckled, "Yes, Rocky always hides when he's scared. He's nothing but a useless fin nipper."

"Rocky, you can do it," Maria said. She gave him a kiss on the cheek.

Rocky hesitated. He was frightened but his resolve was strengthened since Maria believed in him.

He sucked in a deep gulp of water and blew it out. "Okay, I need someone to go with me. There's safety in numbers."

"I'll stay here and protect the females," Flasher quickly said.

After a good deal of convincing on Rocky's part and agreement to share his food for the next month, Rocky and S.H. Rimp slowly made their way to the Dark Zone over rocks and through tunnels. When they entered, Rocky saw that it lived up to its name as he could barely see a fin in front of his face.

They lingered while Rocky's eyes became accustomed to the light and turned into night goggles. S. H. stretched his legs, getting his sensory feelers ready to taste his way through the darkness.

"I don't know, m-man," S.H. stuttered. "There's being brave and then there's being stupid. Are you doing this to show off for Maria?"

"Maybe. She is so pretty. Maria, star of the sea." Bubbles rose out of Rocky.

S.H. smacked him on the head with two of his legs. "Focus."

Rocky sobered. "In any case I think we need to know if there is a killer lurking back here. Anyone of us could be next. Follow me."

Rocky slowly swam toward a large rock. Suddenly, something moved underneath him and kicked up a small flurry of sand. He twisted to one side to get out of the way and pushed S.H. back. After a few seconds, when the sand had settled, he saw a puffed up, well fed red serpent star.

"You look stuffed to the gills," Rocky said. "We're looking for our friend. Eat anything suspicious lately?"

"No way. There's so much uneaten food in here that I don't need any more. But if I get hungry, hungry, hungry I know where to go." The serpent star leered, two of his arms creeping toward them.

They darted out of the way and continued onward through an abyss with high rock walls on either side illuminated by fluorescent tipped hydroids. They were translucent and looked ghostly waving in the darkness. Rocky thought it was hauntingly beautiful.

Since he couldn't see well, S.H. Rimp followed closely behind Rocky. His antenna tickled Rocky's tail, causing him to twitch and accidentally slap S.H.'s face.

"Watch the tail, man."

"Then don't get so close." Rocky flipped a fin at him and swam forward through a narrow crevice.

Suddenly, tentacles from a nearby hydroid waved in the current close to Rocky. He catapulted forward to avoid its poisonous tips.

S.H. felt the water move, ducked and narrowly missed being stung. He scuttled ahead and yelled, "Maybe this is why all our friends have vanished!"

"I don't think so," Rocky yelled back. "The hydroids need to touch a fish in order to sting them. They don't move around and our friends would be stupid to be swimming here."

"You mean stupid like us," S.H. said, dodging more stinging tentacles while following his friend to a safer area.

Rocky stopped abruptly when he reached the deepest, darkest part of the tank that was no longer lit by sporadic beams of light from the surface. S.H. slid to a stop behind him.

"We should investigate inside that small rock cave," Rocky said.

"A cave? Not me. When did you get so brave and become a mighty adventurer? You can explore that death trap by yourself." S.H. folded four of his arms around his body.

"By myself? Well...I'll just take a quick look."

Very slowly, feeling like he was going to his doom, Rocky went to the entrance of the cave and peeked inside. He didn't see or feel anything unusual so he went further in the cave until only his tail stuck out. The interior was quiet and still. He continued to the middle of the cave and looked around. No sign of the damsel or any other creature. Relieved, he turned to leave.

A whirring noise came from ahead. A shiny green body jumped down from a hidden burrow in the roof. A lethal mantis shrimp blocked off the cave entrance and Rocky's escape.

"I was feeling the need for a bite of something tasty," the mantis shrimp said, his large bug eyes focused on Rocky. "Pre-packaged food gets so tiresome." He unsheathed an oversized clubbed claw. Rocky knew that the mantis first hit the water with his claw, making a wave to stun its prey. Then the mantis bashed its victim to death. Rocky wanted to dive under the sand and hide but knew that Maria and the others were counting on him.

The mantis moved his claw and smacked his fist of death in the water. A loud explosion sounded and echoed off the rock walls, the vibration creating an underwater wave that somersaulted Rocky backward. He frantically paddled to keep from being thrown into a cave wall.

His life on the reef flashed in front of him and he realized he wanted a future with Maria and small fry of his own. Taking strength from that thought, he dove and kicked up sand with his nose to obscure the mantis shrimp's vision. He bobbed left then right and swam under the mantis, flipping him up with his tail.

He rocketed out of the cave to S.H. who used his claw to shoot off his pistol. Together they darted off, loud stunning snap waves shrieking from the mantis shrimp interspersed with S.H.'s pistol fire. Rocky blasted through the water while S.H. trotted behind. They dashed by the hydroids, creating a wake that made the poisonous tipped tentacles sway in unison. Then they careened over top of the red serpent star.

Rocky and S.H. emerged from the Dark Zone and abruptly stopped while Rocky's eyes adjusted to the light. They were breathing hard and couldn't talk. Exhausted, they slowly made their way back to their home and friends.

"We didn't think we'd ever see you again," the anthias said.

The convict tang added, "We heard the fire fight."

Maria nuzzled Rocky. "You're my hero."

"Rocky must have dove under the sand a number of times to stay safe," Flasher sneered.

Ignoring Flasher, Rocky gently explained to the damsel that they didn't find her mate. She sobbed but thanked them for looking.

Then he and S.H. shared slightly exaggerated stories about their adventures. All agreed that even though there was a killer mantis shrimp in their world that he wasn't the one eating reef people because they would have heard its club thunder. However, if they ever ran out of food they would need to watch out for the deadly mantis shrimp and the serpent star.

Rocky left the chattering group to think. If neither the mantis shrimp nor any of the other inhabitants of the Dark Zone was responsible for the disappearance of the fish, then who or what was?

Maria swam over. "What's troubling you?"

"I want to show you something."

Fin in fin, Rocky and Maria swam up to the water marker. Rocky explained his scientific observations of the decreasing water level. He pointed out that they hadn't had new water poured into their home since they stopped seeing the five fingered appendage with the net.

Maria frowned and used her fin to wipe the glass clean. She peered out to the vast dry-world filled with strange formations and shakily pointed. "There are water drops on the ground leading from our home to that water and sand filled cube way over there."

Rocky froze then slowly bubbled. "The cube appeared a week ago, just before the water level began to decrease and our tank mates started disappearing. I think the predator lives in that cube."

Rocky and Maria dove down to tell the others of their discovery. They, along with S.H. and Flasher, agreed to stay awake and sound an alarm if there was an attack. As the light faded, the rest of the reef people hid themselves for the night.

After an uneventful evening, Rocky, Maria, S.H., and Flasher nodded off with their eyes open.

"Slurp, slurp, scrape."

Awakened by the muffled sounds, Rocky shook his head and nudged the other three awake. "Listen."

They tilted their heads and listened intently but all was quiet. "You're being paranoid, Rocky," Flasher said.

"Look," Maria yelled and pointed to a large rubbery body with eight suction cupped arms crawling up an outside corner of their home. The octopus moved the lid aside, tipped its large head down and stared at them.

Without warning, one arm quickly unfurled and dropped down into their home reaching for Maria. Chaos erupted. S.H. repeatedly sounded his pistol alarm. Flasher bubbled, "Devil fish," let out excrement and dove under the sand. Rocky lunged and pushed Maria into a hole in the rock, away from the searching octopus arm. She cowered inside as the tip crept closer to her.

Rocky flared his bottom, top and side fins. He shimmied, wiggled and slapped his tail against the suction cupped arm again and again. It drew away from Maria and with a swinging action threw Rocky against a jagged rock. He dropped to the bottom, lay still and began to bleed. The devil fish arm moved toward his motionless body.

Fearing he would be eaten, he yelled, "I love you, Maria." Then a blinding light shone. "I see the light, Maria. I'm on my way to the Big Reef."

Instead, the heavens parted and the fish net swooped in and scooped up the invading octopus.

* * * *

A few days later, Rocky, his body healing from his near fatal fight, and Maria swam together enjoying the clean atmosphere and algae-free walls. The lighting and water flow were back to normal and all the inhabitants were healthy and happy.

The net had once again appeared—this time bringing new residents to Reef Town. They saw S.H. digging a burrow to share with a new goby fish who would take care of the almost blind S.H. The only unhappy inhabitant was Flasher, who now spent most of his time under the sand because of the embarrassing excrement incident.

In the evening, Rocky and Maria stopped and looked out at the infinite world beyond and the distant water cube. They noticed its top now had a large rock sitting on it, no doubt intended to keep the octopus confined.

"It's good to have a safe environment to raise kids," Maria said with a sidelong glance at Rocky.

Rocky bubbled with joy. Together they dove under the sand with their fins and tails kicking up sand dust, shining silver under the now functioning moonlight LEDs.

THE GIRLS IN THE FISHNET STOCKINGS
BY JUDITH KLERMAN SMITH

Fish nets hang from the ceiling, walls and bar of the Calais Club, a speakeasy in mid-town Manhattan. Lorraine, the girl with a new flash bulb camera talking the customers into having a picture taken, continues the pattern. She wears fishnet stockings which make her long legs look extra sexy under a French-maid tutu-length costume. She balances herself on shoes with three inch heels. I wear an outfit like hers but instead of a camera, I carry a tray of cigarettes and cigars suspended from a ribbon around my neck.

Business is booming like it is every night, and both Lorraine and me are kept busy. Lou, the bartender, once explained how come there are no problems with the cops. The right Feds have been greased, and the local bulls are on the weekly payroll. And Lou should know. He's related to the boss, Johnny Remo. He's like a nephew or something. But he doesn't act like it. Not the way his cousin Eddy who also works at the club. Lou's a good guy. He kinda looks out for us girls, like when a customer mouths off or can't keep his hands off me or Lorraine. Lou sets the creep straight, pronto.

I sell my last pack of Lucky Strikes and I'm resting my tootsies in the dressing room when Lorraine shows me the glossy. She's going over the pics she snapped, matching them to the couples. Eddy develops the negatives for the joint. He has a dark room at the club so he can do it right away. That way the customers don't have to wait—not like Joe Public whose got a Brownie camera and has to take his film to the pharmacy.

"Look at this, Gwen," Lorraine says.

I look but I don't recognize the couple and say so.

"No, not the people in front. Look at the next table. In back of them."

Then I see it. "Holy, moley. That gunsel's got a rod on the guy next to him. It looks like he's making him get up and they're leaving. We better tell someone," I say.

"Are you nuts?" Lorraine says. "You want to get us killed? I'm not delivering this pic. I'll tell the customer it got spoiled." Then she takes the picture and puts it on the bottom of her pile of snaps.

I don't feel right about that. But what can I do? I don't know who the people in the picture are or who the gunsel is. Maybe he works for Johnny Remo. Maybe not. And Lorraine's probably right. Asking the boss would be suicide. As it is she's gonna have a tough time figuring what to tell Eddy when she doesn't show up with money for the photo.

But I don't want to argue. My shift is over, and I'm in a hurry to get home so I can soak my aching feet. I change into my street clothes and go home.

I pick up the *Times* on my way to work the next afternoon. Then I know who the guy in the snap with the gun in his ribs is 'cause his dead body is on the front page: It's Henry Harrison Blakely, III, the banking guy's son. Now what am I going to do?

Lorraine is in the dressing room when I get to the club. I show her the front page and she turns white as the club's table clothes.

"What do we do?" I ask.

"I've got to think on it," Lorraine says.

We change into our costumes and get to work.

It's tough keeping my smile on and making small talk, and I can tell whenever I spot Lorraine that she's having a hard time, too.

We both take a lunch break about midnight and meet back in the dressing room. By then I've come up with sort of a plan.

"What did you tell Eddy about the pic?" I ask.

"I told him I spilled a drink on it, and it's spoiled. I can't sell it, and they didn't want to wait for another one. "

"Do you still have the glossy?"

Lorraine nods.

"You need to show it to Lou. He'll know what you should do."

"That's screwy," she says. "I'm not sticking my neck out. I like to keep on living."

The next few hours are tense, but we make it to closing. I try talking Lorraine into asking Lou what he thinks, but nothing I say works. Lorraine is sure it's dangerous to ask. I tell her she has to do something. She wants no part of it.

So it's up to me. She can stay nice and safe. I got to take the chance 'cause if I don't my cop-dad's ghost is gonna haunt me. It's like this. Even though Dad wouldn't like my working in a speak, he'd let it go—he liked a drink now and then himself—but he'd draw the line at letting someone get away with murder. And I do too.

I borrow the picture from her, fold it and slip it into my purse. Then I go talk to Lou. He's still at the bar polishing glasses.

"Lou, got a minute?"

"What you want, kid? I'm ready to call it a night. I'm bushed."

"It's about this picture," I say, showing him the glossy. "Lorraine and I don't know what to do."

Lou studies it. He's quicker than me. He whistles. "Now, that's interesting. I suggest you rip it up and go about your business."

"But, Lou, the guy is dead. It's in today's *Times*," I say.

Lou shakes his head. "My advice is the same. Rip it up and forget about it." He hands back the picture, and I put it in my purse. So much for taking a chance.

I go back to the dressing room and tell Lorraine.

"Lou's right, Gwen. Rip up the picture."

"I can't, Lorraine. Not yet. I need to figure if I can do something." I turn, leaving her with her mouth hanging open, and go home.

The next afternoon as I head into work I've made up my mind. I don't think I can trust the police, and what good would it do to go to the dead guy's family? Lou and Lorraine are right. The guy's dead. Why risk our lives?

I knock on the club door like everyone has to do to get in, and Lou looks through the peephole. He opens the door right away, and instead of letting me in, he slips out, holding the door so it doesn't close all the way. I'm surprised. One of Johnny Remo's gunsels usually mans the door into the speakeasy, and he doesn't step out to talk.

"You're not dead," Lou mumbles just loud enough for me to hear him.

"What's going on, Lou?" I ask.

"Lorraine's dead. Shot. Some bum found her in the alley this morning, still in costume, and called the police."

I gasp. I feel the tears brimming over and rushing down my cheeks.

"That picture," Lou says. I can hear anger in his words.

"But Lorraine wouldn't have told. She wanted to rip it up, like you said."

"Don't matter," Lou says. "She knew."

"Who did you tell, Lou?" My voice trembles.

"I didn't say nothing. It was Eddy. Eddy suspected something when Lorraine said the glossy got ruined. He printed up another one from the negative and took a closer look. He squealed to the boss, and the boss told one of his guys to take care of it. The cold bastard took her outside and shot her." Lou's next words were whispered. "Don't stick around, kid."

"Why?" I whisper back.

"Because Johnny Remo wants you dead, too. Eddy said how you and Lorraine are close. What she knows, you know. So Johnny's muscle is looking for the other French maid in the fishnet stockings."

I turn around and go home, not even taking time to tell Lou thanks for the warning. When I'm back in my room I take the picture that got Lorraine killed and put me on the run out of my purse . The snap is the only thing I got that connects me to Lorraine. I let my tears fall, splashing on the glossy. I'm crying for Lorraine, but for me too. Then, angry, I rip the picture until only tiny pieces are left. That evening I grab a Greyhound for the West Coast. I take my memories with me, but you can be damn sure I don't take my French maid costume or fishnet stockings.

KEEPING UP APPEARANCES

BY JULIE TOLLEFSON

Nick wiped a ring of condensation from the bar and restacked a handful of cardboard coasters. He glanced at Ray, the bar's only patron, nursing his bottle of cheap beer and staring expressionlessly at the muted television replaying highlights of last night's ball game. He dragged his attention back to the papers spread behind the bar, but the buzz of his phone promised to rescue him from the distasteful task. Then he saw the caller's ID. Larissa, his soon-to-be ex-wife.

He considered letting the call roll to voice mail, but he knew from experience that Larissa would call non-stop until he answered.

"Yeah?" He didn't attempt to hide his irritation.

Larissa sighed heavily. "You don't have to act like it's such a chore to speak to me. I'm still your wife."

Nick bit back his response and counted to five before allowing himself to speak. "What do you need, Larissa?"

"I have had the worst day, and I just need to talk. Can you come over, just for a little while?"

"You're kidding, right? I'm working."

Ray chose that moment to drain the last of his beer and heave himself off his barstool. Nick watched his only excuse to keep the bar open walk unsteadily out the door.

"Nettie can't sleep. She wants you to read her that story about the giraffe. She says I don't do it right."

Nick closed his eyes. "It's not fair to keep doing this, Larissa. She's only with you one night a week. Surely that's not too much to ask."

Even as he said it, he knew it was too much to ask. Larissa had made it clear to him when she moved out that she had no interest in being a wife or a mother. She had played both roles for five years, and now she had grown bored.

"You're not here, listening to her whine. It's always the same. 'Daddy doesn't do it that way.' Well, I'm tired of it, Nick. Be here in fifteen minutes."

* * * *

Nick arrived at Larissa's apartment planning to tuck Nettie in for the night and then leave. He had no intention of spending any more time with Larissa than necessary. He knocked lightly, unwilling to disturb Nettie if she had settled down on her own. No response. He knocked more insistently until he was sure he had roused everyone in the building. Finally, he let himself in with the key Larissa had foisted on him "just in case." Until now, he hadn't had reason or desire to use it.

The disarray of Larissa's living room stopped him just inside the door. Her coffee table lay on its side pushed against the too-big TV stand wedged between the door and the kitchen wall. One of the ugly crystal lamps he had always hated lay shattered against the far wall. A dark rusty-brown patch stained Larissa's prized white rug.

"Larissa?"

No answer.

"Nettie?"

Nick's heart contracted. Damn Larissa and her mind games. He edged farther into the apartment. Larissa's bedroom and the spare room that doubled as Nettie's bedroom when she stayed with her mother, and an art studio when she didn't, appeared to be untouched. Larissa's newest painting—a dark, swirling abstract done in shades of deepest blue, pierced by a sharp silver slash with tiny drops of red merging into a black pool—stood in the middle of the room. Its subtext of danger and deception deepened the feeling of unease growing in Nick's gut. The scene was edgy and dark, but he couldn't quite put his finger on the underlying message. Was Larissa predicting the future or reflecting the past with her swirls of navy blue and red-black?

Nick returned to survey the living room more closely. Years of painful personal experience told him Larissa was capable of staging the scene before him to gain sympathy. His wife had a melodramatic flair that had amused him when they were dating. In the intervening years, the constant drama of life with Larissa had worn him down. What had she done this time? He reached for his cell phone, picking through the magazines and toys littering the living room floor while he waited for Larissa to answer. He kicked aside a sofa cushion as the call went to voice mail.

"Where are you? And where's Nettie? Dammit, Larissa, this is …"

A flash of blue under the coffee table caught his eye. He leaned down and drew out Nettie's beloved blue Cat and his heart stopped. His daughter would not willingly leave Cat behind. If Larissa had gone somewhere with Nettie, she wouldn't have left Cat either, and risk Nettie having a very public meltdown. Larissa hated scenes that didn't cast her in the starring role.

Nick opened his phone again, this time calling someone he knew he could count on.

* * * *

Nick paced the length of the living room a dozen times while he waited for Pete Marquardt, his best friend since junior high school, to arrive. He and Pete were inseparable throughout their teen years. They attended the same state college, and after graduation, they both returned to the town they grew up in. While Nick bounced from job to job, Pete became one of the town's most reliable cops.

"This better be good, Nick. The Royals actually have a chance to take the lead...." Pete stopped abruptly when he saw the overturned furniture. His smile faded as he surveyed the chaos. "She never was a very good housekeeper, but this isn't just her carelessness, is it?"

Nick gave Pete a quick run down of Larissa's phone call imploring him to help her put Nettie to bed, then showed him Cat. Pete, who had had spent enough time with Nick and Nettie in the last few months to realize the importance of the abandoned stuff animal, cut Nick off and led him out into the hallway.

"Larissa didn't sound under duress when she called?" he asked, taking the ragged toy from Nick and examining it closely.

"Just self-centered. No different from half a dozen other times," Nick said.

In the early weeks of the separation, he and Pete had argued about Larissa's late-night calls for help. Pete thought his friend shouldn't let her manipulate him, but Nick felt his responsibility to Nettie trumped any temporary victory Larissa might achieve by thinking he was at her beck and call.

Pete dug his phone from his pocket, but the crash of the apartment building's outside door bouncing against a wall caused both men to pivot toward the sound. Gary Lamont, Larissa's on-again, off-again boyfriend, stumbled across the threshold.

"You have no business here, you...you..." Gary, wiry and red-faced, pulled back when he saw Pete reach for his off-duty gun. He raised his hands in front of him, palms up. "Wait. I didn't realize...Oh. My. God. Look at that mess." Gary strained to see past the men, recoiling in horror at the scene in Larissa's apartment. His gaze shifted between Nick and Pete and back again. "What have you done? Divorce wasn't enough for you?"

"What are you doing here, Lamont?" The sight of the man who had replaced him in Larissa's bed broke Nick's tenuous control over the anger that bubbled just beneath the surface of his emotions. He tried not to notice the gleam of Gary's white muscle shirt against his deep tan, no doubt the result of spending long summer days on Nick's boat with Nick's wife. He clenched his fists so tightly he thought the bite of nails in his palms would draw blood.

Gary sidled past Nick in an attempt to appeal to Pete.

"Officer Marquardt, I saw his car in the parking lot. I came to protect Larissa—she's scared of him, you know. She wanted me to be here, to protect her. Oh god, I'm too late. Don't tell me I'm too late."

Listening to the sniveling idiot plying Pete with lies infuriated Nick. All of his frustrations of the past six months, of learning that Larissa was having an affair, of learning how to be a single father, of navigating through the divorce process alone, came to a head. In a flash, he crossed the hall and slammed Lamont against the wall. Nick cocked an arm back and let his fist fly, stopping a fraction of an inch shy of Lamont's deathly pale face. The smaller man's eyes rolled wildly as Nick leaned close. "Stay the hell out of my life."

Nick felt Pete's hands on his shoulders, pulling him away. Gary scrambled backward, tripped, then righted himself and, casting one final look of disgust over his shoulder, fled toward the exit. He didn't get far.

"Not so fast, Lamont." The authority in Pete's voice stopped the man in his tracks. "I'm going to need you to stay right here while I sort out what happened."

Pete released his hold on Nick, pushing him toward one wall and gesturing for Gary to sit on a bench at the far end of the hall. Nick sagged against the wall, struggling to control his anger. "What the hell, Pete?"

Pete glanced back through the open door of Larissa's apartment. "That stain on the rug could be blood," he said, deep worry lines creasing his face.

"She probably cut herself making dinner for him." Nick couldn't keep the bitterness from his voice. Larissa stopped cooking for him and Nettie long before he suspected there was a Gary in the picture.

"Yeah, I know. But I have to call it in."

Nick sank into a crouch, bracing his back against the wall and dangling his clasped hands between his legs. He listened to Pete describe the situation to the sergeant on duty and request that officers be dispatched to the scene. Nick dropped his gaze to the floor, trying to make sense of the evening and wondering how much he should tell Pete about his last few meetings with Larissa. Gradually, he became aware that Pete had ended his call and now stood watching him speculatively.

Nick cleared his throat. "Larissa was supposed to pick Nettie up from school yesterday," he said.

"Didn't show?" Pete asked.

"Nope. No calls, no message. Nettie's teacher called me ten minutes after school closed. Poor kid. She's only five, but she knows her mother isn't like other moms."

Pete grunted. He had never liked Larissa, and Nick's relationship with her was one of the few things the friends had ever fought about.

"I know Larissa's a nutcase. I told you that before you married her. But it sure looks like whatever happened here wasn't her idea," he said.

"What are you thinking?" Nick asked.

Pete hesitated before answering, choosing his words carefully. "Her car is still out in the lot. There's blood in her apartment, which is thoroughly trashed. Did she tell you she called us out two nights ago? Said someone was trying to break in."

Nick shook his head. "She didn't say anything to me."

"She said a neighbor saw someone who looked a lot like you running away."

"What are you saying, Pete?"

"Where were you Sunday evening?"

"Christ, Pete! My every waking moment is spent working or taking care of Nettie."

"Is that what you were doing two nights ago?"

"Of course." Nick stopped. Actually, Nettie had attended a friend's birthday party Sunday. Nick had spent an hour and a half of unexpected free time struggling to complete the paperwork for his divorce. Larissa's betrayal cut deep, and making a list of property they had accumulated together rubbed salt in the wound.

"What aren't you telling me?" Pete asked. "I can't help if you're not straight with me."

Nick rose and paced to the front door, where he could watch traffic fly by. Larissa had chosen an apartment on one of the busiest streets in town, a location totally unsuited for children.

"I told Larissa last week that I planned to seek full custody of Nettie, to have her declared an unfit mother," he said.

For the first time in the twenty years they had known each other, Nick couldn't read Pete's face. "You don't really think I would hurt Larissa," he said.

"I've never seen you so angry," Pete said. "You've been pissed for months, and that thing with Lamont just now? What was that?"

Nick rubbed the back of his neck, a rising tide of conflicting emotions threatening to override his self-control. "What do you want me to say, Pete? Yes, I'm angry. Yes, it hurts like hell every time I see that idiot my wife is sleeping with. Yes, I want to get even with Larissa for the pain she's caused not just me, but our daughter. But no, Pete, whatever happened here, I had nothing to do with it."

He searched his friend's face for understanding, but he found doubt. Pete's suspicions cut almost as deep as Larissa's cheating.

"Look, you know Nettie's better off with me. You know I can provide a more stable home—both physically and emotionally. You weren't even surprised when Larissa walked out."

"This is beyond divorce and a custody dispute, Nick. I'm just wondering why you called me instead of 911. I'm your friend, but I'm also a cop and this is a possible crime scene. You called me, and I have to investigate."

A black cloud enveloped Nick, deadening the rest of Pete's words and sucking the air from the room. "You know what, Pete? I'm sick of Larissa's games. She begged me to come over here tonight, just so I could find this. You investigate all you want. I'm going to get to the bottom of this. You can help me, or you can get the hell out of my way."

"I can't let you leave," Pete said, lunging for Nick as he pushed open the door.

"Don't you dare let him go! Don't let him get away with this!"

The screech from the end of the hall caught both men by surprise. Gary, forgotten in the heat of the argument, leaped off the bench and ran toward Nick with fists raised. Pete stepped between the two, catching Gary by one wrist and twisting his arm behind his back. As Pete pinned Gary to the floor, Nick slipped out the door and ran to his car.

* * * *

The needle on Nick's speedometer flirted with 80 as he flew down Suicide Hill on the back side of Jane's Lake. Nick drove these roads often when he felt troubled, especially at night. In high school, the rush of wind through open windows as his car raced over hills and around blind curves felt daring and exhilarating. Later, the solitary trips gave him the space he needed to think through problems. In the months leading up to Larissa's departure, when he only suspected that she was having an affair, he came here regularly. After every fight, every accusation and counter-accusation. But since Larissa moved out, Nick rarely made the drive. Nettie needed an adult she could count on. He hadn't lied to Pete when he said he spent every waking moment caring for his daughter.

He pulled to the side of the road and cut the engine, hands shaking from an unfamiliar combination of fury and fear. Larissa's disappearance with Nettie had to be punishment for his decision to seek sole custody of their daughter. He couldn't allow himself to think otherwise. So working from that premise, what was her plan? Where would she go and why?

Chorus frogs provided background music as Nick replayed his last conversation with Larissa, hoping to find clues to what was going on in her head.

"Remember the day Nettie was born?" he had asked.

"God, yes. How could I forget?" Larissa shuddered, her face twisted in disgust.

"I knew at that moment, that first time I took our daughter in my arms, that you would be a terrible mother."

Larissa laughed.

"You've never wanted to be her mother, Larissa. To you, she's just another accessory, like diamond earrings and gold bracelets. You use her like you use me, to show the world a picture of a perfect family. You're twisted, Larissa."

"Do you have a point, Nick? Gary's waiting for me. I'm taking the boat out."

"You can have the boat," he said, his anger making him reckless. "But I'll make sure you don't get Nettie. She deserves so much better than you for a mother."

Larissa's eyes had sparked with a maliciousness he had rarely seen, but she had left without saying another word. Thinking about it now, Nick knew where he would find answers.

The wind whistling through the open car windows carried the dank smells of soggy, rotting vegetation as Nick's car plunged through the valley at the bottom of the hill and over the bridge that crossed one of the lake's smaller arms. He slowed as he rounded the north side of the lake, then slowed more to take the turn toward the marina where he kept his boat.

It was dark and quiet as Nick parked and made his way along the dock to his boat slip. By tomorrow, the weekend partiers would be gathering, year-round Christmas lights would sparkle from many slips and the smells of grilling hamburgers and spilled beer would fill the air as laughter echoed across the lake. But tonight, Nick was alone in a stillness that clung to the marina like a dense fog.

He stepped aboard his boat and fumbled in the dark galley until he found a bottle of whiskey and a glass. Back on deck, he poured a generous amount and sat back to wait.

Half an hour later, he tensed as he heard quiet steps on the dock. Not moving, he waited until the steps drew even with his boat and paused.

"You might as well come aboard," he said.

Larissa sank onto the seat opposite him and lit a cigarette.

"You're so damned predictable, Nick."

So are you, he thought.

"What do you want, Larissa?"

Starlight reflected in her eyes. How many nights had Nick found the romance in moments like this? Now, he just felt cold.

"I wanted a grown-up husband, Nick. A grown-up with a real job, not a bartender with delusions of becoming a garage band rock star. I wanted a nice house and nice clothes. I wanted people to see us and want to be us."

She moved next to him, placing one hand on his knee. He suppressed a shiver of revulsion. "But you didn't care about what I wanted. And now, you want a divorce? And you're calling me unfit? Do you know how that makes me look?"

Nick shook his head. "It's always about appearances, isn't it? How can you do this to Nettie?"

Larissa lit another cigarette and remained quiet.

"Gary thinks you're dead, you know."

It was hard to tell in the dark, but Nick thought he could feel her smile.

"Gary isn't very smart. He believes what I want him to believe."

"So what's your plan? You're not dead. Pete…"

"Pete. Pete can be manipulated. He's even more stupid than you."

"Your problem, Larissa, is you've always thought you were the smartest person in the room. But you're delusional. What do you think's going to happen? You'll disappear, start a new life, while everyone thinks you're dead? I'll rot in prison for a murder I didn't commit?"

"That's as good a plan as any, I suppose."

"What about Nettie? Where does she fit in your plan? Where is she now?"

Larissa flicked her cigarette into the lake, watching the glowing end until it disappeared in a soft puff when it reached the water.

"I'm quite sure my parents will be delighted to raise Nettie. They've been obsessed with her since she was born. In fact, she's with them now."

If the situation weren't so ludicrous, Nick would have admired her attention to detail.

"You thought of everything."

"Right down to you seeking solace on this boat. The question now is, how does this end?"

Larissa took the glass from his hands and twirled it between her perfectly manicured nails. The nearly full moon cleared the horizon and cast a pale glow across the lake.

"I have two thoughts, actually." She raised the glass to her lips and slowly sipped the fiery liquid. "Thought one: I walk away now, begin a new life somewhere warm. By morning, Pete will have enough evidence to arrest you for my murder."

Nick shook his head. "Never going to happen."

By the light of the moon, Nick saw her nod and smile. She dipped a long index finger into the whiskey, then touched it to her lower lip as if she were freshening her lip gloss. She tapped the glass. "Yes, too many variables out of my control. So that leaves thought two."

She put the glass down and moved even closer. One hand sliding up his thigh as she put her lips to his ear. "Thought two: You disappear. You sneak out of town under cover of darkness and no one ever sees you again. A clear sign of your guilt."

"I'm not going anywhere."

"I was afraid you'd feel that way. But I've planned for that, too."

A slender, very sharp knife glinted in Larissa's right hand, reflecting the moon as she moved with lightning quickness to place the flat edge along his throat. Her left hand remained on his thigh.

Nick held his breath, fought the urge to swallow.

The knife rested dangerously close to his carotid artery. Larissa had him off-balance, and the chance of being able to overpower her quickly was small. He closed his eyes and thought of Nettie. He couldn't let her grow up thinking he had killed her mother and abandoned her. His only hope was to lead Larissa to outsmart herself.

As if sensing his thoughts, Larissa drew back slightly, at the same time flicking the knife against his earlobe. Nick felt a sting, then the warm stickiness of blood dripping on his shoulder.

"Now, now. Don't get any ideas. Bravado now will only make this more painful."

Nick took advantage of the extra space between them to ease himself into a better position.

"You're the one who's predictable, Larissa. So sure you're smarter than everyone else. Right now, Pete is retrieving the nanny cam I planted in your apartment. He'll see you overturning your own furniture, deliberately cutting yourself." Nick gestured at the bandage on her left wrist. "He'll see you leave—alive. He's not stupid, Larissa. He'll find you."

She laughed again, a tense, strained laugh, unsure whether to believe him. Nick shifted his weight and edged his left arm up toward his lap, steeling himself to take advantage of any opportunity to save himself.

"But you'll be just as dead, Nick. And I don't share your belief that Pete has the wits to catch me."

She brought up her knife hand quickly, but this time Nick was ready. He ducked to the left at the same time as he swept his right arm up to deflect her blow. The knife glanced off Nick's shoulder. Larissa struggled to regain her advantage, but Nick's grip crushed her wrist against the boat's railing. She was strong—and crazy, a deadly combination—but Nick was stronger. Images of Nettie flashed through his thoughts and he renewed his efforts to disarm Larissa. She twisted and nearly freed herself, but Nick used his hundred-pound advantage to immobilize her. He slammed her hand against the rail until she lost her grip on the knife. It fell harmlessly into the shallow water below, and Larissa stopped struggling altogether. Nick groped with one hand for the rope stored among the fishing poles and nets under the boat's seat. He pulled one end free and looped it around Larissa's right arm, then pulled himself up and finished tying her arms behind her back.

Nick collapsed on the deck, exhausted, watching without emotion as Larissa struggled against her bonds. Gradually, he became aware of the buzz of his cell phone. He hesitated for a moment, then punched the answer button.

"Doris, hi," he greeted his mother-in-law. "Thanks for taking care of Nettie. Yeah, are you guys having fun?"

THE HINDI HOUDINI
BY GIGI PANDIAN

The young man in a pristine bowler hat attempted the futile exercise of extricating himself from the twenty-foot fish net that had fallen onto the stage.

The netting was heavier than he'd imagined, causing him to fall to his knees when it dropped. He lifted the knotted rope pressing against his shoulders, shifting his hat in the process. A rose petal emerged from beneath the hat and fluttered to the floor.

"The net isn't supposed to drop until I reach the trunk," he said in a raised voice, ceasing his squirming and readjusting his hat. "Markus, can you get this thing off of me?"

Sanjay Rai, AKA The Hindi Houdini, was practicing for his magic show at the Cave Dweller Winery in California's Napa Valley. It was his first day setting up for his series of shows that would run for the summer tourist season. In his late twenties, Sanjay had already developed quite a following. He liked to think of himself as a magician and escape artist for the 21st century with the sensibilities of previous centuries. He performed in a tuxedo, alternating between a bowler hat and a turban. Either one could hold what he needed for his sleight-of-hand.

"Sorry!" a voice called out from above the stage. After several seconds of shuffling, a wiry stagehand appeared. An oversized dress shirt and jeans hung loosely over his thin frame.

"This net," Sanjay said from beneath his confines, "is heavier than I imagined."

"You're the one who bought it," Markus said.

"And you're the one who dropped it *on my head* instead of on the trunk."

"Let me get William to help me get you out of there."

"I think Lizette is backstage," Sanjay began, but Markus had already left the theater by a stage door.

Sanjay shifted his bowler hat again, making sure it was firmly in place over his thick black hair. The netting was heavy on his neck and shoulders, but his hat was an important prop. Something might have shifted inside. If he removed it now, Markus, Lizette, or William might learn his secrets. And that would never do.

"Got him!" Markus called out from the back row of the theater. The theater's manager William looked worse than the last time Sanjay seen him. A glass of red wine swayed in William's hand as he tottered down the aisle. It was only five o'clock but it was obvious William had already had a few. A theater on the grounds of a winery was probably not the best place for him to work. His handsome face would be permanently ruddy within a few years at this rate.

"I'm sure Markus can handle this on his own," Sanjay said, eyeing William's glazed eyes.

"Ha!" William barked. "Technical difficulties, eh, Houdini?"

Sanjay hated it when William called him Houdini. Coming from most people, it was a sign of respect. But not with William. There was a mocking lilt in his voice as he said it. Sanjay wished the pleasant Lizette had been helping instead, even if it would have made it harder to lift the heavy net.

William set down his wine glass on the edge of the stage and heaved himself up to help Markus. He wasn't a large man, but climbing onto the stage winded him. Sanjay held his hat firmly as the two men lifted the netting. A button on the cuff of Markus's long sleeve caught on one of the knots and the net dropped back down. At least Sanjay wasn't wearing one of his many tuxedos. He wasn't used to working with this particular rope, so he didn't know what its effect would be on fabric. He could have freed himself without dislodging his hat if he needed to—a Swiss Army knife was one of the items concealed on his body—but he hadn't wanted to damage the important new prop.

In spite of a tipsy theater manager and a stagehand in an ill-fitting dress shirt, Sanjay was freed less than a minute later.

"I'll get this back in place," Markus said.

William scooped up his glass of wine and retreated, chuckling to himself. "I'll be in my office for the next hour," he called over his shoulder, "if there are any more magical mishaps."

"You should have asked Lizette to help," Sanjay said, brushing off his knees.

"Did I hear my name?" Lizette's curly auburn hair shone in the stage lights as she stepped from backstage carrying a box of plastic musical instruments that served as props for the show.

"Oh!" she cried out, spotting the net. "Isn't that supposed to fall onto the trunk?"

"I know!" Markus snapped. "I screwed up. I get it."

Sanjay had enjoyed working with the married couple much more the previous season—before Lizette had an affair with William. As far as he knew, the affair had been short-lived, but it still made things awkward. The magician hoped they'd be able to focus enough to help him prepare for his show next week. The Saturday night opening performance was already sold out. Even more importantly, Jaya would be there. He'd only met her recently, but he could tell she was something special. Then again, Markus had probably thought the same of Lizette before he learned she was sneaking off to sleep with William rather than scrap-booking with a girlfriend as she claimed.

Markus struggled to get the net back in place above the stage. Sanjay's on-stage magician's assistant would arrive the next night for several days of proper dress rehearsals. Usually that first day of initial set-up was a relaxing one. Usually.

"Ready?" Sanjay asked.

"I want to make sure I don't drop the net early again," Markus answered from the cat-walk above. "I've got a question for William about the levers before we start." He pulled out his cell phone.

"He's not answering," Markus said after a few moments. "Never mind. I'm sure it's fine. Um. Yeah. Pretty sure."

"You don't sound too sure."

"It's fine, Sanjay. Don't worry. We got the net off you before, we can do it again."

Sanjay couldn't imagine anything he'd like less. "Can you find William?"

"I don't want to lose sight of this lever."

Sanjay sighed. "Let me see if I can find him."

As Sanjay walked around the side of the theater to the winery's administrative offices, he attempted to push thoughts from his mind about what the rest of this season would be like. Markus hadn't always been so absent-minded, but clearly the affair had gotten to him.

Sanjay's knock on William's office door was met with silence. He glanced at his watch and knocked again. Less than thirty minutes had passed, and William had said he'd be there for at least an hour. He was probably drunk enough to forget what he'd said. Sanjay tried the door to the office—locked—before heading back to the theater.

"He's already gone home," Sanjay reported.

"That's odd." Markus tied up a rope he'd been holding and climbed down. "William never goes home this early."

"Well, he did tonight. He's going to crash and burn sometime soon. Have you seen how much he drinks? He locked the door but forgot to turn off the light of his office, too."

"What?"

"The light was on under the door," Sanjay said.

Markus's face flushed. He cleared his throat. "He locks his door when he's inside and doesn't want to be disturbed." He hurried outside to the winery complex adjoining the theater, Sanjay following on his heels.

Sanjay wasn't sure of the big deal. They all knew William would lock his door since he dealt with the money from the theater.

"William!" Markus shouted, pounding on the door. "Is Lizette in there with you?"

No answer. Markus shook the door handle. The door rattled but didn't give.

"You can open it," Markus said, pointing his finger at Sanjay.

"You mean break in?"

"I know you can do it. I've seen your tricks."

"Illusions," Sanjay corrected him.

"Can you open it or not?"

"I really don't think I should—"

"Oh." Markus crossed his arms. "Your tricks are just tricks then. No skill involved. I get it. I always suspected as much."

"Of course I can do it," Sanjay snapped. He ran his hand across his brow. Or so it would appear to any observer. In reality, two fingertips brushed under the edge of his bowler hat and emerged with a thin lock pick. He knelt down and got to work.

A bead of sweat covered Sanjay's brow before the lock clicked open five minutes later. It was a challenging lock. A bolt. Markus's heavy breathing and pacing behind him wasn't helping. Neither was the fact that the indiscrete couple inside was sure to hear what was going on.

Sanjay pushed open the door. He wasn't looking forward to finding Lizette inside with William. Sanjay straightened up and looked inside. His body relaxed. Lizette wasn't in the office. Neither was William. He must have left early after all.

"That's where you two went," a light voice said from behind. Lizette.

"On a wild goose chase," Sanjay said—right before Markus gasped. That's when Sanjay spotted an outstretched arm on the floor behind the office desk.

Markus rushed forward, Sanjay and Lizette close behind.

"Oh, God," Markus said, kneeling beside William's prostrate body. He leaned his head over William's chest.

A broken wine glass lay on the carpet next to his body, the red wine forming what looked eerily like a pool of blood.

"He's not breathing." Markus shook his head slowly as he raised himself up.

Lizette's scream pierced the air. She raised a shaking hand and pointed at the red liquid on Markus's hands. It was too thick to be red wine.

Sanjay moved closer to William's body. He saw why William wasn't breathing: a dark pool of blood was visible next to William's neck. A pair of sharp pink scissors lay on the floor next to his body.

Rather than fleeing the room, nobody moved. Time and motion took on a sticky quality. After what felt like hours to Sanjay but was probably no more than five or ten seconds, Lizette screamed again. The shrill sound made Sanjay's body shake.

"Don't you see?" She cried out. "The scissors. How did they—?"

"Shut up!" Markus yelled. The scream had broken the spell for all of them. His eyes darted around the room.

"There's no one here," Sanjay said. His voice was steady in spite of his nerves shaking inside. As a stage performer, he was used to putting forth a confident voice no matter how he felt inside. "We've got to call the police."

Lizette nodded. She reached for the phone on the desk.

Sanjay held out his arm to stop her. "Not from here," he said. "Evidence."

Lizette shuddered. "I'll go. Our office isn't far." She left without looking back at the scene.

Sanjay let out a long breath and walked to the doorway. He frowned as he looked at the lock he'd picked. He began pacing slowly in the small area at the front of the office, his eyes scanning the walls of the room. He knew there was nobody hiding in the room, but there was something wrong with the scene...

"I can't believe she killed him," Markus said under his breath.

"What?" Sanjay stopped pacing. "Lizette didn't kill anyone."

"I don't want to believe it, either. But those are her scissors she uses to make scrap books. And you and I were together all evening after we saw William alive and well."

"She couldn't have done it," Sanjay insisted.

"Until a few months ago I would have believed you. But after she had an affair... I just don't know what to believe anymore."

"No," Sanjay said. "I mean I don't see how she could actually have done it—how *anyone* could have done it. This type of lock doesn't automatically lock from behind."

"What are you talking about?"

"The lock on the office door—" Sanjay lowered his voice. "The one you had me pick. It was a *bolt*. That's why it took me so long. It wouldn't lock if someone killed him and slipped out of the room. And there isn't a window in the office. I don't see how anyone could have done it."

"That doesn't make any sense."

"No," Sanjay said. "It doesn't."

* * * *

A hush fell over the room for the second time that evening. Sanjay stood without touching anything, twirling his bowler hat in his hands as they waited for the police. He knew he should be thinking about the tragedy of the murder, but honestly he'd never liked William. William was a crass womanizer who'd gotten the job as theater manager because of family connections in the community. Instead of murder, Sanjay's mind instead drifted back to the illusion he was creating with the fish net.

The fish net was a new addition to one of his mainstay illusions. He was to escape from a trunk that was secured by chains, which he'd done before, and he was adding a fish net covering the entire trunk to make the escape appear impossible.

What had gone wrong earlier that day with the timing of the net drop? The theater was a relatively new building, and in spite of William's incompetence as a manager, it was well kept. There shouldn't have been anything wrong with the equipment. There was only one possible conclusion: the timing problem had to have been simple human error.

Sanjay mulled over the phrase in his mind: *simple human error.* He was no longer sure if he was thinking about the illusion or the murder. There was something off about *both*. As if they were both an illusion...

"Markus," Sanjay said. "What had you wanted to ask William about the levers?"

"What?"

"You said you needed to ask him something. That's why we went to look for him. What did you want to ask him?"

"How can you think about your trick—"

"Illusion," Sanjay said automatically.

"It was nothing. He mentioned a change I'd forgotten about." Markus tugged at his sleeves, avoiding Sanjay's gaze. He'd been able to wipe the blood off his hands with tissue, but bloody spots covered the edge of his right sleeve.

Sanjay took a sharp intake of breath just as Lizette returned to the office. He watched her red-rimmed eyes as the pieces clicked into place in his mind.

"They're on their way," Lizette said weakly.

"Lizette," Sanjay said, his heart speeding up. "Did you see any blood on the carpet when we entered the room?"

"I did," she said, "but I thought it was wine."

"There *was* a pool of wine," Sanjay said slowly. He placed his hat back on his head, thinking hard as he ran his fingers along its crisp rim. "But did you notice *two* pools of red when we walked in?"

"No." Lizette sniffled. "Just one."

"Me, too," Sanjay said. "It was only the wine at first. Not blood. Because we had the timing wrong."

"The timing?"

Sanjay's heart was pounding in his chest now. He hoped his voice didn't betray him. Unlike the stage, this was real life—and he was standing in a room with a real life murderer.

"William locked himself into his room," Sanjay said, "as he usually did, and passed out from a drug that had been put into his wine. Markus was adamant I get him into this office—*before William woke up*."

"That's ridiculous," Markus said. "I was with you all evening."

"Except for when you went to get William that first time, when he returned with a glass of wine and was already walking unsteadily. You needed me as your alibi. You knew he always locked his office door—and you knew I know how to pick a lock. You could be with me all evening setting up, and then have us discover the body together. You weren't counting on the fact that the lock of the office being one that couldn't be locked automatically when someone left the office. You wanted to implicate Lizette, using her scissors, and knowing you had a better alibi than her. You had to do it, because you were the one with the motive."

"My scissors," Lizette said, her voice breaking. "You mean Markus—"

"But you said it yourself, I was with you!" Markus said to Sanjay. "I *do* have an alibi."

"Except for the fact that William wasn't *dead* before we walked into that room," Sanjay said. "Only drugged. That's why he was acting so sluggish when he came into the theater. The drug was already in his wine. When you rushed over to him just now to supposedly check if he was breathing, *that's* when you stuck the scissors in his neck. You could easily hide scissors in your hand under that ridiculously long-sleeved shirt—with your alibi standing right here next to you."

"I got blood on my hands when I was trying to save him," Markus said, his voice quivering.

"Then I suppose there won't be traces of a knock-out drug in his system?"

Markus didn't respond.

"You pushed my buttons just right, too," Sanjay said, shaking his head. "Egging me on so I'd go looking for William, and so I'd prove I could unlock this door."

"Markus?" Lizette whispered. "How could you?"

Markus' eyes narrowed as he faced Lizette. "How could *I*? *You're* the one who did this. Did you think I'd let you get away with the affair? That I'd let *either of you* get away with it?"

Before Sanjay realized what was happening, Markus lunged toward William's body. He was going for the sharp scissors.

Standing in the doorway, Sanjay knew he wouldn't have time to reach Markus before he grabbed the scissors. But there was something else he could do. He lifted the hat from his head and flung it at Markus, spinning it like a Frisbee. He aimed for Markus's head. The throw almost succeeded. It hit his neck.

Sanjay cringed as Markus cried out. Pushed off balance, he fell on top of William's desk, just short of where William lay dead. Sanjay ran forward and snatched up his hat. He quickly pulled a piece of rope from inside the hat and bound Markus' hands behind his back.

"What the hell?" Markus asked in a daze, blinking furiously. "What hit me?"

Sanjay finished tying the knot—more tightly than was strictly necessary—and stood back to look at his handiwork. He picked up his hat and knocked his knuckles on the rim of his specially constructed hat. His fingers rapped as loudly as if he'd knocked on a door. "I knew there was a reason I never wanted you to know the secrets of my illusions."

Markus groaned.

Sanjay lifted his magician's hat onto his head.

FISHING FOR JUSTICE

BY HARRIETTE SACKLER

Jamie Keegan sat at a table in an Ocean City pizza joint. The petite young girl looked far too worn for her fifteen years. Her faded jeans and oversized hoodie camouflaged a childlike body. Light brown hair hung limply over downcast eyes. Jamie's hands were clenched in her lap and her face was expressionless. She'd quickly learned to avoid the painful consequences should she fail to do what was expected of her.

Across the table, Mac gobbled down pizza as if it were his last meal, and Jamie could only hope that it was. Crumbs and tomato sauce clung to his hairy face. Everything about him was disgusting: his filthy clothes, his unwashed smell, his bloated belly. They all turned her stomach.

Jamie glanced to the right but didn't dare raise her head. A middle-aged woman at the next table stared at her with a quizzical look, probably wondering why such a young girl was with the likes of the fat and ugly biker type.

"Please," Jamie silently screamed. "Help me!"

But within seconds, the woman returned to the book next to her plate and didn't glance at Jamie again. No surprises there.

Funny, Jamie used to think that her life at home was hell on earth. A junkie mother. Welfare checks that barely covered the cost of food, and that was on good days when the money didn't wind up in a dealer's pocket. The string of crappy apartments that lasted only as long as the rent was paid, then the middle-of-the-night exodus before the marshal came with the eviction order. She vaguely remembered a time before that when life was good, but only now and then did scraps of happy memories surface.

So, when Mac rumbled into Takoma Park, Jamie thought he was a savior, come to take her away from her lousy life. Little did she know.

"You eat now," Mac ordered as he threw two slices of pizza on the plate in front of her. "Make it fast."

Jamie gobbled the food, not knowing when she'd have the chance to eat again. She knew full well that her very existence was dependent on Mac's generosity. He told her when to eat, when to sleep, when to speak. He controlled every part of her life. That's how it was in biker gangs. Women, or more often than not, girls, were property and did what they were told. Or else.

When Mac rose from his chair and headed for the exit, Jamie quickly followed. When he mounted his enormous Harley, she jumped on behind.

She used to think it was a big deal to roar around the country with the Devils, but now it terrified her. She learned real fast that the world she'd left was a helluva lot better than the nightmare she lived in now.

* * * *

That night, Jamie lay on the floor next to the single bed where Mac sprawled. She knew that all the beer he'd consumed and weed he'd smoked probably had put him out for the night. The air in the rundown trailer was musty and stale, the few pieces of furniture soiled and torn but, as she had learned, gang members weren't choosy about accommodations. This place belonged to a guy who'd been locked up for cocaine trafficking and served as a crash pad by bikers passing through the area.

Jamie stared at the stained ceiling listening to Mac's watery snores. As the minutes passed, she decided that if she didn't chance getting away from him now, she probably wouldn't see her sixteenth birthday. Girls who hooked up with the Devils, by choice or not, disappeared within a few years. They were never talked about again. It was as if they never existed at all. No tears. No mourning. No nothing.

Jamie took a deep breath and rose soundlessly from the floor. Since they traveled around the country with only enough belongings to fit in a roll on the back of the bike, they slept in their clothes. She crept into the front room of the trailer, slipping on her worn shoes and wrapping her tiny purse around her wrist. It was the only personal possession she was allowed to keep.

As she put her hand on the doorknob, she felt an arm wrap around her neck. She tried to scream. She clawed at the viselike grip, and blessedly never heard the sickening sound of her neck breaking. Nor did she know that, a short time later, her weighted young body would be dumped into the bay, her little purse floating away.

* * * *

On a Tuesday morning, Eddie Bell stood at the rail of the Route 50 bridge, his line cast into the bay. He came here once a week, not so much for the fishing as for the chance to people gaze and occasionally shoot the bull with the regulars who hung out on the bridge.

For the hundredth time, he reflected on the new life he and Peg shared. When he'd retired after thirty years on the job, they sold their house in Silver Spring, packed up their belongings, and moved down to the Eastern Shore.

At first, Eddie wasn't sure if he'd adjust to a life of leisure after so many years as a cop. He knew too many guys who'd wasted away from boredom after turning over their badges. But truth be told, he never spent a day with nothing to do. Eddie had many interests and an insatiable curiosity that had served him well as a cop.

He also had a love of fishing. He'd become quite an expert and was the go-to guy for anyone who needed advice on all things fishing-related.

And, Eddie had a talent for writing. He kept journals with story ideas and descriptions of people he encountered. He told himself that someday he might actually sit down and write a book about his life in law enforcement. After all, he couldn't say he didn't have the time now.

Several months after Eddie and Peg settled into their new home, he attended a freelance writing workshop at the library. It was taught by the editor-in-chief of the local newspaper, whom Eddie had chatted with at several social events. This fortuitous encounter resulted in an offer of a weekly fishing column entitled "The Fishnet." Eddie's column took off, and he became a bit of a local celebrity.

All of a sudden, Eddie felt a familiar tug on his fishing line. He began reeling in what he hoped would be a good-sized catch. He scooped it up with a net and dumped it on the ground.

"What the hell?" He stared down at a sodden pouch. He picked up a small rectangular plastic purse that had somehow remained intact despite the ravages of the bay. With a bit of effort, he was able to open the clasp and peer inside. He pulled out a plastic comb, a badly rusted neck chain with a pendant of what looked like a caricature of the devil, and a laminated school identification card that listed the name and address of a middle school in Prince George's County, a student's name, and a small photo. The student's name was listed as Jamie Keegan, and a beautiful young girl smiled at him. Eddie stared at the face in the picture for quite a while.

* * * *

The first thing Eddie did when he got home was check for telephone listings for Keegans in the general area of the Prince George's middle school. He placed calls to the few listings, but had no luck. Eddie then placed a call to the local police headquarters. His buddy, Chief Chuck Lewin, took his call right away. After the usual inquiries about family, health, and life in general that begins conversations between friends, Eddie asked if he could drop by to meet with Chuck in about an hour. With no questions asked, Chuck encouraged Eddie to come on over.

When Eddie arrived, he headed straight for Chuck's office. The chief was talking on the phone and gestured for Eddie to take a seat. Considering the number of files piled on his desk, Chuck's office was relatively neat and orderly. But there was no doubt that its occupant was one busy guy. Eddie knew the volume of work that plagued police departments, whether they were in big cities or relatively small resort towns. There was just never enough time.

When Chuck completed his phone call, he turned to Eddie.

"Hey, buddy, it's good to see you. You're looking younger by the day, my man. The good life agrees with you. Now, tell me what you need."

Eddie placed a plastic bag containing the little purse on Chuck's desk. He quickly explained how it had come into his possession.

"I know how swamped you are, but I'd like to ask a favor. I want to follow up on this kid. Her address and number, her family. You know the usual background stuff. I'd also like the necklace checked out to see if it has any significance beyond a young kid's idea of cool."

"No problem, Eddie. I'll have one of the guys get working on it right away. Shouldn't take too long. But I'd bet there's more to this than you're telling me."

Eddie chuckled but quickly turned serious.

"Once a cop, always a cop. And, I'll tell you, Chuck, I've got a funny feeling about this. Let's see what you come up with. Then we'll talk."

* * * *

Eddie headed home with photocopies of the school I.D. and the necklace. He didn't expect to hear from Chuck until the following day and could only hope that any information the chief could provide would be good news.

Just after 6:00 p.m., as he and Peg were about to sit down to dinner, Chuck called and asked Eddie to come over to his office as soon as he could. The summons wasn't a good omen, and Eddie feared what he was going to learn. Ten minutes later, he was again sitting in front of Chuck's desk.

"This is a real hard luck story, Ed. Seems Susan Keegan was a junkie, picked up a coupla times for possession. OD'd eight months ago and her thirteen-year-old twin boys were placed in foster care pending the possible location of relatives. Jamie had left home, whereabouts unknown. No missing persons report was filed. The boys said their mom figured Jamie had run away, and she'd eventually come home."

"Aw jeez…" Eddie whispered .He could feel his heart pounding.

"Now, here's something interesting on the necklace. Seems that exact figure is the symbol used by a biker gang called the Devils. Real rough trade out of Texas, not big, but a nasty bunch of thugs. Travel around the country. We've had them come through here. Mostly into prostitution and drugs. Seems likely your girl got hooked up with a very bad crowd."

As Chuck spoke, Eddie turned pale and shrunk in his chair.

"Shit. How's this gonna be handled?"

"For now, as a missing person. We've contacted the FBI Gang Investigation Unit in Baltimore and are waiting to hear back from them. Our guys are already on the street checking out known crash pads for undesirables that pass through the city. We'll be sending out boats to check the bay. Very little doubt there's a crime here and we're pulling out all the stops. Thank God you found that purse, Eddie. Chances are a civilian wouldn't have known to turn it in to us."

Chuck leaned forward, elbows on his desk. He certainly could tell that his friend was in a lot of distress. But he needed to know why. Sure, this situation would affect anyone. But Eddie was a seasoned police officer and had spent his whole career investigating the worst kinds of crimes.

"Buddy, I need to know the rest. This is personal, and I want you to tell me about it."

Eddie looked at Chuck with tortured eyes. Looking down at his hands, he slowly began to talk.

"One freezing, winter night twelve years ago, my partner and I had the unfortunate task of informing a young wife that her husband had been fatally injured in a car accident. As we tried to comfort her, without any success, a little girl in pink pajamas, clutching a worn teddy bear, came into the room.

"She greeted us, introduced herself as Jamie, and asked who we were. Then glancing at her mother, her face filled with great concern, Jamie wanted to know why her mommy was crying. I explained to Jamie that her mommy just heard some very sad news.

"That beautiful little girl went over to her mother and gave her a big hug. 'Don't cry, Mommy,' she said. 'It'll all be better when daddy gets home.'"

Neither Eddie nor Chuck said a word for several minutes. Anyone who thought that cops weren't affected by the tragedy they saw every day knew shit about police work.

"You know, through the years I've thought about that little girl. I've wondered whatever happened to her and her family. Where was she? Was she doing well? Was she happy? But no matter how many times she came to mind, I never tried to find the answers. I never had the time. I was always wrapped up with the next case, the next investigation. If I had, maybe I could have done something...."

"Eddie, we all have stories about the cases that rip us apart. We're human. We do our jobs as best we can. Protect the public, investigate crime, catch the bad guys. We have to leave the rest to others and hope they do their jobs well, too."

Eddie gave a slight nod but remained unconvinced.

"Okay," Chuck said, "here's what you can do now. Dedicate your next column to Jamie. She's a missing person who is known to have been in Ocean City. Tell your story. Include her photo. Ask anyone who has any information on Jamie to contact you. Keep us in the loop. Christ, I'm preaching to the choir here."

"Thanks, Chuck." Eddie rose from his chair and shook his friend's hand. "I'm gonna head home and get the column to the paper right away."

* * * *

As soon as Eddie's column appeared, calls and e-mails poured in. His readers were touched by Jamie's story and vowed to keep their eyes open for any sign of the young girl. It wasn't until three days later that Eddie hit pay dirt. A call came in from a woman who furnished critical information on Jamie.

"Mr. Bell? My name is Lucille Simpson. My husband and I have a condo up on 125th Street. My husband always reads your column, and he shared it with me this morning. I had to call you right away because I saw Jamie."

"Thank you, Mrs. Simpson. I'm glad you've contacted me. Can you tell me where and when you saw her?"

"It was seven weeks ago. March 29th to be exact. I know because it was the day before my husband's birthday, and I was out shopping for some gifts. I'd stopped at Pizza 'n' Pasta up on Philadelphia Avenue for some lunch. A young girl and a horrid, dirty-looking man were sitting at a nearby table. She looked so sad. And defeated. Her companion was truly disgusting, with long greasy hair pulled back in a ponytail, tattoos all over his arms and, I swear, an evil face that gave me the chills. It just didn't feel right, but what could I do? He could have been her father or uncle. He didn't do anything wrong. But I couldn't get that girl out of my mind."

"Now, Mrs. Simpson, did you happen to notice any jewelry on either of them?"

"The girl had no jewelry on. That man wore a string of earrings on one ear and a leather band on one wrist. Nothing more that I could see."

"Did you happen to notice what kind of tattoos he had on his arms? Were they pictures? Names? Objects?" Eddie was positive by now that Mrs. Simpson was the real deal.

"Well, let me see. To tell you the truth, most of them were too small for me to see from where I was sitting. But you know I was able to see two of them. One was a snake wrapped around a heart with some writing in the center. The other was a creepy creature that looked just like a devil. Good lord, can you imagine?"

"Did they talk, say anything at all?"

"Nothing until he threw some pizza on her plate and ordered her to eat. I tell you, that girl should have gotten up and walked away from that brute!"

"Mrs. Simpson, do you think you would recognize this man if you saw him again?"

"Mr. Bell, there's one thing I know for sure. If I live to be two hundred, I'll never, ever, forget that face."

Bingo! Eddie smiled for the first time in days.

"Mrs. Simpson, I can't tell you how helpful you've been. Now, I ask that you meet me at the police station as soon as possible...."

* * * *

In just a matter of several weeks, a lot of good police work paid off. Chuck Lewin insured that Eddie was included in the investigation every step of the way. Eddie was exceptionally grateful to his friend for keeping him in the loop.

Using the tattoo as a point of reference, the police showed Mrs. Simpson mug shots of known members of the Devils, and she unequivocally identified Lawrence McCarthy, a.k.a. Mac. He had an extensive record and had spent more than half his life locked up. Why he was still on the streets was anybody's guess.

The FBI notified every law enforcement department in the country seeking information on the whereabouts of Lawrence McCarthy. They quickly heard from a town outside of Oklahoma City where a stoned Mac had been arrested for critically injuring a resident whom he had picked a fight with in a local bar. The victim was in critical condition and not expected to make it. Mac was going to be put away for the rest of his life, which would probably end with a lethal injection. Meanwhile, the FBI would continue to investigate the case against Mac for Jamie's death.

The police located an old trailer near the bay that was on their radar because they'd picked up several unsavory characters there for a variety of offenses, including members of the Devils. This discovery pointed them toward an area of the bay where they could focus their search.

When Jamie's body was brought up from the bay, very close to where it'd been dumped, it broke Eddie's heart. With Peg's blessing, he paid for all the funeral expenses and hosted a graveside service attended by an enormous number of locals who had read Eddie's column and wanted pay their respects to the young girl who died so tragically in their city.

* * * *

Six months to the day after finding Jamie's little purse on his fishing line, Eddie sat in his beach chair on the Route 50 bridge. He hadn't been back to the bridge since that day. Eddie had never been a religious man. All the cruelty and evil he'd seen over the years made it hard for him to wrap his mind around the notion of a benevolent god. But Eddie wasn't able to accept that he, of all people, just happened to find Jamie's purse. Coincidence? Maybe, but hard to believe. He figured he might never resolve it in his mind, but who knew?

Eddie hadn't been able to save Jamie, but he had come to the realization that he could do other things. Jamie's brothers were still in foster care and Eddie had gotten approval to visit them once a month as a mentor. They were good kids, and even in light of their hard life, had good futures ahead of them. And, after all, he certainly had the time.

Eddie pulled the school ID out of his pocket and looked into the haunted eyes of a beautiful young girl caught in the net of family tragedy. Then he folded his chair and headed for his car. In half an hour, he was due at a meeting of local leaders who were interested in creating a youth center in a church not far from the bridge. And his copy for "The Fishnet" was due this afternoon.

CLEAN

BY STEVE SHROTT

Pamela rushed inside her apartment and removed her red pumps and fishnet stockings. She tossed the stockings into the sink and began scrubbing the mud off them. It had been a stormy night and when she tried to take a shortcut home, she had gotten all dirty.

She didn't like dirty.

Pamela divided everything into clean and dirty. The day was clean, the night, dirty. People could be clean or dirty and some could start off one way and end up quite another—like her Uncle Ed. He always gave her candy when she visited him, patted her on the shoulder to let her know she was okay. She had always loved seeing him until that day when he came too close to her and…she didn't want to think about that. From then on, he was dirty, dirty, dirty.

Pamela didn't know why she cared so much about such things. Maybe from her dad, a cold alcoholic who punished her if the house wasn't perfectly tidy when he came home from a night at the bar. Then he would tie her up with a torn pair of dirty fishnets and lock her in that dark, damp cellar to teach her a lesson. She'd scream but he wouldn't let her out until the next day.

She would have felt completely alone if not for Jessie.

Pamela removed her hose from the sink and took them into the bathroom. As she hung them up to dry, she thought about Dr. Reynolds. With his white jacket and gleaming smile, he was the cleanest person she knew. The fact that he saw her in the newly painted Warwick Hospital also helped. Pamela called him her mental health professional; she hated calling him a psychiatrist as that indicated she was crazy, and she knew she wasn't. She looked forward to seeing Dr. Reynolds today, to tell him the good news.

She was about to leave the bathroom to get ready when her eyes flickered over to her fishnets. She shook her head.

Not now.

Pamela dressed, headed for the hospital. She walked in, feeling good being around all that fresh white paint. She took the elevator to the third floor, scrunching up in the back, away from the others, trying to be invisible. Then she marched down the hall to the doctor's office. His receptionist, Angela, greeted her with a smile. Pamela intended to smile back as she usually did, but then she saw it—a tiny red speck in the middle of

Angela's white jacket. Was it tomato soup or blood? Pamela turned away in disgust, heart beating fast. She felt nauseated.

Her nausea went away as soon as she sat in the doctor's bright waiting room. A few moments later, he called her in.

She examined the chair that she usually occupied, then, as always, pulled out her cleaning solution. She scrubbed it for a few moments, sat down. "Hi, Dr. Reynolds."

"Hello, Pamela, how are you today?"

"Good." She smiled.

"Are you enjoying being out of the hospital?"

She nodded. "I just had to tell you, Doctor, I met someone new."

The doctor's brow creased. "Oh?"

"Yes, last night. I went to a bar and this man came up to me. He said I seemed nice."

"I see."

"He was very handsome and he took my phone number."

The doctor tented his fingers as if they were a house that could fall apart at any moment. "You know this is wrong, Pamela."

"It's not wrong."

"We've discussed this before. You shouldn't be going out right now."

"Why not?"

The doctor pressed his lips together. "Because of the murder."

"I told you I had nothing to do with it."

"I understand that's the way you feel. But there is going to be a retrial and the court asked me to spend the next several weeks evaluating you." He pushed back his chair, stood up. Pamela's chair screamed as she forced it back. "You know what that means, right?"

"Yes."

"Of course there's no evidence you did anything wrong. However, that girl says she saw you and Hastings together on the night he'd been murdered."

"My lawyer proved she lied."

The doctor took a deep breath, nodded.

The session continued but Pamela didn't say much or listen very closely to what the doctor said. He had ruined it for her. Would she have to keep hearing about this damn case? How many times did she have to explain that she didn't kill that man? Was everyone against her? Where was Jessie?

She did remember the doctor saying she shouldn't go out at night until he gave her the okay. So she went home, watched some TV, tried to write in her diary.

As the day passed from clean to dirty, she couldn't take her mind off her fishnets.

They beckoned her.

She took off her shoes, slid the stockings onto her bare feet, up her long legs. They felt warm. Powerful. The great thing about fishnets was that they made her feel like a new person. A better version of herself. Stronger. Not scaredy-cat Pamela anymore…but fearless Jessie.

After she finished dressing, she took the subway down to The Stadium, a bar near the docks frequented by a rough crowd. She sat at a table in the back and ordered a beer, not caring if it interfered with the medicine Dr. Reynolds had prescribed her.

She chugged the first beer down and instantly felt better. She decided to open one more button on her already open blouse. Jessie liked to show off her body. Then she smiled at the handsome blonde man sitting at another table. He moved toward her.

"Mind if I sit down, sexy?" he said.

She shrugged. Jessie wouldn't answer him directly.

His eyes ran down her body. "So what's your name?"

"Guess."

He paused a moment, then spoke. "I'm Dom. Never seen you here before."

"Never been." She didn't say anything more. Playing with him. Waiting for him to make the next move. He didn't.

She waited another moment, then forced her lips on his—tight. It felt good and evil and scary and wonderful and…dirty. A moment later, she got bold and stuck her tongue into his mouth. They kissed for a while. Hungry mouths.

Suddenly, Dom pulled away from her. "Do you want to go?"

"Where?"

"My place."

"I don't know…"

"C'mon baby, you know you wanna play."

She kissed him again hard and in the next moment they left together, hands roaming.

It happened fast. They entered his room and he tossed her onto the bed. He stared, transfixed by her body. Jessie liked being enjoyed— craved it, yearned for it deeply. He touched her, then slowly peeled off her fishnets.

* * * *

Pamela sat in front of a frowning Dr. Reynolds. He was holding a newspaper.

"What's wrong, Doctor?"

He stared at her, his face white. "Another man was strangled with fishnet stockings last night. The same way as Hastings." He inhaled sharply. "You didn't go out, did you, Pamela?"

Pamela cringed, noticing a smear on the newspaper. Then she gazed into the doctor's bright blue eyes, feeling good, knowing it wasn't her who went out last night.

"No, I didn't."

INSIDE JOB

BY MYSTI BERRY

Ashley cracked her knuckles above the keyboard and waited in the chilly room, computer monitors glowing in the dark. She breathed deeply, pumping oxygen into her brain. When Gary Fish showed up at his island home thousands of miles away, she couldn't afford slow responses. Her enemy, one of the sexiest figureheads of the new technocracy, was wicked smart when he wasn't drunk.

He had started out as her CEO, not her enemy, until It happened. Well, until she understood his connection to It. Now, Mr. Fish was scheduled to arrive in St. Lucia at 3:00 PM local time. Ashley hoped that when she was through with him, he'd wish that he were dead, too.

She stared at the surveillance camera feed from his home security system for any sign of him. It looked like a still picture—green-blue ocean in the background, a crisp new driveway and high fence in the foreground. She stared at the scene, squinting at the sun dogs that sparkled off the shiny brass of the gate. It looked so warm and clean there.

As if hired for their charming looks, a burst of schoolchildren in dark uniforms ran past the rich man's gate to their smaller homes up the road. Ashley had explored the island using satellite maps on the Internet, and discovered that the rich and poor lived impossibly close together. She wondered why the local people didn't rise up and take away the lovely homes and alluring toys of the rich.

They were so few.

A deep green Land Rover crunched up to the entrance gate. Ashley blinked, frozen for a moment. It was actually happening. Everything she'd done up to now could be abandoned. Hacking. Snooping. Writing little blocks of code here and there and inserting them. Using OPP, other people's passwords. But once she started with him, she'd have to finish Gary Fish.

She tapped a key in her darkened office. The monitor changed to the security camera in Gary's garage. He was alone. With a rush of heat to her face, Ashley realized she had no contingency for Gary being with someone else. Her finger hovered over the keyboard, shaking. Had she really thought of everything? Go or no go, as they said at work.

Still unsure, she watched Gary preen at his thinning hair in his rearview mirror. He stepped out of his absurdly large vehicle and tugged off his expensive suit jacket, losing his balance in the process. Pretty jet lagged, or maybe pretty drunk. It must be hotter than hell in that garage,

Ashley thought, watching the sweat flower on Gary's expensive shirt. She saw him jiggle his own tummy, as if trying to decide if he was putting on weight.

His vanity helped her decide. Go.

Gary's garage door slid closed, and fluorescent lights automatically flickered on, just as they had been programmed to. It looked like a movie set—not a tool out of place in the spacious garage. Her fingers danced over the keyboard as Gary moved toward the connecting door to the house. Accessing the new home's computer system, she locked the rolling door and the connecting door to the house.

She heard him swear and stumble as he lumbered toward the connecting door. She quickly tapped a few more keys. This triggered the lockdown feature—any "intruder" trying to get in would feel a shock from whatever door or window he tried to escape through, until the cops came. But of course she'd fixed it so the cops would not be alerted.

"Ouch!" Gary stuffed his shocked hand under the opposite armpit, and swore for quite a while. She waited for him to wind down.

He fumbled for his cell phone but she dialed the number before he could call anyone.

"You are in some serious shit." She used a voice filter, but she needn't have bothered. He had no idea who she was, eight or eighteen levels down. Her boss had told her, "You're one of the ones I don't have to worry about." And given her a few raises or bonuses in her ten years at the company. Because at Fish.net, not causing trouble wasn't really valued.

"Do you know who I *am*? You're in serious shit!"

"You shouldn't have used your company's network to wire your private home's privacy features. Quite the security risk."

"Who is this!" Ragged, savage. This was the Gary she'd heard about, legendary for throwing things—he'd once heaved a laptop at the head of his own legal team, who had been trying to tell him something he didn't want to hear.

"We can't tell you that." Ashley wanted to sound like a force larger than one little employee. She didn't have a lot of experience lying, but she didn't want Gary to realize she was alone.

He snarled incoherently and disconnected. Ashley had a virus ready to install on his phone to kill it the minute he turned it back on. But she didn't have to do that. The bad-tempered man threw the phone at the garage door, shattering it.

She also controlled the intercom system. It seemed like something her ancient aunt and uncle in Santa Rosa would have installed, not a technocrat in the new millennium. Apparently he didn't know that in the last few years, St. Lucia's Internet penetration had soared to 88% of the population. Ashley had learned a lot while preparing for battle.

"Bad flight, Gary?" Her voice, distorted to sound like a boxer's from Brooklyn, snapped Gary out of his temper tantrum.

"Is that Security? The house has gone haywire!"

"This isn't Security. This is the voice of all the people you've crushed on the way up."

"Michael? Is this a joke? I'm just trying to get in the house and get clean."

"It's not Michael or any of your executives, Gary. We've decided it's time to expose you for the information imperialist that you are. Now I'm going to take the shock off your doorknob. I suggest you go inside. If you try to break out, I'll burn your house to the ground. And as your construction team should have told you, the house is designed to keep intruders trapped."

Gary's response was to leap into the Land Rover and rev the engine.

Ashley gasped and fumbled for another control, holding her breath. With a few keystrokes, she killed his engine just as he dropped it into reverse—just before he blew through his own garage door.

The expletives were long and loud as Gary threw himself out of the Land Rover and bellowed in the air. She saw his face bloat with rage, until he waved his hands in the air and then crashed tight fists of rage down on the hood of his own car, over and over.

She waited, grateful for the chance to think.

The humidity and heat of the island must be killing him. She clicked on the air conditioning, hoping he'd respond with a return to rationality. It made her momentarily sick to think she had all the same instincts as a predator working a kidnap victim. She stuffed the thought away, along with all the others.

"Where are you?" Gary asked, his voice raspy from screaming. He looked around the garage wildly. His house was so new, she realized, he had no idea where the cameras were. "If you're smart enough to hack into my house, you're smart enough to know that you are leaving a trail."

"We don't care about that. We care about the people you've crushed. You've hurt too many people." Ashley cut her audio when she felt her voice catch. Breathe, she told herself. Just breathe through it.

"So what?" Gary's face relaxed. He knew how to negotiate. How could she make him feel vulnerable when she kept making mistakes like this?

Gary saw something in the garage, but she couldn't see what as he ducked behind the Land Rover to fetch it. Then she heard the clang of metal on metal. He was prying open runners along the door. If she didn't stop him, he might be able to pop the door off its tracks and escape.

Ashley clicked for a minute to the feed from outside the house. No locals hanging around to hear him. But if another flock of children ran by, they might hear him yelling.

She clicked back to Gary, who had made a small dent in the runner. His shirt was soaked with sweat, and he grunted as he worked.

It wasn't going as she had planned. She had expected to pull digital trick after trick in rapid sequence, to overwhelm him before he could think about who was doing it or how to get out of it. But of course, he was familiar with doing battle, and she was a newbie, stomach churning and nerves shattered. But she'd rather die than let Gary know she was frightened.

"I'm going to push a button to start your house burning, and then I'm going to walk away, unless you drop that and go into the house now." She had no idea how to burn down the house, but she hoped Gary wouldn't gamble on that.

Gary breathed raggedly for a long moment. Then he dropped the heavy metal crowbar and shuffled toward the connecting door into the house. He took one last look around, and then quickly tapped the door-knob. No shock this time.

Ashley switched the camera feed to indoors. She watched Gary grab a cold beer from the spotless refrigerator, and then throw himself onto a couch in the living room area. Normally it was open to the air, but had been shut up and locked against intruders until his first visit. The locks were on the inside, all electronic. She had altered the pass codes.

Gary mumbled something. It sounded like, "I knew this house would kill me."

Ashley felt her throat ache with sudden grief. She trembled, remembering the horrible smell and the twisted, bloated corpse, leaning to one side, in her father's favorite chair. It had taken her father's place, she'd thought at first, shock suffusing her brain.

"Hurry up, I need a shower," Gary said after a large swallow of expensive lager. He still thought she was something he could dismiss.

"Gary, we need you to admit that you've rigged the game. You and your Richie Rich friends. Just admit that you take full advantage. You let the *hoi polloi* believe they have a shot, but these days the pots of gold are all wired with burglar alarms and lobbyists and men behind the scenes, rigging tax laws and all the rest of it. Just admit it and we're done."

"You don't have the balls to start your own company, and then you come after me? There would be no Fish.net without me, no way for thousands of people to earn a living, millions to make their businesses more profitable with our software. Stop this crap now, while you have a short list of felonies to do time for."

"That's your position, Gary? It's a level playing field, and the little guy has only himself to blame?" Ashley trembled with anger and frustration.

A large screen television started up. She had figured out how to send a recorded stream to his set, using the equipment for renting movies installed on his state-of-the-art flat screen.

"So what," was all Gary said, as snippet after snippet of him throwing plates, screaming at underlings, and grabbing his admin's ass played in an endless loop. The images, stolen from his own company's security cameras, were grainy and herky-jerky.

"You look like a convenience-store thief."

"You can't share that without exposing yourself to enough felony counts to go to jail forever—and there's no provenance without your identity," Gary said, and then took a lusty draw from his beer.

"There's a smoking gun, Gary."

A silence stretched between them. She watched as he took a sip from his beer and waited. His cool act was cracking, she thought, watching him scrape the label off his beer bottle.

Ashley waited, knowing he would feel just a little less in control if he spoke first. Finally, he said, "It's capitalism, you spoiled brat. And it's better than coal mining or whatever else you did before I grew a company that can pay you the best wages in the valley. If you don't like it, grow a pair and build your own empire." Gary punctuated his bravado by throwing his empty beer bottle at the television.

"I know someone who did just that. But your style of capitalism killed him. You *killed* him, sure as if you'd pulled the trigger." Ashley fought back the image of her dead father's body, struggled to keep her voice calm. She realized too late that she'd switched from "we" to "I."

Gary swore at her using colorful words, new to her. At last he said, "Who are you talking about?"

Ashley hesitated. If she told him, he might figure out who she was. If she didn't, he might not confess. And then she realized, he probably didn't even know. He had destroyed her father, and he didn't even know.

"One sad old man blows his own head off, shamed beyond redemption because he lost it all on your 'level playing field' and you don't even know who he was." She cut the mike, and cried until she could control her voice again. "You bargained with a man to buy his company, but you never meant to purchase it. He put himself into hundreds of thousands of dollars of debt to make the changes you said you'd need in order to buy his little innovation, but the entire time, you were just trying to get another company to lower their price. Admit it, Gary, you never meant to buy Variable Densities."

"The VD guys knew the risks in a negotiation like that. It's not like I reneged on a contract. I'm guessing you're this guy's son or something. Well, I still say, grow a pair and build your own company."

"How can I, Gary?" Ashley said, savoring the knowledge that he didn't even know her gender. "It's not a level playing field. You rig the elections, you rig the tax code, and you rig every deal in your favor. No matter who it kills. Kills."

Instead of answering, Gary made a break for the garage. He barreled through the door before Ashley could arm the shock mechanism. He grabbed his laptop out of the Land Rover before she could lock the doors.

Panicked, she couldn't remember his laptop network name. She searched frantically, desperate to shut him down. He stood at a shiny new workbench in the garage and typed away. She couldn't think what he was doing, had no idea how to stop him. She hadn't expected that he'd know the nuts and bolts of his own company.

An automated alarm fired a warning message to her. Someone was trying to find her spoofed identity on the network. Gary had gotten close to her in less than sixty seconds. As she worked frantically to log out, retreat, and cover her hacks, his automated detectives rushed through the Internet after her, relentlessly pursuing her. He laughed at her from his garage in St. Lucia, but didn't take any time to make speeches. They were locked in a life and death struggle.

Alarms sounded, dashboards flashed red on her computer screens. Ashley's cave of power was flaming out.

She deployed a virus toward his laptop. She held her breath, but he didn't notice as it downloaded itself onto his laptop. He was on the same technology high that they often were, obsessed with finding and fixing a bug in the code.

"I don't know who you are yet, but I'll find you, and I'll crush you," he growled.

She started his Land Rover. The expensive engine was whisper-quiet. Gary didn't notice, he was too obsessed with finding her in cyberspace.

She said, "Just admit that you take things that don't belong to you. That people die because you feel entitled to everything you want. Do that, and I'll disappear forever." Ashley was still frantically trying to cut Gary off, block his access to the cloud.

"I've nearly got you, you coward. Whoever you're moping about having died, he was a loser. He trusted me because he wanted to, and he should have known better. The world is better off without losers like that mucking up the system. A system that reward men with balls, who go after what they want and let the lawyers clean up the mess."

"Because it's a level playing field?"

"Of course it's not. It never was. It never will be. From Tea Partiers who don't know they've been bought and sold by the Koch brothers to Liberal Dems who keep voting for Senators who keep voting for war, it's all about those who have it. If you choose to believe the fantasy of upward mobility, in the face of all reason and evidence, that is hardly my fault. Nor is it my fault that some stupid moron fell for my negotiation tactics. He should have known better."

Gary stopped typing when his laptop chimed the announcement of a new email message.

"I've been recording our conversation, Gary. That email is a link to the YouTube video of your more colorful behavior, and your last speech." It had only taken a few seconds to upload each sequence to the corporate YouTube portal.

"A fart in a hurricane," he answered, tossing the laptop aside.

"The rich stay rich, when there are so many more of us than you, by never admitting that the game is rigged. Hey, we have a few hundred hits already. I think you're going to go viral, and I think your rich friends are going to cleave unto themselves."

For once, Gary seemed empty of epithets. Ashley continued, "Do you want to turn off your engine or let it keep filling your garage with carbon monoxide?"

"You've locked the car doors! Unlock them!"

"It's a level playing field. You figure it out."

Ashley turned off everything then, and began cleaning the servers. A charity for the aged, her father's favorite, would pick up the equipment in the morning.

When she got home, she would send a shocked email to her boss, with a link to the YouTube video, and resign "under the circumstances." No one would think twice about the quiet geek girl in the aftermath of a technocrat's meltdown.

She doubted that Gary would succumb to the fumes. But he would have hell to pay when the corporate auditors found that hundreds of thousands of dollars of money was missing, apparently transferred offshore by Gary himself. She'd been moving the money around for months. It would take them forever to trace it, long enough for the charity recipients to have spent the money. Like Bernie Madoff in reverse. She had been scrupulous about taking none of it herself.

She smiled at the night watchman as she left the rented office for the last time, thinking of a brief holiday, somewhere tropical, perhaps. The vision of her father's dead body in his recliner, pistol on the floor beside him, had already started to fade.

JOHN CALVIN CAN BITE ME

BY MICHELLE MARKEY BUTLER

"Excuse me, miss." The woman's hand tapped the library counter, then fluttered away. I leaned forward to watch its flight. It landed over the ear of a small child, joining its fellow clapped against the other. "Do you have any books about Easter that don't mention D-E-A-T-H?" She glanced down as she spelled, then glared at me, warning me not to say the word.

What did Easter mean, exactly, without death?

But I'm the church librarian, so what I said was, "Certainly. Let me help you." In a few minutes she was checking out three books, vague about what happened to Jesus but trumpeting the Resurrection.

Sometimes, I loathed Protestants.

All right, that wasn't a particularly Christian thought.

True, though, despite how acknowledging it made my soul squirm. I grew up Catholic. In our Passion Week services, death and suffering were center stage, followed by the glorious burst of the Resurrection. Easter among the Protestants was like preschoolers eating dinner unsupervised, ignoring the broccoli and reaching right for dessert.

I'd gotten dragged into this church by my boyfriend a year ago. I'd quickly ended up as the church's librarian. Doug had been introducing me to the Executive Pastor when the prior librarian had come to tell Pastor Bob she needed to step down to care for her elderly mother. Doug said, "I bet Annie could do it." That was that. But it turned out I liked it.

Most of the time.

The Easter-without-Death question wasn't the strangest I'd gotten. Maybe not even in the top ten. "Excuse me, miss,"—it's always miss— "where are the books about the myth of evolution?… about feminists destroying the family?…about why God hates gay marriage?" And a personal insulting favorite: "…about how to evangelize Catholics?"

I'd learned pretty quickly not to talk politics. Or mention my background. "Catholics worship the Pope," I'd been told. Once a little old lady patted my hand sympathetically. "It's not your fault you were born into a cult, dear." *Cult?* As far as I was concerned, at the core we shared a faith, and I liked helping people deepen theirs. It made up for the other stuff I had to deal with.

Like church politics. As disturbing as the disdain toward my upbringing and secular politics was, finding myself in a smothering web of internal church machinations was even worse. It was ironic how few people here believed in evolution because the situation was decidedly Darwinian. Several bigger fish had their sights on my library.

One swam in. Pastor Clark, the Facilities Pastor, came by every Sunday to see how many people were using the library. A free market zealot, he'd championed putting in a bookstore and was still angling to replace us. Hence the surveillance, hoping to gather evidence the space was "under-utilized in its current capacity" or some other corporate-efficiency lingo he'd picked up from his father, a Toyota executive. Let yourself get sucked into a conversation with him and you could count on at least one mention of how Toyota's management principles could be applied to running a modern American church.

Running a church like a business? God help us.

I put my head down and typed, trying to look too busy to talk. Not difficult. Running a church library wasn't for wusses. New materials to process, donations to sort (thanks so much for your decade-old copies of *Christianity Today*!), returned items to scan and shelve, books to repair, and scratched DVDs to salvage or scrap. Not to mention keeping things tidy, which was harder than it sounded since half the patrons were pint-sized.

The second service ended. The library filled with kids clutching Veggie Tales DVDs and Angel Wars comic books. Excuse me—*graphic novels*. Men planted themselves at tables for this week's installment of "how liberals are ruining America." Women chased little bodies scattering among the shelves like leaves in a strong wind.

A woman scooted to the counter before the line got long, *Left Behind* book #8 in her hand. "I just *love* this series."

"I'm glad you enjoy them, Lisa."

"I mean, *what* a witness."

"Some people find them very moving." I scanned the barcode and gave back the book. She beamed and turned away, tucking it into the bulging bag slung over her shoulder. If the pattern held, she'd be back next Sunday for #9.

Barcodes. I watched the line grow as I greeted the next person. How many church libraries had barcode-enabled computerized catalogs? I'd installed it.

As always, when the line was a dozen deep, the head of Children's Ministry approached the counter. Between second and third service was our busiest time, so naturally that was when she wanted to talk to me. You'd think a woman who worked with children, looked like a fairy, and sounded like a southern belle would be a gentle person. You'd learn better.

Another thing I'd learned was not to keep her waiting. Throwing an apologetic look down the line, I turned to her. "What can I do for you, Clara?"

Her eyes narrowed. Suspicion seemed to be her default mode. "The children's books get very messy during the week," she said. "Can't you do something?"

I swallowed a sigh. She complained about this at least once a month. "I have a job." Medical data entry wasn't a great job, true, but I had to pay the bills.

She looked at me like I was a bug. One she was about to squash, or one already mashed on the bottom of her shoe, I wasn't sure. "Doing God's work should be the most important thing," she said, oozing televangelist-grade fervor. I suppressed a shudder. Religious conviction was fine but Catholics tended to be reserved about it. The first time I'd see someone in church with their hands in the air, swaying to the drum beat, I felt like I'd landed on another planet. "And I'm going back to graduate school."

"Oh, my," she drawled. Which meant, *Aren't you the uppity girl?* Evangelicals, I'd learned, distrusted higher education. But volunteering in the church library had shown me what I really wanted to do with my life. I was going to be a real librarian, and grad school was the way to get there. "Does Doug know?"

"Not yet."

"Oh, my," she repeated, this time with an oily tone that both confused and concerned me. "Why ever not? Shouldn't a girl's fiancé hear good news first?"

"Doug's in India for three weeks. For the bank."

"They don't have email in India?"

"He doesn't like me to bother him when he's on a business trip. He says he needs to concentrate on the job. I understand. Besides, I want to tell him personally."

"I see." Again the smug tone, like someone watching a skunk about to walk over a cliff. "Yes. That's definitely the way to do it."

Her tone implied the opposite. But Clara liked to mess with my head where Doug was concerned because her younger sister had dated him before me. She always seemed like she was wondering what he saw in me.

Actually, I wondered the same thing. I pictured his face, his serious expression at odds with his drop-dead looks. Brown hair, sun-streaks making him look more surfer than banker. Ghirardelli-chocolate eyes. Well-muscled shoulders I wished I'd seen more often than at two church pool parties. I was the pudgy geek girl, in the corner at every dance but the front row in every classroom. What *was* he doing with me?

Now," Clara tipped her head, blue eyes fixing me with an icy glare, "about those messy shelves. Couldn't you just pop in once or twice a week?"

I lived half an hour away, and her After-School Program made the mess. Did that matter? Apparently not. "I have to work."

She waited. I tried not to squirm under her stare.

It was obvious as the Georgia in her voice that she wanted me to offer to train one of her assistants to handle the library during the After-School Program. I didn't dare. Once her assistant knew how to run it, *gulp!* Children's Ministry would gobble up the library. She'd argued for it four times already in Leadership Meetings.

"Well," she stretched the word to six syllables, "if you *really* can't do anything."

"Not a thing." I hoped my relief at escaping her scrutiny didn't show.

She turned away, striding like a pixie warrior back to her office. I tackled the now-muttering line—typing, swiping, smiling.

When the last patrons left, I sat back, pulling a deep breath, heart pounding like I'd been running. I got that sense of victory every time I made it through the peak. Books in hands, DVDs in bags, patrons happy. I won again.

When my heartbeat slowed to normal I dusted my hands on my skirt and left the counter. After the busy time the library looked like a horrid bookish disaster—volumes on every surface, board books land-mining the carpet, emptied displays, DVDs catawampus on the slat wall.

As I bent to straighten a listing line of books, a finger tapped my shoulder. "Excuse me, miss?"

I jumped. "Yes?"

"Oh, sorry," the tapper said unconvincingly. "There's a problem I hope you can help me with."

Uh-oh. Problems could be anything from "Why don't we have the new $25 hardback in the Amish fiction series?" to "I demand you remove all books by that heretic Thomas Merton *right now!*"

"How can I help you, Brenda?" I tried to call people by name. I read somewhere it calms them.

No such luck. The frown deepened. "Where have all the evangelism books gone?"

I hadn't gotten to that shelf yet. It was around the corner in the Coffee and Conversation area. "Hmm," I said. "Let's go see." Gesturing for her to follow, I headed towards the gleaming chrome beacons of caffeine.

Sure enough, the shelf that should have been crammed with titles like *Sharing Your Faith—and Loving It!* and *Seven Simple Steps to More Effective Evangelism* was bare.

What the…? It was full when I put half a dozen new books there earlier that morning.

"What's happened to them?"

"I don't know." I stepped closer, not quite believing what I was seeing. Seriously, where were they? It was like aliens had beamed every book vaguely connected to the Great Commission into outer space.

She stopped frowning long enough to preen. "I'm head of the Fish Nets." She tossed her hair. "We donated half a dozen evangelism books both this month and last."

The Fish Nets is the Women's Missions Committee. Did they intend the double meaning? I don't know. It's hard to imagine them *not* realizing it, but on the other hand, this is a gingham-and-plaid crowd, so maybe. It invoked Jesus telling his disciples to be fishers of men rather than fishermen—that's what Missions was all about. But maybe, like the original punning command, they meant that and more. If so it was a pretty clever, and funny, name for the Women's Missions Committee. I'd never asked. What if only the gospel reference was intended, and even knowing what fishnet stockings *were* was a sign of heathenness?

"So what's happened to them?" she asked again.

"I don't know," I repeated.

Hoping to avoid another conversational loop, I started back to the counter. "Let's check the computer."

She tapped her fingernails while I typed. We all know women who look like they iron every piece of clothing they put on—pulled together, but uptight? That's Brenda. The longer she stood there, the more nervous I felt. It didn't help that none of the new evangelism books came up as checked out.

"Anything?" Scorn dripped like an ice cream cone in July.

I shook my head.

She rolled her eyes. "You're supposed to be a librarian."

"We're not the Carnegie Library," I said. "We don't have a security system. Sometimes people borrow things without checking them out."

I could hear her foot stamp. "It's *your* responsibility. My committee *was* planning to donate more books but if you can't keep them on the shelves," she fixed me with a basilisk glare, "we'll have to go to your supervisor."

"I'm a volunteer," I muttered as she stomped away. But her threat wasn't an idle one. It wasn't a job, but I could be fired. Or, rather, "asked to step down." I'd never led anything before, my day job was torpefying and lonely, and I really did like helping people even if I didn't always agree with them. I didn't want to lose this.

After the last service, I straightened up the library once more and left. But I didn't go home. Sometimes people took books and set them down somewhere else in the building. It was a long shot since so many were missing, but it couldn't hurt to walk around the church and look.

The church wasn't a building so much as a complex of buildings. There was the main building, which held the sanctuary, expanded three times over the two decades; a smaller pair of buildings for staff offices; and across the street, the building that housed ministry activities like kids' Sunday School classes, the ear-numbingly loud Teen Worship service, the After School program, and the library. Each had little waiting areas, with two or three corporate-looking chairs, the kind that look like they'd be comfy but aren't, and a small table beside them.

That's where I found the missing books. Not all in one place, but sown among the waiting areas. I collected them until my arms were full—figuring I was on a fool's errand, I hadn't brought a bag—took them back to the library, and returned for another pass. It took three trips to get them home. It was awkward, carrying armloads of books while wearing a skirt. I still wasn't used to wearing skirts all the time, but Doug preferred women not wear pants so I hadn't since we starting dating seriously.

Whew. That was weird. But I had them back. When Brenda saw the well-stocked shelf, would she apologize for getting snippy? Probably not.

* * * *

Next Sunday, I checked the evangelism shelf first thing, and was relieved to see the books still in place. Which was more than I could say for the children's books. Someone, or more likely someone's assistant, had "cleaned up," rearranging books by size and color. It made a striking image on the shelf but was useless for finding anything. It took me an hour to re-alphabetize them.

After that the morning ran on rails. As usual, the time between the first and second services was brisk but not busy. During second service, people began trickling in, making a beeline for the coffee. True to form, towards the end of second service, Lisa the *Left Behind* Lady checked out Book 9, her heavy bag perched this time on her hip. Clara dropped by when fifteen people were in line, but it was a perfunctory visit, her flicking gaze making clear she was really there to see what I'd done about the children's books, nostrils flaring when she saw it already fixed. Oh well. Just another round of survival of the fittest.

I was basking in the post-rush glow when Facilities Pastor Clark came to the counter. "Why is there an empty shelf in the Coffee and Conversation area?"

"What?" I was out of my chair in a tick.

He frowned. "If you're not able to make good use of the space…"

I made a beeline for the shining pots. There was my evangelism shelf, buck naked. I bit down on an unchurchly word.

Pastor Clark had followed. "This area…"

"Again?"

I found Brenda at my elbow. Another unholy thought burst through my brain.

"She's not doing her job," she hissed at Pastor Clark.

"I know—"

"I'm head of the Fish Nets—"

"This is prime real estate—"

"My committee donated those books—"

"Right by the coffee pots—"

"Out of our own budget—"

"I knew a bookstore was a better—"

"Incompetent—"

"Ought to be replaced—"

"Ought to be *fired!*" Brenda wagged a finger under my nose. She was gone before I could blink at the too-close manicured nail.

"So this shelf's been empty for a while?" Pastor Clark nodded to himself. "*Very* poor use of space." He tsked. "Room is too tight to give any over to inefficacy. Just like Toyota."

I kept my teeth together until he was gone.

* * * *

Someone was out to get me.

This time I brought a bag, and it was full to groaning by the time I collected the evangelism books, scattered once more around the campus like grass seed.

Someone was removing the books and distributing them hither and yon. A person who borrowed without checking out only took a few books, and took them home, intending to bring them back. The rare outright thief took some, but not so many. A prankster bent on random destruction would drop them into trash cans, not end tables.

Somebody was trying to make me look bad.

It was disheartening how many prospects there were.

Maybe I could set up a webcam and catch the culprit. But did I really want to stay when someone was trying so hard to get rid of me? It'd be creepy, like watching over my shoulder at a haunted house, waiting for the next ragged creature to jump out. And what if it didn't work, but they found out I'd tried? Much better to go quietly and with some dignity intact.

How long before my Ministry Supervisor asked me to resign?

At least Doug would be back soon. Just a week left. I made dinner reservations. I'd tell him about grad school, and we could celebrate his homecoming, my new career, and me getting fired all at once.

* * * *

Next Sunday the evangelism books were still there when I arrived. I wasn't reassured. That'd been true last week and they disappeared before the last service. But the morning was butter-smooth.

Just before the between-service rush, Pastor Clark went pointedly to the Coffee and Conversation section, then walked past with a stiff look on his face that told me the shelf wasn't empty. Clara made a perfunctory complaint about the "messiness" of the DVD slat wall, which turned out to mean three cases were upside down.

As I was reshelving during third service, Brenda flounced by. Just like Pastor Clark, the look on her face told me everything I needed to know. As third service ended, I checked the shelf again. All was well.

The morning was nearly over. The books were still there. Thank goodness.

Whatever had happened, it was over now. I felt a twinge of guilt at having suspected sabotage. Fortunately, guilt is a specialty of Catholics. I whistled softly as I headed back to the counter and began entering new materials into the catalog.

Left Behind #10 slapped down right by my nose.

"Oh!"

"Sorry!" Lisa panted. "I wasn't sure you'd still be here. I *really* wanted to get the next one." She hiked her monstrous bag further up on her hip.

"No rush," I said. "I'm always here for about half an hour after the last service."

"Ooo," she breathed. "That's good to know. I usually go to second service but I slept in this morning and had to come to third."

I swiped the book and handed it back to her.

"Thanks!"

"No problem. Have a good day."

"You, too!"

In a few minutes the library was empty. Once everyone was gone, I gave in and whistled openly while I typed. Sometime later the custodian stopped by. "You gonna be much longer? I'm turning lights off."

"Would another ten minutes be okay? I'd like to finish these last two books."

"Sure. I'll lock up the other buildings and come back." He paused. "Is that empty shelf an extra? I could get rid of it for you."

I froze. "Empty shelf?"

He pointed towards the coffee area, his ring of keys jangling.

I was wheeling around the counter, skirt flapping, before his goodbye faded.

The evangelism shelf *was* empty again.

I thought something so vile I'd never heard a real person say it, just characters in movies.

How had this happened? All the suspects were at the library that morning but the shelf had been full when they left. Could one have slipped back without me noticing? But I'd been watching. I hadn't seen any of them.

And—why had the books disappeared so much later this week? Brenda, Clark, and Clara came through at their usual times. If one of them took the books...why the change?

Understanding rang in my head like Eucharist bells.

It wasn't any of them.

It was Lisa.

There wasn't a plot to discredit me. Just a woman's *Left Behind*-inspired attempt to save souls before the Rapture. I could picture it as clearly as if I'd seen it. Lisa's enthusiasm, the bulging bag when she only checked out one book at a time. Scattering the books around the church's public areas, trying to encourage the faithful to go forth and convert the lost before it was too late. Honest, earnest Lisa, wanting to save the world.

I blew out a breath, wrestling my irritation. No doubt she hadn't meant to cause me problems. Next week I'd explain how her well-intentioned attempts to goad her fellow congregants were making me seem disorganized. I could suggest she join the Fish Nets as an outlet for her evangelistic fervor.

The door opened. I turned, hoping it might be Lisa coming back but expecting the custodian.

It was Doug.

I wasn't expecting him until evening. He must have caught an earlier flight. I beamed. I wanted to run to him and hug him but he disliked public displays of affection, so stayed where I was.

He gave a thin smile, grave as always. "Hello."

"How was India?"

"As expected."

Now I did come to him and, unable to resist, touched his hand. "I have good news!"

"Your acceptance to graduate school? I heard."

I took a step back. "You heard?"

"Clara emailed me."

"*Clara?*" I shook my head. "But you said you don't like to be contacted on a business trip."

His hand flicked impatiently. "Not for trivia, of course, but it is acceptable in an emergency."

"*Emergency?*" I took another step back. Grad school was an emergency?

He gestured to the table. "Please sit. We need to talk."

I sat.

His face fell into deeper lines. "You can't."

"Yes, I *can*. I got a fellowship." Giddy relief swamped me. "Is that what you're worried about, the money?"

"No...I have a Bachelor's degree."

"Um...okay...?"

"God doesn't want the woman to be more educated than the man."

I resisted the urge to dig at my ear with my little finger. "What?"

He said it again.

It still didn't make any sense. "Where in the Bible did you get that?"

He coughed. "It's not in the Bible, per se. It's my interpretation of the writings of John Calvin."

I stared. Was he joking? A little welcome-back ridiculousness?

Doug never joked.

"You mean," I said slowly, "I either give up grad school or you'll break up with me?"

He nodded as if pleased with my quick understanding.

My eyes flooded. I blinked, trying to keep wetness from spilling out. He hated emotional displays of any sort.

Something snapped.

Why did I care what he liked or disliked?

I'd given up Mass and jeans for him. The centuries-old splendor of the Liturgy, prayers etched in memory since childhood, the dignified plainchant of the priest.

Jeans were insignificant in comparison. Except they weren't, when you realized, as I saw now, what they represented. Ease of movement. Freedom. Men and women dressing the same.

I shivered, as if I'd suddenly noticed a pit I'd almost tumbled into.

"Doug," I began softly, then stopped.

It wasn't his fault. Not entirely. If he'd tried to put me into a box, make me into his idea of a nice little Protestant girl, I'd let him. Most of my friends from college were already married. A few even had kids. Desperate for a boyfriend, I'd gone along.

"Doug," I said again quietly.

Quietly.

No. Not quietly. I'd been ready to walk away from the library quietly.

That was the coward's way. And I *was* a coward. Not only was I too afraid of being single to challenge Doug's controlling ways, I sniggered at people in my head who I was patently afraid to confront. Like Clara. Who clearly wasn't at all afraid of me. I was even too much of a wuss to say a swear word out loud. I liked to think of myself as bold, even edgy, but that's exactly where my courage began and ended—in my head.

I'd obeyed when he told me to sit, like a well-trained puppy. Now I stood. "You can bite me."

He blinked.

"And John Calvin can bite me. I quit."

"Quit...?" Surprise shivered across his face, more emotion than I'd ever seen there. Anger followed. "You're breaking up with me? *You're* breaking up with *me?*" His face reddened. "I should have known. Ungrateful papist. I tried to *save* you."

Ten minutes earlier, learning that Doug shared his congregation's all-too-common view about Catholics would have upset me. Now it stoked my resolve. His arrogance had wanted to mold a girl into his ideal wife. A Catholic girl was even better—what a spiritual coup. But it'd been helped along by my craven unwillingness to stand up for myself or anything else. No more. Not ever again.

I started for the door.

"Where do you think you're going?"

"Mass." I pulled the door open. "Then grad school. In jeans."

FISHING FOR MURDER

BY TERESA HEWITT INGE

Detective Dexter McKane watched from the Rudee Inlet Bridge as the crane operator lowered a silver pick-up truck onto a barge in the Virginia Beach inlet. Two crewmen the size of small mountains stood on the barge deck, guiding the operator.

"Any sign of the driver?" Detective Katie Whitaker asked Dexter as they stood near a team of accident reconstructionists gathering readings and measurements of impact, skid marks, and speed calculations on the bridge.

"No." Dexter turned toward the Virginia Beach dive team onboard a police boat floating near the barge. The team had finished an underwater search and rescue for Mac Seagraves, driver of the pick-up truck who was nowhere to be found. However, his fishing partner, Bobby Harrison, had been riding shotgun and was found safe and sound after swimming to shore. Dexter and Katie exited the bridge and made their way down a slippery, wet embankment and onto a dirt path under the bridge. They walked past a group of rubberneckers eager to find out about the truck that had tumbled off the bridge. The detectives stopped to talk with an officer posted at the beach for crowd control.

"Well, well, look what the sand drug in. I see the brass called in the experts," the officer teased.

Dexter grinned, sporting a new set of veneers that covered teeth discolored from years of smoking. The veneers were part of his self-induced makeover to help him look and feel better alongside the young, fit detectives in the unit. He'd already given up cigarettes, the hardest part of his journey. "Detective Whitaker and I will be working with the crash team."

The officer nodded toward the attractive brunette detective.

"Whatcha got?" Dexter asked.

"What I've got is an open and shut."

Dexter's eyebrows arched, heavier and darker than the thinning gray hair on his head. "How so?"

"The passenger, Bobby Harrison, stated Mac Seagraves lost control of the vehicle in the rainstorm while on the bridge. They hit the jersey wall and took a nosedive into the water. Simple as that."

"Where's the passenger?" Dexter asked the officer.

"Over at the fishing pier near the ambulance. He's wrapped in a dark-green blanket." The officer pointed toward a sandy haired man.

"Any other vehicles involved?" Dexter said.

"Nope."

"What about witnesses?"

"Two fishermen were packing up their gear on the north bank when the crash occurred but they didn't see anything due to the downpour," the officer said.

"What about relatives?"

"There's a daughter. Name's Abbey Seagraves. She's the pretty young blonde in the red parka. She's sitting on a bench at the fishing pier with her boyfriend, Tyler Logan, an all-star wrestler at Virginia Beach High."

"Any other relatives?" Dexter said.

"No. The mother died a few years back. The father was raising the daughter by himself in a cottage on 9th Street."

Dexter waved. "Thanks for the info."

"Hey, McKane. Rumor has it you're on your way out. Is that the reason for your new sidekick?"

"Don't believe everything you hear and only half of what you see." Dexter was not pleased he had a young female partner assigned to him. Her gender had nothing to do with his frustration. From what he'd seen she didn't know which end was up.

"What was that about?" Katie asked.

"Smart-ass cop. Thinks he knows everything. Just follow my lead so you don't get yourself in trouble."

Katie snorted. "I'll have you know that I am quite capable of assisting you with this investigation."

Dexter turned toward her. "That's right. The operative word here is assist. And don't forget it."

He made his way toward the fishing pier with Katie trailing behind. He tried to button his coat to shield himself from the chilly, mid-March air, but the twenty pounds he packed on last year when he quit smoking made it difficult. Losing weight was also a part of his makeover.

"I'll talk to the passenger first, then the daughter," Dexter said to Katie as they walked toward Bobby Harrison.

"Mr. Harrison, I'm Detective McKane and this is Detective Whitaker." Dexter put his hands in his pockets and jingled some loose change around, a habit he'd picked up since quitting smoking.

Bobby nodded.

"I'm sorry to hear about your friend," Dexter said to the grim faced man with bloodshot eyes. "I understand you swam in frigid water?"

"Rough is more like it."

"Have you been checked out by the paramedics?"

"Yes."

"The accident must have been pretty frightening for you?"

"I feared for my life," Bobby said.

"What did you and Mac do today?"

"What do you mean?"

"What happened before the accident?"

"We worked on the fishing boat."

"What time was that?"

"We got on the water at five o'clock. The fish weren't biting so we came in around noon."

"Besides the accident, did anything happen outside the norm today?"

"No. We went on the boat, fished a little, then came in. Simple as that."

Dexter's eyebrows knitted together. That's twice he'd heard the words "simple as that." One thing he'd learned during his thirty years on the force is death is never as simple as that.

"Did you or Mac drink any alcohol today?" Katie asked.

Dexter glared at Katie.

"We had a couple of beers on the boat."

"Only a couple, Mr. Harrison?" Katie pressed for another answer.

Bobby hesitated before responding. "I'm not sure what all these questions are about. The bottom fell out of the sky and Mac lost control of the truck. We hit the wall and flew into the water."

"What happened while you were in the water?" Katie asked.

"I couldn't see anything but I reached over for Mac. He didn't budge. I unhooked his seatbelt but he never moved." Bobby's voice was shaky.

"And…" Katie urged.

"I rolled down the window and swam out."

"Did you go back down to try and pull Mac out?"

Bobby's face caved in. "No, the current was too strong so I swam to shore."

"Simple as that," Dexter said.

Bobby hunched into the blanket. "Look, my best friend is missing and I almost drowned. I don't want to answer anymore questions." His voice was firm as he staggered down the pier with the long blanket dragging behind him.

"He's lying," Katie said.

"And you came to that conclusion because…?"

"Women's intuition."

"We work investigations based on solid leads and forensic evidence, not on women's intuition."

"Well, my intuition tells me he drank a lot more than he let on."

"How so?"

"My theory is this. Bobby and Mac gulped down several beers because the fish weren't biting. By the time they reached the bridge, they were drunk. Bobby's eyes and the staggering support that."

Dexter shook his head. "If that's the case, why doesn't Bobby just tell the truth? Especially since he wasn't driving."

"I don't know, but my intuition tells me there's more to this than a rainstorm. Let's go check out the daughter." Dexter frowned as she led the way toward Abbey.

"Ms. Seagraves, I'm Detective Whitaker and this is Detective McKane. We're sorry to hear about your father's accident."

"Did the divers find Daddy?" the girl cried.

"No ma'am, but we're working on it," Katie said.

Abbey nuzzled her face near Tyler's shoulder. She muttered the words, "I feel so bad about last night now."

"What about last night?" Dexter said.

Abbey lifted her head. The wind blew her long blonde hair into her eyes and Tyler smoothed it back, exposing her pink cheeks to the brisk air. Dexter noticed Tyler's left cheek had two long scratches on it.

"My dad and I got into an argument." Abbey's eyes filled with tears.

Katie reached into her pocket, pulled out some tissues and handed them to Abbey. "What was the argument about?"

"Just a silly argument, that's all." Abbey dabbed at her eyes.

"Anything you want to talk about?" Katie asked in a concerned, motherly tone.

"No."

"You didn't see your father this morning?" Dexter asked.

"No. I wasn't awake when he and Bobby left for work."

"Does Bobby live with you all?"

"He rents a small apartment behind our cottage."

"Are your dad and Bobby close?"

"Bobby keeps to himself most of the time." She began to cry again and Tyler put his arm around her.

"We'll do our best to find your father," Katie said.

* * * *

The temperature jumped to a high fifty-five degrees on Monday. Dexter and Katie drove back to the fishing pier where Mac's crackly old boat was docked. Abbey's name appeared on the back of the boat in large black letters. Dexter and Katie made their rounds on the pier but got resistance from the local fishermen. No one wanted to talk about Mac Seagraves until Dexter made reference to several out-of-date fishing permits. Word had it a territorial-waterway war was going on between Mac and fishing newcomer, Juan Hernandez.

Later that afternoon Dexter and Katie drove to the police compound to check out Mac's truck more closely.

Dexter squatted at the side of the pickup and pointed toward the left rear truck bed, heavily damaged with white paint.

"The white paint didn't come from the bridge," Katie said.

Dexter's knees cracked as he stood up and faced Katie. "What does your intuition tell you this time?"

"That another vehicle hit them on the bridge."

"Have forensics take scrapings of the paint for matching and I'll touch base with the crash team," Dexter said.

* * * *

On Tuesday morning, Dexter and Katie visited the Seagraves cottage. Tyler answered the door, running his hand through his wavy blonde hair in a nervous gesture. "Did you find Mr. Seagraves?"

"No. We're here to see Abbey," Katie said.

"She's not feeling well. She's in the back room sleeping." Tyler held the screen-door halfway open.

"Shouldn't you be in school?" Dexter tried to peer around him.

"I'm here to comfort Abbey," Tyler said boldly.

"Ask her to give me a call when she's feeling better." Dexter handed his card to Tyler.

"Something's not right with that kid," Katie said as they walked toward the car.

"Is this that women's intuition thing again?" Dexter asked.

"Yeah something, like that. Let's grab an early lunch and talk about it. I'm starving."

"Okay, but I'm trying to drop a few pounds. I'll get something light." Dexter patted his belly.

After eating a grilled chicken salad at Big Sam's Inlet Café, Dexter and Katie paid another visit to the fishing pier. This time, they discovered Juan Hernandez straightening fishing nets on his boat.

"Mr. Hernandez, I'm Detective McKane."

"And I'm Detective Whitaker."

"My permits are all in order," Juan said. His almond skin glistened in the March sun.

"Do you know Mac Seagraves and Bobby Harrison?" Dexter asked.
Juan hesitated. "I do."

"I take it you heard about the accident they were in."

"I heard. Did they find Mac?"

"No." Dexter paused. "Where were you around two o'clock this past Saturday?"

"I was fishing."

Dexter looked around the parking lot. "Do you still own a white Chevy van?"

Juan frowned. "Yes. My cousin has it right now."

"Was your cousin driving your van on Saturday afternoon?"

"What's this about?"

"Were you and Mac Seagraves having a dispute over the waterways you fish in?" Katie asked.

"Let's just say that I operate on a first-come, first-serve basis," Juan said.

"Meaning?"

"Meaning, whoever gets on the waterway first, gets the fish."

"Tell me about your relationship with Bobby Harrison," she said.

"What relationship? He was lucky to have a job with Mac."

"And why is that?"

"Because he's a lousy drunk."

Dexter shot a quick glance at Katie. "You plan to keep working in Virginia Beach, Mr. Hernandez?"

"Fishing's good. Money's good." Juan placed the nets over the side of the boat and shrugged his shoulders. "I'll probably stay a while. Anything else? I have a lot of work to do."

* * * *

The next morning Katie plunked down two manila files on Dexter's desk. "Got em' from forensics last night. They were taken by the cameras installed along the bridge and captured the images well, despite the rain."

Dexter looked up at Katie then opened the first file. He pulled out four 8x10 photos. One by one he viewed pictures of a silver truck being hit by a white two-ton truck on the bridge. "Did you run the white truck's plates?"

"Yeah. They belong to a Buick. The owner is a seventy-eight-year old woman who reported her plates missing a few days ago."

Dexter opened the second file. His eyebrows shot upward. "According to this report, Bobby Harrison had a high blood alcohol level when the accident occurred."

"Yep. I told you he was drunk. Probably too drunk to realize that someone hit him and Mac," Katie said.

"He must've sobered up quickly when he hit the cold water."

"His adrenalin probably kicked in when he swam to shore. Of course the alcohol was still in his blood stream when the paramedics checked him out," Katie added.

"Do you have the forensic results?"

"Yep. Paint matched the same make and model of the utility truck on the bridge. How about the accident report?"

"Results confirm two vehicles were involved when Mac's truck went over the side." Dexter's phone rang. "This is McKane."

"Detective McKane, it's Abbey Seagraves."

"Yes, Ms. Seagraves." Dexter pressed the speakerphone button.

Katie stepped closer to hear the conversation.

"Have you found out anything about my father?"

"No, but I would like to talk to you about the investigation. Will you be home in the next half hour?"

"Yes."

Dexter grabbed the photos. "Let's go, Whitaker."

* * * *

Abbey greeted Dexter and Katie at the door. She looked worn and tired. "Have a seat." She extended her arm toward two white couches with overstuffed pillows and blue throws strewn across the back of each sofa.

"I can't bear to put it away." Abbey glanced at the fishing equipment near the door as Dexter and Katie made their way past the gear.

"Are you okay, Abbey?" Katie asked.

"No. I haven't been feeling well the past few days."

"Is there anything I can do for you?"

"Well, unless you can give me something for morning sickness…"

"You're pregnant?"

"Yes. That's one of the reasons I called Detective McKane. That and to talk about the argument my father and I had. I didn't want to talk about this in front of Tyler."

"Go ahead." Dexter leaned forward in his seat.

"Well, when Tyler and I told my father I was pregnant he went ballistic and threatened Tyler. They had a huge fist fight and Daddy told me I was never to see Tyler again."

"Is that why Tyler's face is scratched?" Dexter said.

"Yes."

"I can understand a parent being upset over news like this, but why did he threaten Tyler?" Dexter asked.

"They didn't like each other to begin with and this made Daddy like Tyler even less. Tyler cheated on me and I always had to pay for mine and his way to the movies and dinner. Daddy felt Tyler was a deadbeat."

"I thought Tyler was an all-star wrestler with a good future ahead of him," Katie said.

"That's true. But he also has a rotten side. When I turned eighteen last week, I told Tyler I would get a big insurance payoff from my mother's estate. Tyler began making plans for the money and Daddy found out. And when I told Daddy about the pregnancy it was like the final straw. That's when we had the argument." She began sobbing. "I miss him."

"Abbey, the search and recovery effort has been called off for your father." Katie's tone was soft.

"We also have some photos from your father's accident to show to you. They may be disturbing for you to see." Dexter pulled the pictures from the folder and handed them to her.

"Do you recognize the driver and the vehicle?" Katie asked.

Abbey gasped. "Yes, it's Tyler driving his father's truck. I recognize the custom blue pinstripes down the side."

Katie scooted next to her on the couch. "I'm sorry, Abbey."

"He said he was going to get even with my father, but I didn't believe him."

The front door swung open. Tyler stepped into the living room, his eyes full of rage as he looked at Abbey. He spotted the photos in her hand and the rage turned to panic.

Detective McKane leaped to his feet. Tyler dodged him, trying to escape. McKane thrust his body against Tyler's, plunging both men to the floor. Tyler wriggled away and grabbed a fishing net by the door. He slipped the net over McKane, flipped him over onto his back and pressed his chest against the detective. He grabbed McKane's neck and pinned him to the floor. The detective extended his arm sharply, faltering Tyler's grip and wrestled Tyler off of him. McKane shoved both hands through the net then under Tyler's armpits from behind. He linked his hands behind Tyler's neck, forcing his head forward.

Katie stood over both men with gun in hand. She pulled the tangled net off Dexter. "Impressive wrestling skills, McKane."

Sweating profusely, Dexter grinned. "Virginia Beach High, Class of 79' All-Star Wrestling Team."

Fifteen minutes later, two uniformed police officers led the hand-cuffed Tyler Logan into their patrol car. Katie turned toward Dexter. "My intuition paid off on this one."

"Actually, it was good ole fashioned detective work." He hesitated. "But your intuition did help."

"Yep, it's as simple as that," Katie said.

Sherian —
Enjoy!
Teresa Inge

IN SEINE

BY KATHARINE RUSSELL

"He stinks," Tracy said.

Her mom swiveled in the passenger seat of the station wagon. "That is a rude thing to say, and a rude way to say it."

"She's got a point, Margaret," Franklin Tilghman said as he guided the Pontiac down the dirt road. "Captain Billie wears the same pair of long johns all winter."

Margaret sighed. "I know how hard it is for people without indoor plumbing, especially older folks, but you, young lady, must learn to be generous of spirit with those who are less fortunate."

"I don't think he's less fortunate, he just doesn't want to take a bath." Franklin winked at his daughter.

"Frank, you are not helping." Margaret poked her husband in the arm. "Tracy, you can go out in the backyard after you greet Captain Billie. Plenty of fresh air out there on the river."

"Are you kidding? With the fish heads and the muskrat guts?" The girl plopped her chin down on the back of the bench seat.

Franklin guided the station wagon off the state road down the lane to Captain Billie Huckabee's ramshackle property. He eased between a listing fence supported by honeysuckle vines and an ancient wagon propped up on cinderblocks.

The March wind worried the lapels of her jacket as Tracy followed her mother up the path to the sagging porch steps. Ahead of them, carrying the two crab nets he had brought, her father threaded between the stacked firewood and heaps of empty crab traps to the door. He tapped and entered.

"When was the last time this place was painted?' Tracy whispered.

"Before you were born. Now hush." Her mother held her hem as she crossed the threshold to keep her new tweed coat from brushing the splintered frame.

A wave of too warm air redolent of kerosene, wet wool and wetter dog assaulted Tracy's nostrils. She dragged her sleeve to her nose as she bent to pat Brick, the ancient Chesapeake Bay retriever who limped to her and snuffled her crotch.

"Whitecaps all the way up to Wicomico Corners this morning, Captain." Franklin shook the old man's hand.

Captain Billie sat in his rocker, a creaking leather affair, black with age. He was so close to his stove, the right side of his face glowed from the heat, and his wispy hair danced in the up currents. The yellowed edge of his long johns peeked out at the collar of his faded flannel shirt.

"I brought you some of my sugar cookies," Margaret said. She frowned at the surface of the dining table, trying to find a place she could set her parcel among the dirty cups, piles of unopened circulars and rolls of twine.

Franklin held his nets for the Captain to see. "These need redoing. Thought I'd bring them over early. No use waiting until the season is upon us."

The old man fingered the webbing and cocked an eye at Franklin. "They could go another season."

"I know. You make 'em strong, but I don't want to take the chance," Franklin said. "Margaret's brother's boys are coming down, and kids are rough on things."

The captain nodded in silence.

"May I take Brick out back, sir?" Tracy already stood by the kitchen door.

"Sure, go on along."

Tracy closed the door behind her and surveyed the back porch and yard. This porch was more orderly than the front one, because this was where Captain Billie made his gill nets. Dowels affixed to the face of the house held a half-woven specimen, and a bucket brimmed with cork floats waiting to be fastened to the lead edge of the net in the last stages of production.

From the rafters hung the finished nets ready for sale. Tracy thought the porch resembled the stage at the high school she would attend next year, with its rows of curtains and scenery.

The dog sniffed the surface of a sawed-off tree trunk the captain used for gutting fish. The captain's ancient scaling tool rested on the top. Finding no fish heads, Brick snorted and padded off down the path to the dock.

Tracy followed, her fists stuffed in her jacket pockets. Dad said there wasn't much left of Captain Billie's net business, because most people now bought synthetic gear. Fortunately, there were a few traditionalists left who preferred natural fibers and hand-knotted mesh for their gill, fish and crab tackle. The captain also had a partnership with Widow Morgan. He made string carry-alls and she dyed them pretty colors, offering them for sale at Barbour's General Store.

Captain Billie also made hammocks. Margaret was arranging for him to deliver two in time for the church bazaar. Craft items were popular with the city people who came down to Wicomico Corners to eat country cooking and buy preserves, quilts and driftwood carvings.

Tracy walked the length of the dock and looked back at the shore. Smoke from the captain's chimney drifted westward on the breeze. Across the mouth of Hayden's creek and up the steep bluff to the east rose the imposing facade of Cramleigh Hall. The great barn of a house had been fixed up—no, Tracy corrected herself—restored by the Montgomery family. More important, from Tracy's point of view, they had added a stable.

"Yoohoo, Tracy, we're going," Tracy's mother called from Captain's Billie's porch.

* * * *

"Do you think he bought the bit about your nephews coming?" Franklin gunned the Pontiac after reaching the macadam road at the end of the dirt lane.

"Hope so. He's too proud for charity," Margaret said. "I've got to come up with an argument for why he has to take money when I pick up the hammocks for the church."

Just tell him I've got enough of an income to need the tax right-off." Franklin waved at the driver of a Cadillac that barreled past them, its fins sparkling in the sunlight. "Look, there goes Brandon."

"I don't care how much he makes selling real estate. It's obscene to buy a new car every year," Margaret said. "Is he turning?"

Tracy swiveled around and watched the big sedan slow and turn left onto the dirt road, sending a fishtail of dust in its wake. "Yep."

Franklin's expression turned stern. "He should leave that old man alone. Captain Billie doesn't want to sell. Just wants to be left alone to die in his own house."

"Brandon Holt simply can't resist a drop-dead view. A city buyer could level that old cabin and build himself a pretty little summer place," Margaret said. "Brandon would have it sold in a week."

Tracy frowned and leaned forward. "What would happen to Brick if the captain died?"

"Don't you worry, honey," Franklin said. "The captain isn't going to die anytime soon. Too tough."

* * * *

The car wash was a fundraiser for the volunteer fire department. Tracy watched as two high school boys dried the Pontiac with chamois. Her father was talking to the fire chief.

"Why would anybody want to own a British car down here?" Chief Burch asked. "Her insurance bill must be an eye-popper."

"Beats me. Nobody around who knows how to repair foreign makes," Franklin said.

As Tracy studied the long, low sedan with the jaguar hood ornament, its owner approached the boy lathering the top of the vehicle.

"Young man, you take care not to make any scratches." Mrs. Montgomery wagged a finger at the boy. A big woman to begin with, her jodhpurs and boots gave her a threatening appearance.

"If Freddie Copsey weren't such a hell-raiser, I'd go to his defense," the chief said under his breath to Tracy's dad.

"She's a force. Look, his jellyroll is actually quaking," Franklin laughed.

Freddie backed away, clutching his sponge as Selina Montgomery inspected her car's forest green paint with a scowl.

"You probably haven't heard Selina's latest." The chief motioned to get Franklin to move farther away. Tracy followed as the men strolled behind the department's sparkling red tanker. "Selina is trying to convince Captain Billie to move into the Veteran's Home."

"Bet she'd love that. His cabin is right smack in the middle of the view from her tarted up manor house."

"Exactly," the chief said. "She tried to place his name on the waiting list, but we explained he has to do it himself."

"I forgot you're on the board. He'll never do it, though."

"Correct. I mean, he has every right as a veteran of the Great War, but he'll never leave that house of his."

"Here's your key, Mr. Tilghman." The taller of the boys who had washed the Pontiac handed Franklin his keys.

Franklin waved goodbye to Chief Burch, slung his arm over Tracey's shoulder and headed for his car.

"Dad, why is Mrs. Montgomery meddling in the captain's business?"

"She's family. Selina Huckabee Montgomery is Captain Billie's niece."

Tracy stared at him, mouth open.

"I know they seem about as far apart as two human beings can get. Fact is, though, she's probably his only living relative. His son died at Guadalcanal. Selina was raised up in Washington, and only came down here during the summer."

"Then, if she's kin, why does she want to put him in a home?"

"Can you picture him up at the big house? I seem to recall your remark about his, ah, aroma. Besides, he'd be miserable."

"I know, but to throw him out of his home, because you want a better view…"

"Let's not repeat that observation, okay? We need to be fair. Selina might just believe her uncle is no longer safe living by himself at his age." Franklin slid behind the wheel of the wagon and slammed his door.

Tracy tore around the hood to the passenger side and got in. "He's not alone. There's Brick."

Franklin smiled and turned the key in the ignition. "Yes, Brick and memories."

* * * *

Margaret and Tracy stood on the porch of Captain Billie's cabin. They had come to collect the hammocks for the church bazaar, but there was no answer to their knock.

"I wonder if he's down at the dock." Margaret clutched the handles of her purse.

"Then Brick would be with him, not up here." Tracy patted the dog who had been stretched out on the front porch when they arrived.

"Look who's coming." Margaret pointed as the Montgomery's foreign car pulled into the disheveled yard.

"Mrs. Montgomery is driving Captain Billie!" Tracey blinked.

Captain Billie sat in the back. Despite the chill April morning, both the front windows of the elegant sedan were all the way down. The car eased to a stop, the rear door opened, and with effort, Captain Billie got out and stood upright.

He limped forward a few steps, and turned to wave. Without reciprocating the gesture, Selina pulled away, and the car's windows returned to the closed position.

"Well," Margaret stammered. "It's a lovely morning for a ride."

Tracy didn't think Mrs. Montgomery was much on giving people rides. "Captain Billie, did you need the doctor?"

The captain offered a gape-toothed smile. "Naw, been over to Cramleigh Hall doing a little consulting."

Margaret, Tracy and Brick followed the old man into his house. The captain shrugged out of his peacoat, hung it on the rack, shuffled across the room and lowered himself into his rocker before continuing.

"Seems Selina has a muskrat problem."

"At Cramleigh?" Margaret pulled over a dining chair and sat.

"Yes, you'd think the critters would show more respect." Captain Billie winked. "She had that fancy reflecting pool dug, but to a muskrat, it's just the same as a farm pond."

"Water's water." Tracy leaned against the stove.

"Right, girl. Her front lawn looks like the trenches at Verdun."

"Holy-moly. Selina is due to host the Garden Club's June gala." Margaret's hand flew to her chest.

"That so? Didn't mention it to me, but what do I know about shindigs?"

"You can help her, though?"

"I gave her an idea or two." Captain Billie rose and walked to an old hope chest where a large parcel rested.

He patted the package. "Here are your hammocks. I threw in a few string bags. Had time on my hands last week during that rain."

* * * *

Aloysius Dennis pushed back from the table and patted either side of his stomach. "I shouldn't have helped myself to seconds on the ham, but the All Saints Supper only happens once a year."

"You'll work it off pacing back and forth during your interminable summations," his wife said. "I'm going upstairs to the crafts tables."

"Don't buy any more watercolors. We're out of wall space." The lawyer stood and pulled his jacket together over his paunch.

Tracy leaned around him to collect his empty plate and silverware.

"Where's your dad, young lady?'

"In the kitchen carving hams," Tracy said. "He's just staying ahead of this mob."

"Great turnout. I'll just have a word with him." The lawyer sidled down the aisle.

"Aloysius, I'd shake hands, but I'm all over grease." Franklin finished filling a platter which was whisked away by a server.

Aloysius waited for the server to recede before speaking. "Listen, Franklin, I need to bring you into the picture on something I got wind of down at the court."

"Something to do with me?" Franklin stopped carving.

"No, with Billie Huckabee." Aloysius lowered his voice. "Selina Montgomery plans to have him declared incompetent."

"You mean become his conservator?"

"Yes."

"He's a little eccentric, but he's as sane as I am." Franklin wiped his hands on a towel.

"Yes, but she could set him up. She might not have even told him about the hearing. She could dump him in the middle of a courtroom in his fishing duds. He'd look foolish and be confused. Have no time to prepare."

"Anybody would look bad. Doesn't the court have to notify him?"

"How often do you think the Captain picks up his mail?"

"I'll take care of it, Aloysius. I'll go over after church tomorrow, and when the hearing happens, Margaret and I will drive him."

"It will be in about two weeks. I'll call you with the date and time." Aloysius sneaked a small slice of ham, downed it and exited the kitchen, licking his fingers.

* * * *

A week later, Tracy leaned her bike against Captain Billie's porch, happy to see he was outside. She could avoid the odor of the cabin's interior. She had delivered her mother's Easter cookies to the Widow Morgan, the shut-in Marla Thompson and now the captain. She had a ham bone for Brick.

Captain Billie was hauling gill nets down to his pier. A boat waited, not a wooden skiff like his or her father's, but a modern shell with a center console. Selina Montgomery's commanding voice boomed up as Tracy approached. "Why do you want me to stand?"

"Because that way you won't tangle them." Captain Billie settled a coiled net over her right shoulder. Her other shoulder was already engulfed in another.

"They're heavier than they look." Selina steadied herself, resting a hand on the console.

"Yes, one more should be all you need." The captain draped the last gill net around Selina's neck. "Garner'll help you out of these when you reach the Cramleigh dock."

Garner Montgomery reversed the engine and backed away from the wharf.

Tracey reached the captain's side. "What's Mrs. Montgomery going to do with all those nets?"

"Told her she might discourage her muskrats from tunneling by draping nets on the bank." Captain Billie limped down the dock toward the shoreline.

Garner put his engine in forward and headed for the channel, his acceleration carving a deep wake in the quiet river.

"His motor sure is noisy."

"Too much horsepower for a boat that size." Captain Billie stepped onto the path. "But you can't tell city folk anything."

Tracy looked over her shoulder at the receding boat. Mr. Montgomery had steered the craft in a wide arc and was aimed up Hayden's Creek. His brisk speed pushed the prow of his boat out of the water. Cramleigh's large wharf gleamed in the late morning sun.

When their bow reached the eddy that marked the mouth of the creek, the stern of the boat shuttered and dipped, and the bow jerked upward.

Garner Montgomery pitched forward over the helm. His chest bashed the port side of the skiff as he flipped head first over the side.

"Captain, look!" Tracey screamed.

Teetering under her burden of nets, Selina tried to get a firmer grip on the console. The boat slid back in reaction to the loss of Garner's weight, but surged forward again, struggling to free itself from something beneath the water.

Selina was thrown aft, then forward with the thrust of the engine. Losing her battle to stay upright, she disappeared over the starboard side.

"Run, child, run to Widow Morgan's and use the phone." Captain Billie tugged at the rope to his skiff. "I'll go to them."

As Tracy tore up the path, she saw Garner Montgomery thrashing in the tide next to the foundering boat.

* * * *

Assisted by an usher, Garner Montgomery sidled into the front pew of All Saints church. His black coat was draped over his shoulders because he couldn't get it on. He was wearing a brace for his broken collarbone.

Tracy watched from the rear of the nave as mourners filed in. A noise attracted her attention to the open church door. The hearse was backing toward the end of the brick walk, so the casket could be removed and carried in for the service.

Spotting her father standing with Chief Burch on the porch, she dodged past an undertaker carrying a mammoth floral tribute, and reached his side.

"Couldn't bring her up. Had to call for Navy divers." The chief shook his head.

Her father looked confused. "I know she was a big woman, but…"

'Wasn't her, it was the damn nets. Weighed all hell, wet like that." Chief Burch cringed and blessed himself. "Sorry for the cuss word. The nets pushed her down deep in the bottom mud."

"Garner was lucky," Franklin said. "He could have passed out before Captain Billie got to him."

"Right. We might have had two funerals today." The chief stepped back as the undertakers brought Selina Montgomery's coffin up on the porch.

Tracy saw her reflection in the polished mahogany as the men bore the casket into the church.

* * * *

"If they identify the owner, he will be fined under the ordinance. Untethered gill nets are a hazard to navigation." Tracy's father set the newspaper aside and reached for another biscuit.

"So the propeller got tangled in a drifting fish net?" Tracy put her fork down, her breakfast plate empty. "Why couldn't they see the corks bobbing?"

"Garner Montgomery is a weekend sailor, not skilled in looking for hazards," Franklin said. "Besides, a strong current can pull a net under, corks or not."

Margaret returned to the table with the coffeepot. "So, the verdict is negligence, not murder?"

"Murder? Don't be silly."

"Why?" Margaret said. "Half the Garden Club wanted to kill her. Most of the library committee, too."

Franklin held his cup for Margaret to fill. "Seriously, the sad thing is it was a handmade net. Probably one of Captain Billie's. Most of the ones still in use are his."

"That is sad." Margaret set the pot on a hot pad.

Tracy frowned. "Isn't Mom's idea at least possible? Couldn't somebody put out a net and let the tide carry it into the mouth of the creek? Only wharf up there is Cramleigh Hall's."

Margaret considered her daughter's idea as she slid into her seat. "A working waterman would know the tidal flows like the creases in his palms."

"What's the motive? Selina refused to buy somebody's bluegills for one of her fancy parties?" Franklin said.

"I just thought…" Margaret's voice trailed off, her fingers worrying the edge of her doily.

"Way too farfetched. Like those television shows you watch. How could you orchestrate the collision of the boat and the net? Only Fate and a careless fisherman could do that." Franklin popped the last of the biscuit in his mouth.

* * * *

Tracy waited at the entrance to Captain Billie's lane as Brandon Holt backed the big Cadillac out of the rutted road. She saw Mr. Holt grimace when the car's underside scraped the rocky surface. He straightened the car and shot forward, leaving Tracy in a cloud of grit. She rubbed her eyes, spat and guided her bike up the lane.

Captain Billie was cleaning fish when she rounded the house, and settled on an old crate in the middle of the yard. His gnarled, expert fingers flew along a limp torso, sending scales dancing in the air where they sparkled in the afternoon sun.

"Captain, I've been thinking," Tracy said.

"'Bout what?" The captain placed a fillet in a nearly full enamel pan.

"About Mrs. Montgomery's death."

"Child your age shouldn't dwell on death. Time enough for that when you get old, like me."

"It isn't that."

"What, then?"

"It's her muskrats."

Captain Billie stopped scaling, put his tool down and looked hard at Tracy. "Doubt she thought of them as hers. Now, you've put it that way, though, she did like to control things."

"But you can't control muskrats, sir." Tracy stood and walked closer. "I mean, you can't tell 'em what to do, and not to do, like people."

"You can't, and that's a fact." Captain Billie's lip curled slightly, revealing a hint of the gape-toothed smile.

"Muskrats can chew underwater."

"Always said you were a bright one."

"And you know what else?"

The captain rose, took the pan and headed for the porch. "No, what?"

"They don't have any respect for gill nets."

Captain Billie disappeared into the shadow of the porch, laughing. "You sure have a way with words, young lady, but that's the thing."

"What is, sir?"

"No matter what words are at hand, there are just some things you don't bother telling city folks."

Tracy could barely make out the silhouette of the captain as he stood in the door of his kitchen, in the shabby cabin that despoiled the view from Cramleigh Hall.

LAWN BALLERINAS

BY BETH HINSHAW

I'm at the cabin. It feels different now, serene and warm. The wood stove is new, made of beautiful gray soapstone. I look at the tableau above the mantelpiece, then my eyes shift to the mantelpiece itself. I know what I will find.

It's been two years, six months, 22 days and 12 hours—give or take—since my husband died. I remember this as I look at the last photo of him. He was laughing, holding the fishnet with a monster steelhead trout showing through the netting. He was so proud of his stinking fish. So happy. Such a flaming asshole.

I do have to admit he was in his element and looked the part. Four hundred dollar pole, hip waders, fly fishing vest with lots of pockets, and polarized sunglasses so he could see the fish coming at the fly.

I remember that day. Sitting on my riverside log, out of the corner of my eye I saw that he had hooked one. The tip of his pole jerked. He started reeling it in, slowly, expertly. Let out the line, let the fish really latch on. Let him fight his way to his death. As my husband brought the fish near, he scooped it into the fishnet. The steelhead flopped and writhed and struggled. My husband grabbed the fish by the gills and, showing no mercy, yanked the fly out of its mouth. I could see the thing in the net gasping for water, its mouth and gills opening and finding none.

My husband came out of the river onto the bank, his hip waders squishing all the way, grinning from ear to ear. "Take my pic, hon."

I turned my back on him and went to the catch-all stump that served as a riverside table, found the camera. "Smile," I said as I turned back to him. Dutifully I snapped the digital photo so everyone could see in twelve megapixels his slimy prize. Not to mention his slimy self.

"Clean this thing for me, will ya?" It wasn't a request. He took the fish out of the net. "And make sure you do a proper job of scaling and gutting this time. Last time I nearly gagged on some scales you missed." He basically threw the damn thing at me, all eight pounds or so, and waded back into the river with his fly fishing gear.

All I could think of while cleaning that fish was how much I'd rather be gutting *him*. But I did clean that steelhead with great care. I knew what could happen if I didn't pay attention.

It was March in the Northwest and it was our semiannual camping, fishing, getting out into nature trip. My husband's family had been coming to this twenty-five acre piece of land on the Rogue River near Galice,

Oregon for generations. They own it. No one dared trespass, not with all the signs posted. It's in the National Forest but had been grandfathered in. There is a small cabin on the property. His family calls it a lodge but if you ask me it's more like a shack or a hovel. At least it has rudimentary amenities like an indoor toilet and a kitchen sink.

The focal point of the cabin was his fly tying desk, complete with barbs and brightly colored feathers and hair, beads and eyes. He had a clone of the desk at home.

He was an avid fly fisher. Some would say he was almost rabid in his pursuit of the wily fish. He had made a study of fishing beginning in his childhood—his grandfather had taught him all the tricks.

The trip was never scheduled; rather, we had to go when the weather was warm and dry after a couple days of rain, and when the fish were noted on the Web as coming in from the sea. He'd watch the weather like a hawk. When conditions were right he would be champing at the bit. I had to be completely ready to go on his order. It was a lot of work, but after twelve years of marriage I was used to it. I would watch all indicators as well, and start getting ready, occasionally up to a week earlier. Then we would drive two hours to the cabin.

* * * *

During the spring steelhead run the banks of the Rogue were lined with fishermen vying for a few square feet of space in the river. Every year there were accidents with lures due to poor casting, falls due to slippery rocks and fast running water, and usually a couple of drownings due mostly to stupidity. Of course, stupidity reigned supreme as far as I was concerned. Anybody who spent the time, money and discomfort to catch a fish was a blatant idiot, my husband not excluded.

These fishermen spent tons of money; the license alone is $45 for a year. Not to mention all the gear: poles, reels, creels, nets, waders, vests, tackle boxes with every known lure, you name it. There are all these rules, too. In Oregon fishermen cannot keep native fish, just hatchery fish which have had the top fin cut off. If you're caught with a native fish there's a hefty fine and you can lose your privileges for many years. Native Americans are the only ones who can catch the indigenous steelhead, but only in certain areas.

Steelhead salmon are prized for their fighting spirit. They're a crafty lot. And picky. Some call them trout but they are, in fact, a species of salmon native to the Pacific Northwest. The term steelhead is used to distinguish between rainbows that stay in fresh water permanently and those that venture out to the ocean. Both rainbow and steelhead trout will return to the place where they hatched in order to spawn. Unlike salmon, steelhead and rainbow trout can spawn numerous times before dying. Lucky for them.

And so we were set up there on the banks of the Rogue. We brought with us a ten by ten foot canopy which was pretty much useless when it decided to rain. We parked ourselves there almost all day, even when the weather was cold and wet and gray, like any spring in Oregon. The only things that made it bearable for me were the plentiful bald eagles, osprey, deer, and colorful spring wildflowers. The Oregon trillium were in abundance that week. One year we saw a bear in the fall with her cubs. I remember being sorely tempted to cover my husband with lard and let the bears have at him.

After catching his limit we would pack up our gear and take the fish back to the cabin. Then came the second part of the ritual—the hunting and picking of the mushrooms! As obsessed as he was with fishing, he was even more obsessed with mycology. He meticulously recorded in a mushroom journal as well as on camera, his finds and their precise locations. Then he would take his discoveries, and sometimes the mushrooms themselves, to what I refer to as his mushroom support group. I occasionally went with him. It was just about the only time we went out together.

Anyway, he had to have his fresh mushrooms for dinner. He would make me go scrabbling with him through the forest, up muddy slopes, hanging onto spindly saplings to keep my footing. We knew where the Chanterelles thrived on the property, but it was slow going sometimes. That afternoon was particularly messy. The dense forest hadn't allowed the sun to dry up the mud and I slid down a leaf strewn slope. This was extremely unfortunate because I had the Nikon. The lens got muddy and I was blamed for not putting the lens cover on. He complained bitterly for the twenty minutes it took him to clean the lens to his own exacting specifications. It didn't matter that I had seriously scraped my shins and had blood oozing through the knees of my jeans. I thought he was going to hit me right there but I guess he didn't want to hurt his camera.

We found the scattering of mushrooms amid some Douglas firs. Chanterelles favor Doug firs. It took him an hour to pick a little over a dozen. I held the remote flash for each of them, from four separate angles, illuminating the stem, the caps and their profiles and then finally the gills. He marked every single one of them down in his journal, along with the photo number. He also recorded the GPS coordinates. He checked his mushroom field guide each time. It didn't matter that each looked the same as the previous one, the one next to it and the one right next to that. He had to make sure they were correct and, for instance, didn't show any webbing on the undersides which is often a sign that the mushroom is poisonous. When he was satisfied he took his pocket knife and carefully harvested the mushrooms at the base of the stems, leaving part in the soil, and then gently placed them in a paper bag. The rule of thumb for any mycologist, amateur or expert, is if you are not 100% sure of what you're seeing, throw it away.

When we finished picking we trudged our way back to the chilly cabin. While he lit a fire in the wood stove I got out of my bloodied jeans and cleaned myself up in the bathroom. I put on a fresh pair of pants and then started cooking. It was family tradition—and I use the word family loosely—that I would prepare the evening meal. It was always the same. Steelhead filets with whatever mushrooms he had found.

"Make sure you follow that chef's recipe from that restaurant we went to in Portland. What the heck was it called?" He spoke to himself but I knew I needed to answer. It was part of his game.

"The restaurant is called Ned Ludd's and I have the recipe right here. It's really quite simple. Rub the fish with some curry salt, sear over high heat in a little olive oil. Then in a separate sauté pan, gently cook the mushrooms in butter, take off the heat and add heavy cream. Serve over fish with a side of rice pilaf." I was reading from the recipe I had brought with me. "Even I should be able to make this."

My husband scowled at me and sat down at his fly tying desk while I began my attempt to make a perfect meal over some rather imperfect kitchen appliances. The stove was antediluvian but at least it was propane powered. He came over when he heard me open his precious bag of mushrooms. He had to watch me slice them, and make sure one more time that they were edible.

"Too bad you're allergic to mushrooms. These are fresh, earthy and spectacular." He made sure they were sautéing correctly before he started back to his desk. He had decided that his nymphs had to have more flashy colors. The fish seemed to be fashionistas.

In truth my allergy to mushrooms was aversion. I hated anything that he loved, including his precious fish. Terrified of his retaliatory nature, it would take every ounce of intestinal fortitude for me to choke the fish down.

I put the sautéed mushrooms aside after a few minutes. "I'm starting the fish now, would you please get the wine?" Unhappy with this interruption, he nevertheless scraped his chair back and stomped out to fetch the bottle he had left cooling in the river. For him the timing of wine and fish had to be perfect. Not chilled enough or overdone would ruin the meal.

While he was retrieving the wine, I removed the *Cortinarius* mushroom paste from the small baggie that I had concealed in my pocket while changing earlier. I stirred it into the sauce, along with the heavy cream and tossed the baggie into the trash. I started humming a little ditty. I was so happy that I was finally going to do something about his abuse. When I heard his heavy boots on the cabin steps I plastered a neutral look on my face, but the song continued in my head.

* * * *

Really, it was his fault for starting me down the path to his demise. Last fall I had asked what kind of mushrooms we had growing in our front yard. He brought out his books, studied them, and finally stated that they were *Cortinarius*. "This genus is not well documented. It's notoriously difficult to differentiate these species. But I am certain. They're terribly poisonous, nearly always fatal." He then had me go to Home Depot for a lawn fungicide to kill them. He worried that neighborhood kids or dogs might get sick and die from eating them. But it had rained and he had to wait a few days for the lawn to dry out before he applied it. This gave my lover and I plenty of time to perfect our plan, starting with a spore print for propagation.

As it turned out my lover, botany professor at the University of Oregon, possessed a number of dried *Cortinarius*. "Did you know, my darling, that some *Cortinarius Orellanus* specimens have retained toxicity for over sixty years?"

I smiled when I heard that tidbit of information. "Where did you get them? Are they legal?"

"If I tell you where I got them I'll have to kill you!" Laughter. "And no, it's nowhere near legal. We botanists like to keep close tabs on poisonous mushrooms. We wouldn't want anyone to die."

My lover and I needed to make sure that if somehow I was accused of murdering my husband there would be *Cortinarius* growing nearby, which he could have picked by mistake. Planting the spores was really just a precaution: Reasonable Doubt. We knew the general timing of the fish runs. We knew where on the property the spores would flourish and how much beforehand to plant them. It was easy to make a few tablespoons of mushroom paste in the botany lab late one night.

* * * *

My husband set the wet bottle down on the table. "This is a $55 bottle of wine here so you need to enjoy it. *Clos Electrique* from Dundee. Good Oregon wine. Cameron Vineyards, neutral oak, nice mineral tones, buttery, a little pear and apple. I'll open it this time. Last time you mangled the cork and it ended up in the bottle."

I just smiled at him and slid the perfectly cooked fish onto plates. His got the mushrooms; mine just some extra butter from a clean knife.

He gobbled up his dinner, belched loudly, and told me that I'd done okay. A rare compliment. I told him it was the great recipe. He humphed at me and went back to his desk. I cleared the table and scraped the remnants of dinner into the trash. We always deposited the trash in the dumpster at Park Headquarters on the way home. I washed the dishes and pots, and retired for the evening.

I lay in bed that night speculating as to when the symptoms would appear. Would it be three days or twenty? Would he feel terrible at first and then begin to recover? Would the end be excruciatingly painful? One could always hope.

I had a sudden, terrifying thought as I drifted off. Did he write in his journal that he had found the *Cortinarius* on our front lawn? What if my lover and I were caught? I had to have a look at that journal. I had to know.

The next morning we set up on the riverbank and my husband went back to fishing. He would catch his limit, put the fish on ice in the cooler and we would head home.

I eventually excused myself and went back to the cabin. I found his journal and opened it with unsteady hands, dreading what I might find. There it was. *Cortinarius speciossissimus*. He had even made a note of its common name, Deadly Lawn Galerina. God! What had I done? My actions couldn't be undone. His death was highly likely if not inevitable. Would they even suspect foul play? Could I do something to prevent my getting caught? I had to think.

I went back to the river, sat on the log, and watched my husband fish. Think! After strenuous mind-numbing thought, a perfect solution came to me.

* * * *

About a week and a half after that fateful night I had a sudden, severe case of the stomach flu. Nausea, diarrhea, splitting headache, aching in my back and joints. Of course my husband told me it was nothing, that I really wasn't very sick at all. Even when he saw the contents of my stomach in the toilet he wasn't convinced. Typical. No sympathy. No kindness. He called me a hypochondriac. I was ill for a good week.

Around day fifteen he began feeling the effects. That's the beauty of the *Cortinarius*. It takes an exquisitely long time for the poison to manifest itself in the human body. He thought he had caught my little bug. We went to the doctor, who sent him home with an antibiotic and orders to rest and drink plenty of fluids. This he did and he started to feel better after a few days. He hypothesized that he was in such robust health that, unlike me, he could fight it off more quickly. He went on about his business.

The following week the Mushroom Club had a scheduled field trip to our property on the invitation of my husband. Seven members went: three other men, two women and one teenage girl with a bad case of acne. I came along and helped out as needed. They found lots of different kinds of mushrooms: Golden Chanterelles, Morels, King Boletes and a handful of American Matsutakes. The pimply girl was near the Chanterelles when she noticed the patch of *Cortinarius*.

"Ooh! What are these?" she asked no one in particular.

"Don't touch it!" the group leader barked. "It could be poisonous!" The others were too intent on the Matsutakes to pay any attention to the ugly urchin.

The Tuesday after the mushroom hunt, nausea, headache and diarrhea attacked my husband with a vengeance. He thought it was the flu coming back. He began to have an almost insatiable thirst. I was shocked at how much he drank. I was amazed by his output, so to speak. He was in the bathroom more than he was out of it, it seemed. Then he stopped urinating altogether. He became very fatigued and was in bed for another week before he admitted that maybe he should go to the emergency room. They immediately admitted him to the ICU.

What happened next was a rapid deterioration of his bodily functions. His kidneys were so far gone that it was too late for dialysis or even a kidney transplant. It never occurred to my husband or anyone else that his illness had anything to do with mushrooms. Such an arrogant bastard.

One night the doctor told me that the end was near; death would be within the hour. There was nothing they could do for him. I went to his bedside, took his hand in mine, gently spoke his name. His eyes fluttered open and he focused on mine. I suppose he thought I had come to tell him that he was everything to me, that I would miss him and love him always. Tears glistened in his eyes.

"Honey. I have some things to tell you." My voice was calm and even. "I don't regret what I have done. I couldn't take your abuse anymore. I was sick of your incessant criticism. I was terrified of retaliation if I crossed you. I could take the occasional physical beating, but the constant psychological beating I took from you was too much." I looked at him and discovered fear in his eyes. For once, he was listening to me.

"My lover and I talked for a long time about how to get rid of you. Then, when I found the *Cortinarius*...."

His eyes widened. "Yes, sweetheart, we poisoned you. I put *Cortinarius* in that lovely mushroom sauce. The one you complimented me on. We knew that there was a latency, but we also knew the general time frame for the symptoms to show. It was really quite simple for me to fake a case of the flu. Headache, nausea. I gave myself ipecac to induce vomiting and drank bottles of Milk of Magnesia so you would see that I was sick. I waited a week and a half after our trip to the Rogue. Then I got my 'flu.' The timing worked well."

He was terrified now. I let this realization sink in for a minute and then I added the perfect last jibe.

"I thought you'd like to know the identity of my lover." I told him the name. I stared at him as he lay helpless among the restrictive tubes and machines. His jaundiced face turned ashen. He clutched at the ventilator tube, all the while gasping for air like one of his fish caught in a net. Alarms went off. The nurse and a doctor came running in. They shooed me out of the way. I went down to the cafeteria for coffee.

The ICU nurse found me twenty minutes later, telling me he had died moments before. "We took out the ventilator to make him a little more comfortable. Without that tube he started talking up a storm."

A practiced tear ran slowly down my cheek. "I should have been in there," I uttered, feigning just the right amount of grief.

"Don't feel guilty about being out of the room, sweetie. I've seen many of the dying wait to take their last breath until their loved ones leave. At the end some of them don't want to burden their family."

"What did he say?" More tears flowed from my eyes.

She chuckled, "You know, I think he was enjoying himself. He was talking about ballerinas on the lawn."

I gave her a quizzical look. "He must have been hallucinating."

"Oh, honey. I've heard it all." She placed her hand gently on my arm. "Sorry for your loss."

I turned away. I took comfort in the thought that he had had twenty minutes or so to suffer with my deathbed confession.

* * *

My lover and I are at the cabin. We've made some improvements so it's now quite livable: all new appliances in the kitchen, updated bathroom with a claw foot tub and two-person sauna in an ell that we added on. New blinds cover the windows, artwork adorns the walls, new furniture, a Persian rug. The old desk is gone, replaced by an antique secretary. Yesterday we hung my husband's rod, creel and fishnet over the mantelpiece. We like the irony; perhaps I like it more. The photos of my husband are all there too, lined up like toy soldiers. My little shrine.

I head to the kitchen island. I deftly open the bottle of *Clos Electrique*, pour two glasses and give one to my lover. I am taken aback by the beauty of the graceful hand that accepts the wine. Her nails are perfectly manicured. The glow from the wood stove highlights her auburn hair.

We raise our glasses, clink and tip them ever so slightly toward that last photo. We silently toast the fact that it's been two years, six months, 22 days and 14 hours—give or take—since my husband died.

DON'T TAKE THAT CHANCE

BY KATE FELLOWES

"Hi, Danny," Robin Bauer greeted the package delivery man waiting at the back door of her gift shop, Robin's Nest. "You're early today."

She juggled her morning coffee from one hand to the other, punching her access code into the security panel with one well-manicured finger.

Danny shook his head and looked as forlorn as a six-foot tall blond ever could, even one on the wrong side of forty. "You would not believe how many stops I've got scheduled for today. I won't be finished until eight o'clock tonight."

"Bad luck! Eight hours work is plenty for me."

She pulled the door open and let him bump his over-laden dolly across the threshold into the storeroom/lunchroom/office.

"But maybe those days are numbered," she said with a smile, tapping the fresh morning paper sticking out of her tote bag. "I haven't checked the lottery numbers from last night yet, and I've got a good feeling!"

Danny began unloading boxes onto the stainless steel shelving along one wall. "You say that every Monday morning," he said, laughing.

Robin took a moment to admire the view as he bent, lifted and swung one box after another. "Hope springs eternal."

The back door opened, admitting the rest of the Robin's Nest staff. Angie, a retired office clerk who now ran the cash register, lagged behind Jason, a recent college grad working his first full-time job.

"Hey, guys," Jason said, looking up from the cell phone he carried like a talisman.

Crossing the small room, he stowed his lunch in the ancient refrigerator in one corner. "We have got to clean this thing out," he complained, nose wrinkling.

Angie added her crisp brown paper bag to the fridge then lifted out one wrinkled apple and half a sandwich, the bread blue with mold.

"Who leaves this stuff in there?" she wondered aloud, eyeing the back of Jason's head.

Robin caught the look and bit her lip to keep from smiling. Angie chucked the rotten food into the big plastic garbage can underneath the bulletin board, dusting her hands and clucking her tongue.

Danny heaved the last box onto the shelf with a grunt. "That's it," he said to no one in particular.

He parked the dolly beside the door in front of the big landing net Robin used to capture birds in the summertime. Since the shop was located right across from the park and Robin insisted on keeping the front door propped open with a sandwich board all day, birds were regular visitors.

"Why don't you just keep the door closed?" Danny had asked her once and she'd pouted.

"We get more business if it's propped open. Folks can just wander right on in. And the net doesn't hurt the birds. I can snag 'em and get them right back out." She pantomimed her net-swishing technique. "Haven't lost one yet!"

Now Danny held out the electronic clipboard for a signature. "Who will do the honors?"

The crowded back room held not only the lunch table, refrigerator, microwave and shelving, but also Robin's desk over near the only window. She came out from behind it to sign her name with a flourish.

"There!"

While Danny keyed in the letters of her name, Robin spread the newspaper across the lunch table and turned to the page listing winning lottery numbers. The shriek that split the air seconds later caused everyone to freeze.

"We won!" Robin cried. "We won! We won! We won!" She grabbed Angie by the forearms and jumped up and down. Angie, stunned, jumped, too.

"No way!" Jason rushed over, looking down at the newspaper. "Are you sure?"

"Yes! Yes! We play the same numbers every week, silly. And I get the ticket. 2-7-14-23-28-31," she recited the numbers by heart as Jason followed along, dragging his finger across the newsprint.

"We won!" he shouted when she finished. "We really did! We're rich! We're rich!" He and Danny high-fived and clapped each other on the shoulder.

"Congratulations, you guys. That's amazing!" Danny whistled. "What was the jackpot? Do you know?"

"Eighteen million dollars," Robin stated with certainty. "At least, that's what the board at the gas station said." She pulled out a chair and flopped onto it. "I can hardly believe it."

"My heart's just pounding!" Angie said, collapsing onto the chair beside Robin's. Her eyes swam with tears of surprise.

"How long have we been buying tickets, Ang?" Robin asked. "Two years or three, since those factory workers hit it big?"

"All I know is you've been docking my pay since Day One," Jason teased.

"Oh, we started playing the lottery way before you hired on! And aren't you glad?" Robin asked, laughing. "Bring me the ticket. It's right there on the board." She pointed at the scrap of orange paper posted next to the week's schedule, a calendar and some coupons for the sandwich shop on the corner.

Jason plucked the ticket down and read the numbers off slowly. "3-9-11-22-30-41. Um, boss?"

"What? That can't be right!" Robin snatched the paper from his hand. "We always play the same numbers. It improves the odds."

"Actually, statistically—" Jason began in his grad school voice.

"Always. The. Same. Numbers," Robin interrupted.

Danny glanced at his watch. When Robin looked over at him, eyes wide, he suggested, "Maybe the clerk at the gas station gave you the wrong ticket."

"It was really busy in there that day," Robin said, thinking out loud. "And I didn't really look at the slip." She sighed. "We'd never prove it, though." The corners of her mouth turned down, her brows knit together.

"Could be she gave you two slips stuck together," Angie said. "That happened to me once. I got two credit card slips instead of one in my bag at the Big Mart. Well, I must have spent half an hour looking up that other person's name in the phone book to call and tell them. You can't be too safe with your receipts, you know!"

Robin gasped, feeling a little surge of hope. That had happened to her at the Big Mart once, too. "Then the right slip might still be in my purse!" She was already on her feet heading over to the file cabinet where she stashed her purse.

"Or maybe it's somewhere in that mess," Danny said, pointing at her desk. "I'm sure it will turn up somewhere. And when I come with the afternoon delivery, you'll be serving all your customers champagne."

"I hope you're right," Robin said as he clattered his dolly outside. Danny did have a point. Her workspace was a bit of a mess. It would be easy to lose a little piece of paper somewhere among the invoices and sales receipts.

Tipping her purse upside down, she dumped it out onto the lunch table. Her lipstick rolled off onto the floor as she sorted through the rest of the contents, first quickly and then with more care. Mints, wallet, comb, change purse, envelope full of bank deposit slips, coupons, pen, hankie. But no lottery ticket. Next, she tackled the pile on her desk. Picking up every single paper, smoothing it flat, she examined them all, front and back. Nothing.

Angie was picking carefully through the contents of the garbage. "Maybe it fell off the board," she said, even though a ticket had never fallen off the board before.

Eventually, Robin sat down heavily and Angie shook her head. They exchanged a solemn look.

"Easy come, easy go," Angie said unconvincingly, patting Robin's hand. She blinked back fresh tears. "Eighteen million dollars."

Taking the cash drawer from its resting place on the corner of Robin's desk, Angie headed for the front of the store, her shoulders slumped. Jason set to work opening the boxes Danny had brought, silently checking their contents off the packing slips.

"I can't understand it," Robin said aloud, fingering the losing ticket. She read the numbers on the paper again in disbelief, double-checking. Then, she blinked, looking again.

The date printed at the top of the paper wasn't right. She'd gotten the ticket on Saturday, for Sunday's drawing. This paper was dated Thursday! The clerk would never have handed her a two-day old slip by accident.

How could an old ticket have ended up where their new ticket should be?

Robin's breath caught in her throat.

There was only one way.

The papers had been switched. The winning ticket had been replaced with this old loser.

But, how? And, who?

Could a customer have slipped in back and swapped them? The door to this workroom was rarely closed and never locked. But, no. The lottery drawing had been Sunday night and now it was Monday morning. No customers could have come in.

Robin stood up quickly, tossing things back into her purse at random. She heaved her wallet in with some force, not liking the new direction of her thoughts.

Dropping back into her chair, she rubbed at her temples, trying to push the idea away. But it kept coming back.

Jason?

Angie?

Both of them could use eighteen million dollars. Well, who couldn't?

Robin bit her lip, tapping the paper against the table, thinking. It would be time to open the shop soon. Time to act normally while wondering which of her employees had stolen the winning ticket. Picking up a pencil, she doodled more hearts and flowers next to the existing ones on the desk blotter.

Whoever had switched the slips had to know she knew. Angie had said, "Easy come, easy go," but there had been tears in her eyes. Of anxiety? Or of genuine loss? Jason hadn't said a word, just turned away to work. Because he thought she'd been mistaken all along? Or because he was guilty and couldn't look her in the eye?

Pleating the losing ticket as she thought, Robin considered the logistics of the crime. Whoever did it would have had to come into the shop late the night before or earlier that morning. They would have used their access code to unlock the door, crept across the room in darkness and slipped back out, resetting the code. She could just call the alarm company and find out which code had been used.

"Say, Jason, could you run down to the post office and pick up some stamps for that sale flyer going out next week?"

Jason looked up from the packing slips. "Right now?"

"Uh huh."

Robin heard him sigh and set down the paperwork.

"How many should I get?"

"Two hundred," she said, handing him money from the Petty Cash box in her top desk drawer.

He gave a little salute, finger to temple, and set off.

Robin knew he'd dawdle all down the block, probably stopping to pick up a cup of coffee on the way. He'd be gone, out of earshot, for at least ten minutes.

But she didn't need anywhere near that long to get an answer from the alarm company. The polite, businesslike voice on the phone told her the back door of Robin's Nest had been opened at 6:15 a.m. and relocked at 6:17 a.m. that morning.

And the access code used was Robin's.

Stymied, Robin hung up the phone and, for the first time, felt angry. She'd always paid a fair wage to her workers, even when it meant she took home a bit less in a week. How dare one of them betray her this way?

She drummed her fingers on the desktop, wondering what to do next. They would have to have a meeting. One of those "just put it back and there will be no questions" kind of meetings. And they'd have it right after closing time, before they even balanced the till. Then she could dust her hands, just as Angie had done when she walked away from the stinky garbage. Robin lifted her head, feeling a bit better. In just a few hours, she'd be finished with this stinky business.

* * * *

Late that afternoon as the shop was closing, Robin got to work. Tidying her desk, dumping the garbage, she set the stage. She'd spent several hours anticipating this showdown, thinking out every possible scenario. No matter what happened, she'd rehearsed the exchange in her head.

Jason came through the door leading to the front of the shop, carefully balancing the cash drawers from both registers. "Busy day," he said, smiling. "We made some money—but nowhere near eighteen million dollars." He set the drawers down onto the table, ready to count the day's profit.

"Don't get started right away with that," she said. "We're having a staff meeting."

"Cool." Jason hooked a chair with one foot and yanked it out, then sat.

Just as Angie entered the room the back doorbell rang.

"Got it!" she said, pulling the door wide and stepping back to let Danny trundle over the threshold with the afternoon delivery.

"Hello, all," Danny greeted them. "Just a few more things for you today." He looked up, at Robin. "Any luck finding that ticket?"

"Not yet," Robin said, not moving from her desk.

He unloaded boxes onto the shelving and stepped toward her, clipboard extended.

As Robin signed, she dropped her voice low so he had to lean close to hear her. "Could you stick around a few minutes? I may need a witness." She shot her eyebrows up and glanced at Jason, engrossed in his telephone.

"Sure, sure," Danny agreed. "I'll just take my break."

Danny frequently took his break in their back room, eating some fruit or a sandwich over the garbage can, gulping some old coffee from the pot on the counter. Now, he filled a chipped ceramic mug with the last of the brew and pulled an orange from his jacket pocket. Robin saw him look at Jason and then at Angie, who was rinsing out the empty pot.

"Angie, we're having a brief staff meeting now," Robin said, rising.

"All-righty," Angie said, easing into the chair across from Jason.

Robin took a deep breath, steeling her nerves, focusing her energy. "I've been thinking a lot about that lottery ticket incident from this morning," she began.

Jason looked up. "Incident?"

"Yes." Robin strode slowly around the room, doing her best Perry Mason imitation. "You see, someone swapped our winning ticket for some old losing ticket."

Angie gasped, one hand hovering over her throat. "Who would do that?"

"Did you call the cops?" Jason set his phone down.

"I don't think it was a customer or a burglar," Robin said slowly. "I think it was an inside job." She let the sentence hang there in silence for a few seconds.

"You don't think I did it!" Angie said, breathless.

Jason crossed his arms over his chest defensively. "Well, don't look at me." He stretched his legs out, frowning.

"Look, I don't care who took it. I just want it back," Robin said. "We're a team here. We buy our ticket as a team, we'll split the money the same way." She stood over near the door now, hands on her hips.

Across the room, Danny stuffed another orange segment into his mouth as if it was popcorn and he was watching a movie.

"I know you used my own key code to get in here," she said, letting her gaze drift over Angie. "And I know you used it to lock up again, too," she added, shifting her eyes past Jason. "Pretty clever."

She lifted her head, narrowing her focus.

"Of course, you've watched me key in those numbers a million times. At least." A brief smile flickered across her lips.

Danny swallowed hard, spit a seed into the garbage can. "Are you talking to me, now?" he asked.

Slowly, sadly, Robin nodded. "Sure am. I just couldn't think any of my loyal staff would rob the other two blind by switching those tickets. You're the only other one who might know my key code."

"Geez, Robin!" Danny's cheeks flushed. "I can't believe this. How could you possibly think I—"

"Because you stand there every day, eating your lunch by our bulletin board. Those same numbers are posted every week. You had to have seen them. Memorized them!"

Danny threw the rind of his orange into the garbage. "I'm not going to stand here and listen to this malarkey. I've got work to do."

He took two steps toward her, stationed at the back door like a bank guard, then turned, ready to sprint into the shop and out the front entrance.

But he never made it.

Jason pushed his chair backward, blocking the path, forcing Danny to veer around him. Robin grabbed the big landing net from beside the door, telescoped the handle with one swift twist and used her practiced swishing technique to drop the net over Danny's head and shoulders.

"Call the cops, Angie," she ordered calmly.

Trapped between Jason and Robin, the delivery man stood without struggling.

"Why'd you do it, Danny?" Robin asked with genuine interest. "Did you think I wouldn't notice?"

Danny smiled, teeth bright in his handsome face, and shrugged. "Hope springs eternal," he said.

THE LURE OF THE RAINBOW

BY GLORIA ALDEN

The spring peepers fell silent at eleven thirty-five. Carl glanced at the windup alarm clock. Probably a raccoon prowling, he thought. His wife, Dotty, God rest her soul, had wanted a goldfish pool beside the house so they could hear water running over rocks. He smiled. It seemed silly since their cabin was on Red Fern Lake. Every year they stocked it with feeder goldfish and restocked it again the following year. Only a few fish survived the cold winters or the raccoons. Probably some spring peepers fell prey to raccoons, too. That's all life is about in the end, he thought. Living and dying.

He sighed, rolled over onto his back and put his hands behind his head. God, how he missed Dotty, even after ten years. Maybe he should sell the cabin. It'd be different if Abby would come, but she hadn't come by since she got married. I thought when she married a fly fisherman they'd spend some time here, he thought. Hadn't happened.

He thought of those summers when the three of them enjoyed the lake, the woods and each other. As soon as school was out, they'd head for the cabin and stay all summer. Abby took to fly fishing like a natural. He'd started her out fishing for brookies in the creek that ran into the lake. They were easier to catch. Dotty didn't fish, but she loved it here, too. He smiled remembering her excitement over every fish they caught—rainbow or brown trout, or sometimes bass or perch. But it was the rainbow trout they most liked to fish for. Great fighters they were. How delicious fresh fish tasted when Dotty fried them, but not anymore. Could be my cooking or more likely eating alone, he thought. Maybe I can coax Abby to come for a few days this summer. She could cook our catch the way her mom taught her.

Car lights flashed through the window. Who'd be coming this late? He turned on the outside light then opened the door when he recognized the visitor.

"What are you doing here this time of night?"

"Sorry I'm so late. I had a few days off. Thought I'd do some fly fishing if you can put me up."

Carl shrugged. "Come in. You can have the spare room." He nodded in that direction. "Helluva time for someone to come. If you want anything, get it yourself," he grumbled. "I'm goin' back to bed. See you in the morning." Frowning, he went to his room and closed his door, leaving his visitor to settle in on his own.

* * * *

On her way to the cabin, Abby stopped at Red Fern General Store to fill her gas tank and pick up a few groceries. Few people remembered a time when the Gilberts didn't manage the store. Mrs. Gilbert hasn't changed much although her hair is whiter, Abby thought when she walked in and saw her behind the counter.

"Hello, Abby," Ida Gilbert greeted her. "I'm sorry about your dad."

Abby nodded and swallowed. Tears were never far away since he'd died last week.

"Everyone thought so highly of Carl. We're all upset."

"Thank you. I just wish I'd come up here more often to be with him."

Ida reached across the counter and squeezed her hand. "It happens with young folks.

They get busy. I see it all the time."

Abby nodded and wiped her eyes. Ida went on. "Your dad kept us up to date on what you were doing. Heard you're a nurse now. He showed us pictures of your wedding. You were a pretty bride. He was happy you married a fly fisherman. Said you'd probably be up here a lot. Don't think I ever met your husband. If he came in here, it had to be without you or your dad.

Is he coming up later to be with you?"

Abby gave a weak smile, not about to tell her Brad had never come to the cabin. He said fly fishing in mountain streams out west was enjoyable, not some small lake in the east.

"No, he had to work." She wondered if he was really at some casino. "I'm on my way to the cabin and thought I'd pick up some food to tide me over a few days."

"Let me know if you need any help."

Abby wandered the aisles of the old store with wooden floors and shelves stocked exactly as she remembered them—not a lot of selections, but everything necessary. She'd loved coming here as a kid. It was always busy with campers, cabin owners or renters, and the permanent residents of Red Fern. She picked up a loaf of bread, a quart of milk, and a dozen eggs. With this and the food in her car, she'd have enough for several days.

Ida totaled up Abby's groceries. "You remind me so much of your mother with your black hair and blue eyes. Quite striking."

Abby gave her a polite smile. The pain of her mother's death had softened over the years. Maybe because it had been a natural death, not like her dad's.

"That reminds me, I have some mail here for your dad. Let's see. Ahh. Here it is." The Gilberts maintained the post office for Red Fern in their store.

Abby took the mail and thanked her.

Ida's eyes radiated sympathy. "Can't be easy going up there alone. If you want, I can get Ed to take over while I go to the cabin with you."

Abby shook her head. "Thank you. I appreciate your offer, but ...." Her voice trailed off.

"I know. Some things are best done alone. Here's our number." Ida handed her a card. "Call me if you need anything or just a friendly shoulder to cry on."

Giving a brief nod, Abby went out the screen door onto the front porch. She didn't notice the man sitting in one of the rockers until he stood up and spoke.

"Hi, Abby."

Startled, she turned his way. The man wore sunglasses and a deputy sheriff's uniform. She gave a tenuous smile. "Greg? Greg Gearhart?"

"Yes." He took off his sunglasses and smiled. "It's been quite a few years."

"You joined the army, didn't you?"

"Yeah. Then went to college, finished and eventually ended up back here."

"You're with the sheriff's department, I see."

He nodded and his face sobered. "Sorry about your dad. I liked him. When I had a few days off, I'd often spend it at his cabin fishing and shootin' the breeze with him."

She searched his face. "I didn't know. He never told me."

He was silent a moment before answering. "Maybe he didn't want you to feel guilty. He talked a lot about you, you know."

Feeling her eyes well up again, Abby glanced away, biting her lip for control. Why had she put off coming here to visit these past few summers?

They stood in silence then he said, "I'll be up later to make sure everything's okay."

She nodded and hurried to her car before he'd see her tears of regret over lost time not spent with someone she loved more than anyone else. A rumble signaled a storm approaching, and soon rain started pouring down. Abby switched on her wipers. Even with the rain sluicing off her windshield, every curve of the road was familiar and brought back memories. Half way up the drive to the cabin was the big rock she'd sit on waiting for her dad to return when he'd gone somewhere. He'd stop for her and let her steer the car and even drive when she got a little older.

The cabin came into view as she pulled into a clearing—a simple cabin but enough for the three of them. She looked beyond the cabin to Red Fern Lake, the lake that had claimed her father's life.

Abby ran through the rain to the door and unlocked it. Once inside her eyes roamed over the room that took up half the cabin. An aerial view picture of the cabin hung over the stone fireplace. If one looked closely, a small person could be seen on the dock. She'd waited forever for the plane to fly over, her small arm growing tired from waving. A comfortable couch and chairs with reading lamps were in front of the fireplace.

At the other end a table, chairs, stove and refrigerator made up the kitchen. Her heart seized when she spotted a solitary cup with a picture of a rainbow trout at the end of a line setting on the kitchen counter. His favorite cup. She picked it up, holding it against her heart for long moments before rinsing out moldy residue of unfinished coffee.

When the rain stopped, she carried her suitcase to her old bedroom. The bed was stripped of bedding. Only a bare mattress remained. Perplexed, she stared at it. Her parents always kept it made up for her or other guests. She felt a pang, wondering if her dad had given up all hope of her coming. She fell on the bed and sobbed. She'd come too late. Maybe she should have put the cabin up for sale without returning, but she knew she needed to be where he'd spent his last days.

Finally, she went to the large wooden chest holding clean bedding. It still held a hint of the lavender her mother kept in there. There weren't as many sheets or blankets as usual and only one set of twin sheets. Abby smiled when she took out the well worn sheets with Peanut cartoon characters. She hadn't used them in years.

After she made the bed, she fixed a cup of instant coffee, sat down at the table and picked up the mail. There was a letter from Uncle George dated several days before her dad died. She opened and read it. He wrote he'd be coming to visit this weekend, do some fly fishing. That would've been last weekend, she thought. Dad was found Saturday. I wonder if Uncle George came to the cabin or changed his mind. He didn't mention it at the funeral. She read on. He expressed interest in buying the cabin, wrote he'd be willing to make a good offer for it. She put the letter down. Uncle George. Her father's younger brother. They'd never been close. She'd never like how he bragged about his money, as if he was superior to her teacher parents. She didn't like his wife, either. A snob. If I sell to him, she thought, he'll probably tear it down to build a big fancy one. She tossed the letter in the pile of junk mail before going outside.

Abby stood by the railing on the back deck and stared at the dock near where she'd heard his body was found. She couldn't understand how her father could've drowned. The coroner ruled out a heart attack. He had contusions on his face and head so the coroner thought maybe he'd had a dizzy spell and fell, hitting his head on the dock before ending up in the lake. Was he getting ready to take the boat out? He liked to fish where the creek entered the lake and the water lilies grew. Looking out, she felt hatred for the lake he'd loved so much and had claimed his life. But then she heard her father's voice in her mind, "The lake is a thing of beauty that brings peace if you let it." How often she'd heard him say it, especially in the years following her mother's death. She watched ducks swimming near the shore. An eagle soared over head. She caught her breath as it swooped and rose again with a fish in its talons.

"Oh, Dad, I wish you were here to share that with me."

The sun parted the clouds, and she held her breath when she saw not just one, but a double rainbow. She felt peacefulness enter.

"Maybe you are here with me," she whispered. "Maybe you are."

She heard a car drive up, but was reluctant to see anyone, not wanting to destroy this moment. Maybe they'll go away. When she heard someone coming around the corner, she turned and saw Greg Gearhart, a box of pizza in one hand and a six pack of beer in the other.

"I looked in the door and didn't see you so I figured you might be back here."

She smiled at him then turned back to the lake. "It's peaceful in spite of what happened." She took a deep breath and released it.

"I love this place, this lake. It's one of the reasons I returned to live here."

"And another reason?" she asked, not really caring that much.

"A girl. I brought pizza. I figured you probably weren't eating much. Beer, too."

She nodded at him then turned to continue staring at the lake. "Did you marry her?"

"No. It was a long time ago. Old news. I'm hungry and didn't want to eat alone, so I came here. Want some?"

"Psychology. You're feeling sorry for me and trying to get me to eat."

He gave a sheepish smile. "Was it that obvious?"

She nodded. "I'll have one piece and a beer." She started to go inside.

"Stay here. I'll fix it." Soon she heard him getting plates and glasses out of the cupboard.

He didn't open up several cupboards looking for things. He obviously knew his way around. She wasn't sure how she felt about it. Grateful her father had a friend, or a little envious he'd taken her place, or guilty because she should've been here? Of course, she never had much time off. The drive was rather long, too, and Brad never wanted to come here or have her go without him.

Greg brought out the pizza, paper plates, napkins and two tall glasses of beer and set everything on the table. He held a chair for her before sitting down.

"Thank you. You seem to know your way around in the kitchen."

"I meant it when I said I liked your dad. He was one of those special guys willing to listen and not pass judgment. I miss him, but not as much as you do, of course. I'm sorry I couldn't make the funeral. I couldn't get the time off. We've been short handed lately."

"I'm glad you were here for him, especially since I wasn't." She swallowed.

"It was easier for me because I live in Red Fern, and I'm single. No encumbrances. Now eat your pizza while it's still warm."

She picked up a piece and took a bite. She was hungrier than she realized.

"Is your husband coming to join you?"

"No," she said without explanation. Greg saying no encumbrances resonated with her. Is that what Brad is? Not for the first time she realized what a failure her marriage was. They argued over everything. She glanced at Greg. He was staring at the lake. The sun had dropped behind the pines, leaving a reddish glow on the lake.

"Were you here when they found him?" She wanted to know but dreaded his answer, too.

"I answered the call about someone floating. I called for backup and raced straight here."

"And?" she prodded when he didn't go on.

He closed his eyes. "I pulled him in."

Abby heard the pain in his voice and started to cry. Had she ever stopped crying? It didn't seem so. He took her hand, held it tightly and let her cry. When she finally stopped and freed her hand to mop her face with the tail of her shirt, she glanced at him and saw tears on his face, too.

"He really did mean a lot to you, didn't he?"

"He did. I don't think it was an accident." There was anger in his voice.

Her eyes widened. "You don't?"

He shook his head. "No. I think someone killed him. He wasn't some doddering old man. He was healthy and spry."

Abby took a deep breath as pain shot through her. "No, that can't be true. No one would want to harm him. The coroner's report said he drowned."

"There was a bruise on the back of his head. He could've been knocked out first."

"But it could have been an accident, couldn't it?" She wanted that to be true. An accidental death was bad enough, but she couldn't bear the thought of someone deliberately killing him. "Did you tell the sheriff about your suspicious? What did he say?"

He shook his head. "He didn't believe it was murder."

"He won't consider it at all?"

"You have to realize he's retiring and heading for Florida at the end of this season." Greg's face showed his frustration.

Abby felt anger wash over her. If he was murdered, would the murderer get away with it just because the sheriff didn't want to be bothered? It was hard to believe. She thought about the bare bed and wondered if the murderer had slept there, and shuddered.

"I wondered about the bare bed and missing bedding."

He looked at her, waiting.

"Dad always kept the spare bed made up in case someone came. There's only a bare mattress now. It made me wonder if he'd given up on me," she said in a small voice.

He reached for her hand again. "No, he always thought you'd come. And the bed was always made up and waiting, even the times I showed up late at night."

"Late at night?" She looked at him with a question in her eyes.

He shook his head and didn't look at her. "Not for a long time, but when I first came back I had a bit of a drinking problem."

Briefly she wondered about the girl he didn't marry and thought about what he'd said about her father being non-judgmental. Then she closed her eyes in pain as the thought of her dad's possible murder washed over her again. "The only sheets for the bed were some old ones with Peanut characters."

He stared at her with narrowed eyes. "That can't be. I can't remember what the sheets looked like, but they sure as hell weren't cartoon characters. I'd remember that."

"Could someone have taken the sheets because of DNA?"

He nodded. "If someone slept on them, they might've worried about DNA. I can't think of any other reason someone would take the bedding."

"There was only one used coffee cup on the counter."

"I noticed. It was your dad's favorite cup. If someone was here, they washed whatever else they used."

"There was a letter from my Uncle George. He wrote he was coming for the weekend. Wrote about wanting to buy the cabin. Was he here when they found Dad? He didn't say anything about it at the funeral."

"Not that I know of. I recognized most here that day except for a few curious boaters. No one mentioned being related to him. Do you think your uncle is capable of something like that?"

She bit her lip. "I never liked him, but it was because he always bragged and acted like he was big stuff. Even if he wanted the cabin, I can't see him killing for it."

"Abby, I don't like having you here alone."

"I'll be okay. We don't know for sure he was killed, and I really don't want to believe it, to tell the truth." Her voice trembled. "Besides, only you and the Gilberts know I'm here."

"I'm putting my number in your cell phone. If you hear anything, or even feel nervous and afraid of being alone call me."

She nodded and looked away.

"I mean it. If I think you won't, I'll sleep on your porch."

She gave him a weak smile. "I will. I promise, but you may be sorry."

He smiled reassured. "Never. Someday I'll tell you about the crush I had on you when we were both twelve years old."

"Really?" She looked at him in disbelief.

"Really. I liked what a tomboy you were, not afraid to bait a hook, and you did a mean cast with a fly rod."

"Didn't I manage to hook you once when I did a wild cast?"

He nodded. "I still have the scar, too."

Suddenly she felt exhausted. "I'm getting tired."

"I'll be on my way. Make sure you lock up and keep your phone handy."

Abby made sure both doors were locked after he left. She was afraid she'd lie awake for hours but in spite of everything, she fell into a deep sleep and didn't wake until dawn. Lying in bed she thought of what Greg said. Who'd want to kill her father? Maybe they were both imagining things. If he was murdered, could it be Uncle George? Maybe he wasn't as rich as he pretended.

After her first cup of coffee, Abby decided to go fly fishing in memory of all those times she'd fished with her father. She got together her dad's fly fishing gear: the tackle box with his hand-tied flies, his rod and fish net. She added an apple, a leftover piece of cold pizza and a bottle of water. She carried everything down to the boat, and then rowed into the morning mist toward where the water lilies grew.

Soon she got into the groove of casting and felt at peace as if her dad was with her. Abby felt a fish grab her fly and held on as it took off. When it leaped into the air, sparkling in the first rays of sun, she knew it was a rainbow trout. Even without seeing it, she'd have known by the fight it put up. The battle went on and on until her arms felt they couldn't hold on much longer. Finally, she could feel the fish tiring. When she brought it closer to the boat, it made a final run before becoming too exhausted to fight any longer. Slowly she reeled it in and carefully lowered the net. She sat breathing hard, looking at the beautiful fish in the bottom of the boat. It had black spots on its back and dorsal fins and a reddish pink stripe down its silvery side. She reached to remove her fly before releasing it, and noticed another fly hooked in its mouth, too. Someone had caught it recently since any flies not removed eventually come loose on their own. Carefully she removed both lures and released the fish over the side and watched as it lay quietly for a few moments before swimming away.

Abby picked up the old fly, and a shock went through her. She examined it closely, noticing the metallic gold thread tied just so and the yellow parakeet feathers, not the chicken feathers usually used. Tears of anger filled her eyes. She now knew who killed her dad. But could she prove it? She rowed slowly back towards the dock, her arms tired from the fight with the rainbow trout.

Halfway to the dock, she saw a man walking in the sunshine. Him. She stopped rowing, not sure what to do, then punched in a number on her cell phone

When she saw a car pulling in, she continued rowing until she reached the dock.

He held out a hand to help her. "I thought I should be with you. Nice place here."

She didn't take his hand."You killed my Dad. Why?" She stared angrily at him from the boat.

"What are you talking about? You're crazy."

"It was your gambling debts, wasn't it? Were you hoping to get the money from what my dad would leave me?" Tears streamed down her face.

"He killed my father," she said to Greg, who walked up. "I found this fly in the mouth of

a rainbow I caught. It's a special fly only my husband makes. He wanted me to believe he's never been here, but he has, and recently."

* * * *

A week later Abby returned to the cabin. She was on the deck when Greg came around the corner bringing sub sandwiches.

Abby gave him a weak smile. "The bearer of food."

"Someone has to look after you. I don't think you've been eating much lately." His eyes showed sympathy and still a touch of a twelve year old kid's love and admiration.

"Thanks for coming so quickly after I punched in your number."

"I wasn't far away."

They sat quietly on the deck looking at the lake, drinking coffee and thinking their separate thoughts.

COVER STORY

BY ELAINE WILL SPARBER

The toe bugged me.

Not that it was an unusual toe. Well, aside from being a dead toe. Attached to a dead body. Rather, what bothered me was the fuchsia-polished nail poking through the gaping hole in the white fishnet stocking, and the way the toe peeked out from under the azalea bush with the purple blossoms. I almost missed it because of the purple blossoms.

I had pulled into the Beakman-Bryce Publishing parking lot just after nine, the way I always did on Monday morning, and headed straight for my usual spot in the last row by the back fence. As I nosed into the space, the purple azalea blossoms caught my attention, as they did every May. But today, something else did, too. Something glinted, and when I investigated, I found the toe. And the body. I never did see what glinted.

"You really think you dropped part of the manuscript when you screamed?" asked Rina Valencia, a publicist and my best friend. We were standing at my office window, watching the police activity outside.

"I'm afraid to check," I answered, "but the thing does feel a tad lighter now than it did when I left my house. I dropped the box when I screamed, and I think some pages may have fallen out and blown away. After I called 911, I picked up the box and fixed the lid without looking inside. I was really shaky."

"You had good reason," Rina said.

I just looked at her. I was an acquisitions editor and I had spent the weekend editing the manuscript. It was a good manuscript, but the author was new and I had done quite a bit of slashing, moving, and shoving.

"You can print the missing part out again and try to reconstruct," Rina suggested. When I didn't answer, she finally turned toward me. "Harley Amelia Rose, at least you're not dead like her."

She had me there.

* * *

The last thing I expected to see was another pair of fishnet stockings. These were black, however, though the legs they encased were as pale as a dead body's, and the polish on the toenails was black, too, instead of fuchsia. Fiona Sullivan, who had the perky disposition usually associated with her natural red roots and freckles, sported dyed black hair, black-lined eyes, and a black-on-black ensemble straight out of *The Vampire Diaries*. Her black-polished, black-fishnetted right toe bobbed up and down as she finished her telephone call.

"I am *so* sorry," she said, dropping the telephone receiver into its cradle and hopping up to grab the manuscript I was hugging to my chest. I may have lost part of one project today, but I finished preparing another and was delivering it to Fiona, the production editor who would shepherd it through copyediting, typesetting, and proofreading. She eased it out of my stranglehold, apparently mistaking my gawking at her fishnets for a post-traumatic stress reaction to this morning.

"Sit," Fiona ordered, guiding me into her visitor's chair. She stepped around to her own chair and plopped down, thankfully removing her fishnets and toenails from my sight. "Excellent," she commented, sliding the thick rubber band from around the package and flipping through the forms. "And three weeks early!" She glanced up at me and smiled. "We'll probably have to wait for a copyeditor, though. They're usually booked weeks in advance."

I just nodded.

"I can't believe what happened in the parking lot," Fiona said, now riffling through the manuscript. "A dead body. And first thing in the morning. A Monday morning, no less!" She shivered. "You poor thing." She slipped the rubber band back around the package and dropped the bundle into her letter tray.

"It definitely wasn't something I expected to see," I said, "but I'm fine. I just keep feeling like I've seen it before. *Déjà vu*, you know?"

"On TV maybe? The eleven o'clock news? Or in the newspaper? Or online?"

I shook my head after each suggestion.

"A book cover, then?"

I started to say no, but stopped, mentally turning what I had seen into cover art. Something niggled at me.

"See, this happened to me about two months ago." Fiona leaned forward on her elbows. "I didn't find a body, but I saw a news photo of one, and it looked just like the cover of one of our books. And it was here. On Long Island. Near Jones Beach."

I shook my head.

"It was a woman's body, naked and wrapped in a fishing net. You know, the kind fishermen use?"

I groaned.

"I didn't really work on the book, so I don't know the plot—all I did was make some corrections to the proofs—but I did get the printer's shipment and passed around the copies. That's why I got to know the cover. I inherited the book after Mitchell Turner left. You know, next door?" She pointed at the wall behind her.

I smiled. Mitchell and I had produced several successful books together.

"Hold on." She jumped up, spun around, and reached up to a high shelf. Pulling down a paperback, she gave the cover a quick brush and held the book out to me. *Murder on the Beach* was the latest entry in one of our popular mystery series. Other books in the series were *Murder in the Desert* and *Murder in the Valley*. I wondered what would happen when the author ran out of terrain.

"Here's the news photo." Fiona rummaged around her desk and found it under a four-inch pile of paper. She unfolded it, then held it next to the book cover.

"Oh my goodness!" I sputtered. "They *are* identical!" The photo was a long shot while the book cover was a close-up, but the similarities were clear: the fishing net wrapped around each body; the bodies' distance from the water; the bodies' angle against the shoreline. I skimmed the article, which said the real body was that of a woman, naked, age not yet determined. The body on the book cover was also a naked woman, but clearly young, with flawless skin, impeccable makeup, and shiny blond hair blowing in the breeze. The artist obviously had never seen a real dead body. Or even a real dead toe. I thought of the white fishnet stocking, the fuchsia nail polish, and the purple azalea blossoms, and I wished I hadn't, either.

* * * *

"I can't believe she told you that!" Rina sat back in her desk chair and shook her head. "That was just so—"

"So nothing," I cut in. "There's nothing wrong with what she told me. It's not like the body I found was someone I knew. I didn't know her."

"It was still a shock for you," Rina said. "But since we no longer have to tiptoe around you...Have you heard anything? Who the woman might be? What the police think?"

"No, I just know that the detective told me to 'stay available,' whatever that means. He did interview me twice, though. He can't suspect me, can he?"

I had stopped by Rina's office to give her a copy of the manuscript I had just delivered to Fiona so Rina could begin preparing publicity materials. She flipped through the manuscript without removing the rubber band, then placed it on top of a pile tottering next to her desk. "I wonder if those murders are connected," she said.

"I don't know. Why would they be?"

"Oh!" Rina gulped. "You didn't hear, of course." She looked like a guppy about to be scooped up in a little fish net. Eyes wide, she stared at me for a few seconds. Then, eyes returning to normal, shoulders relaxing, she opened a desk drawer and pulled out a book. She studied the cover before slowly turning it toward me. "Recognize this?"

I took the book from her. A paperback, its cover featured a young woman sitting in a swing, raven hair falling in waves around her shoulders. She was leaning to one side, eyes closed, cheeks shiny.

"Is she dead?" I asked. I looked closer. "No, she can't be. She's crying." A garland of white lilies and pink roses floated above her, ends dangling, with the book's title, *Por un Beso*, in red script above the garland.

"*For a Kiss*," I translated. "One of Natalia's books?"

Natalia Lopez had been the executive editor of the Spanish-language romance line until last fall, when Beakman-Bryce had suddenly killed the imprint and laid Natalia off. She had not been happy.

"Yes, one of Natalia's. It's been making the rounds in Publicity today. It seems that a month ago, a body was found posed just like this in a playground not far from here."

I looked at the cover again. The woman was in a swing, but that was it. She was alive. I cocked an eyebrow at Rina.

"From what I'm told, a police detective talked to our esteemed publisher a few days after the body was found. A garland of fake white lilies and pink roses was wound around the top of the swing set, with the ends hanging down and framing the body."

"Like on this cover." I took a deep breath and started to return the book, but then pulled it back. "Has anyone told the detective about this?"

"I don't think so," Rina answered. "I guess we should," she added sheepishly.

"Yeah. I'll take this to him," I said, thinking I should also double back to Fiona's office and get a copy of *Murder on the Beach*.

I studied the *Por un Beso* cover as I left Rina's office. At least the woman wasn't wearing fishnets.

* * * *

My grandfather had been a book editor. In fact, he was an editor with Beakman-Bryce when it was just Beakman, "publisher of fine fiction for the modern reader." His discoveries included some of the most esteemed authors of the 1960s, '70s, and '80s, and a few of the books he edited grace every "100 Best Books of the Twentieth Century" list published. He cared about his authors, and he rolled up his sleeves and worked elbow to elbow with them on their manuscripts. Quentin Zarek wasn't like that.

Quentin was our premier editor. As executive editor, he helmed all the mystery and thriller imprints. Quentin was also one of the new breed of editors—a businessman first, a wordsmith second. Therefore, when I rapped on his doorframe, I wasn't surprised to find him with his nose in a spreadsheet instead of a manuscript.

"Just dropping off some reading matter," I said when he looked up. Every week, journals and magazines with noteworthy articles and reviews of Beakman-Bryce books were circulated among the staff. I slipped the pile into his letter tray. "Do you have a minute?"

Quentin dropped his pen, pulled off his glasses, and rubbed his eyes. "Yes, please." He pointed at his visitor's chair. "These numbers are painful—financially and physically. I could use a break."

"You heard I was the lucky one to find the body this morning?" When Quentin nodded, I said, "I've had this feeling all day that I saw that scene before. The azalea bush with the purple blossoms, foot sticking out from under it, white fishnet stocking, fuchsia nail polish—"

"Like this?" Quentin dug to the bottom of his letter tray and pulled out a file folder. Inside was a cover flat, which he tossed across the desk to me. When it came to a rest, I gasped.

Earlier this year, I had been called in to the monthly art meeting to discuss several of my covers. I hated those meetings. The artists were there, plus the publisher, the two editors-in-chief, all the executive editors, and the interested department heads. As a result, the discussions were often long and loud. When I entered the conference room that particular morning, I hit the jackpot. It seemed as if everyone was yelling—about the cover that now sat before me and featured an azalea bush, in full purple bloom, with a white fishnetted foot with fuchsia-polished toenails peeking out from underneath. The only thing missing was me, standing in front of the bush, eyes closed, screaming, manuscript pages floating away on the wind.

Quentin scowled. "We had to scrap this cover. The manuscript was in proofs when the author discovered a major plot problem and had to cut this victim. The nitwit production editor used a freelance copyeditor who obviously didn't know what she was doing. Thank goodness Fiona took over. She quickly got a handle on the problem and kept the damage to a minimum."

"Fiona is good," I said, cringing at the slam of the original production editor, "but I wonder why she didn't mention this when she told me about the *Murder on the Beach* cover."

"I've heard some babble about that cover. Interesting."

"You didn't, by any chance, tell the cops about any of this, did you?"

"No, why would I? It's bad enough a dead body was found in our parking lot. This company could use publicity, but not that kind." He picked up the cover flat and dropped it back into the file folder, then started to slip the folder back into his letter tray, but stopped. Holding the folder mid-air, he mused, "I wonder if we can turn this into good publicity." He began tapping the folder on his desk, in sync with the gears that seemed to be grinding in his brain. "We could turn this into a book. *The Book Cover Killings*. And I know just the writer."

I closed my eyes and prayed: *Please don't assign it to me.*

"But for now, I have to get back to my numbers," Quentin said, eyes gleaming.

"And I to my manuscripts," I responded, scurrying from his office. And to my phone, where I probably should put the detective on speed dial.

* * * *

Pam Reynolds sipped her cappuccino, rolling her eyes heavenward. "My, this is good. They make these so well here."

"They do have the touch," I agreed, and took a sip of my own.

Pam was a literary agent who handled the subjects I acquired. We met for lunch every few months to discuss projects of hers I had bought and was working on and new projects she thought might interest me.

"So, tell me," Pam said, "is it true a dead body was found in the Beakman-Bryce parking lot?" She settled her cup back in its saucer.

I put my own cup down and nodded. "I was the one who found it."

"Oh for Pete's sake, Harley—"

"I'm fine, really. I mean, I was shook up when it happened, but that was a month ago. I'm fine now. Although, I don't park in the same space anymore." I smiled.

Pam picked up her teaspoon and slowly stirred the milk foam and cinnamon decorating the top of her drink. "I heard there might be another body connected to Beakman-Bryce."

Again I nodded, but this time I didn't smile. All around us, people were talking, laughing, and enjoying their food. One table over, three women broke out in giggles. I rubbed my arms. Leaning forward, I whispered, "There might be two more bodies. One was found at the beach about three months ago, and one at a local playground about two months ago. They both seem to be connected to books we published."

"Are you serious? How?" Pam also leaned forward, her eyes wide. "Do the police have any theories? Any suspects?"

"I have no idea what the police think. However, most of the people at work are worried. Some are scared. The first book was a mystery: *Murder on the Beach*. The second was one of Natalia's romances: *Por un Beso*. The way the bodies were left, well, they looked like those covers."

"I know those books," Pam said. "*Murder on the Beach, Murder in the Desert*—those are mine. The author's been a client since the first book in that series. My partner handled the other book. They're sure the covers were copied?"

"I saw a photo of the beach crime scene held next to the *Murder on the Beach* cover. They looked identical. And the police say the other crime scene almost perfectly matched Natalia's cover."

"How did Natalia react?"

"I have no idea. Natalia was furious when Beakman-Bryce killed her imprint and laid her off, and she hasn't stayed in touch."

We sipped our cappuccinos in silence. Deep in thought, neither one of us heard the waitress approach. When she plopped our check on the table, we both jumped.

Recovering first, Pam asked, "And the crime scene in your parking lot also looked like a book cover?"

"Yes. At least, I think so. It's weird, but it resembled a third cover, one that was never used. It's another mystery, and according to Quentin, there was a problem with the plot and the victim pictured on the cover had to be cut. The proofs had to be corrected and a new cover made."

"I heard about that," Pam said. "The production editor is a freelancer now and does work for me. Talk about not being happy with Beakman-Bryce, Mitchell's another one!"

"You mean Mitchell Turner? I thought he left for another job."

"No, ma'am," Pam said, shaking her head. "He was fired. For that book with the plot problem and new cover. Luckily, he landed on his feet. He's nonstop busy. But he always manages to squeeze me in within a couple of days. He's a doll."

After we finished our cappuccinos and paid the check, I slipped my pocketbook strap over my shoulder and scooped up the four proposals Pam had convinced me were right up my alley. Lunch had been productive.

* * * *

The escalator creaked as it carried a lone woman down from the raised Long Island Rail Road platform. I watched as she stepped off and looked around. No one was waiting to pick anyone up, and the woman settled into a bench by the closed ticket office and pulled out her cell phone.

Above, beeping warned that the train doors were closing. When it stopped, the escalator, the ground, and the pillar I was leaning against all began to vibrate. A rumble and a whoosh, and the train was gone. Silence dropped again.

Loud footsteps echoed behind me. I swung around and saw a man in jeans and a T-shirt approaching the ticket vending machine. Clanking made me jump and turn again. Another man, this one in shorts and a tank top, pushed his bicycle into the bike rack and started fumbling with a chain.

The station clock showed eleven twenty. The morning rush was over and the afternoon rush still hours away. I fanned myself; the calendar claimed early July, but the thermometer argued mid-August. A crick stabbed my shoulder and I adjusted my briefcase, checking to make sure the manuscript box was still safely tucked inside.

I swept my gaze along the length of the parking area on the south side of the station. As I turned to scan the north-side parking area, I found Mitchell Turner's nose just inches from my own. I squealed and jumped back.

"Hey, Harley. Thanks for meeting me here. I'm just not ready yet to go back to that building."

"No problem. I totally understand." My heart thumped, and I patted my chest to calm it down. "It's so good to see you!" I leaned forward and hugged Mitchell. "I had lunch with Pam Reynolds yesterday, and I was floored when she told me what had happened to you. However, she also told me you were doing well, freelancing and all. So, when I got back to my office and found this rush project dumped in my lap, I thought of you."

"You have it with you?" he asked. When I nodded yes, he said, "Well, let's have a look, then."

I unzipped my briefcase and pulled out the manuscript box. Holding the box in front of me, I explained, "As I said on the phone, it's a creative nonfiction crime book. The writer finished it as far as possible; now we have to wait for the cops to make an arrest. They say they're close, though. And we're hoping that when they do, we just have to slap on a chapter or two about the arrest and add some photos. The author's done a great job writing this while the investigation's been going on, but I need someone experienced with crime to edit it. Make sure it flows. I just don't have the time to do it myself."

Mitchell shifted his weight and slipped his hands into his pockets. "Isn't this a little unusual? Nonfiction crime books usually aren't published until the trial's over. What's the rush here?"

"Believe it or not, it's about a series of murders targeted at Beakman-Bryce. And you know our Publicity Department. Gotta wring out every last promotional drop."

Mitchell looked down at the manuscript box, but instead of reaching for it, he slowly moved his gaze back up to my face. "Bull," he said, so low I wasn't sure I'd heard him correctly.

"Pardon me?"

"Bull." A little louder. "You know," he growled, stepping forward, his abdomen pushing the box into mine. Before I could respond, I felt something hard poke into my ribcage. I looked down and gasped. A gun. "How?"

Closing my eyes, I sucked in a calming breath and slowly released it.

"It was simple," I said, trying to keep my voice steady. "We all see all the covers as they're passed around in batches for corrections. You, however, were the only one who never knew that one of the covers you'd seen ended up being replaced. You were fired before that happened. The azalea bush cover.

"I then saw Pam Reynolds, who mentioned you were freelancing. She said you were always able to work on her projects immediately. I pictured you sitting at your desk, twiddling your thumbs, thrilled to get her phone call. In other words, *not* doing so well.

"You were screwed, Mitchell. As a production editor, it wasn't your job to content edit. That also wasn't the job of the freelance copyeditor. It was Quentin's job, and he screwed up and he used you as a scapegoat. You had production edited a ton of Quentin's mysteries—"

I suddenly hopped back and batted the gun away with the manuscript box, surprising both Mitchell and myself. The gun fired into the air as it flew out of Mitchell's hand. Pigeons napping in the nooks under the tracks above flapped and took flight.

"Drop it, Turner." The man from the ticket machine aimed a gun at Mitchell, while the man from the bicycle rack pulled me to safety. "Get down on your knees. You're under arrest." As the woman with the cell phone rushed past me with her own gun drawn, the manuscript box slipped out of my hands, and I watched as the manuscript pages wafted away on the breeze. This time I didn't care, though. The pages were blank.

* * * *

Later that day, when the police were finally done with me and Rina was satisfied I was okay, I settled in at my desk. I reread the memo from Quentin and punched the number it included into my telephone.

"Hi. It's Harley Rose from Beakman-Bryce. I've got a book that needs a writer. A creative nonfiction. Working title: *The Book Cover Killings*. Interested? The cover's already done."

THE RUNAWAY

BY E. B. DAVIS

I awoke in darkness. The blanket I'd found in a storage compartment had gravitated to my feet. Pulling the blanket to my chest, I wrapped it around me. The cold must have awoken me, but then I heard voices coming from outside the cabin. Alarmed, I jolted in the berth.

The soundness of my decision to stowaway on the sport fisher *Runaway* this afternoon was now a moot point. The name had attracted me since I'd run away from home. After walking all of a half mile, I had detoured into the same marina where my AWOL father kept his fishing boat, also missing since he and his buddies had taken *Shannon Kathleen*, named after me, to Mexico for a fishing tournament. I knew the gate access code. Mom had made me so mad that I slipped through the gate without a thought.

It was too late to rehash my convoluted thinking. Being caught aboard someone else's vessel would prove embarrassing. I imagined my mother chiding me for my indiscretion, as if she weren't acting like a juvenile delinquent herself.

The *Runaway* wasn't the cozy place I had imagined when choosing it for lodging. Many of the marina's boats were luxury cruisers or sport fishers, having amenities that assured a comfortable stay over the long President's Day weekend. The marina's security gate and the Coast Guard Headquarters, located down the road, assured my safety, or so I had thought.

Easing off the bed, I felt the cold penetrate my soles. I slipped on my socks and sneakers, picked up my backpack and swung it over my shoulders, pulling the straps tightly so it wouldn't swing, then tiptoed to the cabin door. Lowering myself into a crouch, I cracked it open.

The pole lights on the dock illuminated the aft deck of the boat. A middle-age man and woman stood facing one another, frozen like a paused DVD. Anger and confrontation emanated from their expressions and stances. He wore preppy wire-rimmed glasses. The woman, a trim brunette, wore jeans and an unzipped down jacket with a turtleneck top. The video resumed when he spoke.

"I don't have to put up with this crap, Linda," the man said. He spoke with force, but in a subdued voice as if trying to avoid anyone overhearing.

"Why not, I put up with your crap," Linda replied.

"But I don't have to."

"You will unless you want your wife to find out about us. Fork over the cash, Jim."

"Money. That's what this is about? I thought you loved me."

"Like you love me?" The woman's laugh chipped the icy night like a pick.

"You were the one who mentioned love, not me, Linda. I've been straight with you."

"Yes, I've appreciated your honesty," she said, her words bitter with sarcasm. "I wish you'd appreciate mine. Fifty-thousand, Jim, and your wife won't know. The lawyer alone will cost you that much, and a division of assets will be *how much*?"

"Fifty-thousand. You're out of you mind if you think I'll give you money. Haven't you heard about the economy?" The man advanced, backing the woman against the gunwale.

"I think about the economy all the time, Jim. Perhaps I should ask for sixty-thousand."

"Really funny, Linda."

"You like funny, I'll give you funny." The woman changed her stance, moving her right foot forward. "In the morning, it will only take one phone call. Or, maybe I should wait for her at the office. Wasn't it her money, Jim? Oh yes, I forgot, it was her daddy's money."

"You bitch."

"Now you're getting the picture."

The man grabbed the woman by the shoulders. I closed my eyes, afraid to witness their fight, but I heard feet scuffling and felt the boat rocking.

"Stop right there, Jim. You don't think I'm stupid enough to come here without a gun."

Gun? I opened my eyes. The woman was pointing a handgun at the man. In a boxer's snap, he punched the woman in the face. I winced, hearing the crunch of her nose cartilage. The gun clattered onto the deck as her hands flew toward her face.

The impact of his punch sent her into a backward fall onto the deck. Her scream burst through the quiet night like a fire siren, and she continued screeching. Sprawled on her back, she held her nose with one hand and tried to raise herself with the other. He hovered over her, looking around as if wondering who might hear her screaming, then he grabbed a bait knife out of the livewell and stabbed her in the chest. The woman's body went slack.

Her silenced scream echoed in my mind like the aftermath of gunfire. Shocked by the man's violence, I watched catatonically as he opened the stern's built-in fish box, picked up Linda's body and stuffed it inside. He replaced the fish box cover, then took the knife, opened a water cooler, swished the knife clean and pocketed it inside of his jacket like a ball-point pen. He emptied the cooler over the side and wiped it dry.

After locating the gun on the deck, he dropped it into his jacket's outer pocket. Then he leapt onto the dock and uncoiled a hose provided by the marina management, jumped back onto the deck, and sprayed the entire aft deck, including the outside of the fish box. The bloody water drained out the back through the scuppers.

He looked down at his jacket. Blood had spattered the front. Unzipping it, he took off the jacket, turned it inside out, folded it around the knife and gun and held it like a football. His carnage had been quick, and now the evidence was disappearing like a mirage—except for me. He turned in a circle as if wondering what incriminating evidence he'd missed.

If he entered the cabin, he'd probably kill me, too. When he turned his back to spray the deck again, I took advantage of the spray's noise by closing the cabin door and scooting to the head, which contained the only door within the cabin. I pulled the door shut behind me and latched it. The stall was small. When the boat rocked, I figured that he was returning the hose to the dock. My backpack impeded any movement, so I leaned forward against the opposite wall on my palms, closed my eyes and prayed.

The pounding in my ears dissipated as minutes passed without hearing a sound. My legs trembled and twitched as I tried to keep still. I mentally commanded the adrenalin to stop pumping, quieting the physical riot my fear instigated.

Maybe ten minutes later, I decided to chance it by opening the head's door. I crept to the cabin door and inched it open, hearing only a quiet splash in the distance. A fish jumping, maybe? No one appeared to be on the aft deck.

I dropped to my knees, crawled out the door and peered around the cabin. The forward deck was empty. No one was on the port side. I reversed and checked the starboard side. No one appeared to be on the boat. But as I rose to my feet and took a few steps, I remembered too late that the tuna tower could hide someone. Looking up, I saw no one there and continued to walk toward the dock.

Before leaping off the boat, I stopped. The woman might still be alive. I opened the box. Perhaps my mental panic caused visual distortion. It appeared as if I were looking through a tunnel from a great height. The dead woman lay at the bottom of the box surrounded by fishnets. Her turtleneck was ripped and bloodied. Her eyes were open. I couldn't save her. She was dead. Some fancy artist like those I learned about in art class would paint the scene in an impressionist style and give it a title like, *"Dead Woman on Fishnets."* But what I saw wasn't a surreal painting. Her body was evidence of the murder I witnessed.

I catapulted onto the dock. The *Runaway's* stocked galley should have made me suspicious. The killer must have planned a tryst with his lover. His plan for the weekend had gone awry. Mine too.

Anger replaced my fear. I got mad—at Mom. In retaliation for Dad's fishing tournament, leaving her alone, Mom dropped some Ecstasy and called her rave friends. I hadn't stuck around for long. If I heard Nirvana or Moby one more time, I'd explode. What hurt the most was that in a few short hours I'd turn eighteen. Happy f'ing birthday.

I ran blindly down the boards, picking up speed, and turned onto the central walkway. When I rammed into something, I bounced backward but kept my balance. Focusing on the obstruction in my path, I saw a man. He emitted a whoosh, like a deflating raft. I started to scream, but he cut me off.

"Hey, what the hell's wrong with you?" the man asked, looking me in the eye. He wasn't the killer, but a large, burly older man blocking the walkway. "What's going on? Haven't I seen you before?"

"Maybe, my father moors his boat here. Frank Greely. I'm Shannon Greely."

"Yeah, I know your dad. What's got you so riled up? You're out too late, there are curfew laws."

"I can't talk about it. I have to get away from here."

"Not so fast. Frank's boat is in Mexico. Did you break into anyone's boat? You and your friends partying?"

"Do you see any friends? Leave me alone. I don't want to talk."

"I'm a cop, and I also do security work for the marina management. Don't tell me, I'll tell you."

I debated telling the cop about the murder, but he seemed to assume that I had done something wrong. He probably thought I was a criminal. I wondered if he would accuse me of the murder if I told him. I also didn't know where the killer was. If he heard me telling the cop, the killer would know that I'd witnessed the murder. Would he come after me? I looked around trying to determine if the killer was nearby listening. The cop must have thought I was ignoring him.

"Did you or did you not break into a boat at this marina?"

"Yes, but—"

"Okay, I've heard enough. Let's call that mother of yours."

"You know my mother?"

"Heard about her."

If he'd heard about my mother, it was no wonder he thought I was a criminal. "I need to get out of here."

"Just try it. What boat did you break into?"

"It was open."

"Don't give me that. No one enters a boat without the captain's permission. You ought to know that much." The cop blocked my way, crossing his arms over his chest.

"The *Runaway*," I admitted.

"The owner's a friend of mine, Jim Cooper, and I got you dead to rights."

"What's that supposed to mean?" I asked. How could I tell him now? The killer was his friend. Would he cover for him? Maybe he would try to pin the murder on me.

"It means that Jim has digital cameras running inside his cabin in case anyone breaks in. Smile, you're on candid camera." The cop looked at me as if he'd made a joke or a pun. I didn't get it, but I understood that if the killer played the disc, I probably wouldn't live another day.

Counting on surprise, I shoved him, enabling a quick retreat, and ran back to the *Runaway*. Finding the DVD recorder and destroying the disc was my only chance. Of course, the cop would finally catch me, but as long as the disc was destroyed, the killer wouldn't know that I had witnessed the murder.

"Hey, you're adding resisting arrest to breaking and entering as well as violation of curfew," the cop yelled.

I jumped off the dock, landed on the aft deck and ripped open the cabin door. When I had previously entered a glimmer of daylight remained. Now, I saw the tiny green lights of the cameras in the dark. One was mounted above the galley, the other over the main berth where I had slept. But where was the recorder?

A cushioned-lined bench ran along the inside of the cabin. If this boat was anything like my father's boat, the base was hollow for storage. I threw the cushions aside and lifted the bench seat. Hinged, it rounded upward revealing a cavity beneath. Inside held the DVD hardware, recording my movements even now.

The boat lurched as the cop jumped aboard. I punched the button on the DVD recorder, ejecting the disc. As the door flew open, I stuffed the disc down my pants. He looked down and noticed the empty carriage.

"We'll get the disc. I'll take you down to the station and one of my female colleagues will search you. Come on." Holding the door open, he grabbed me by the elbow and pushed me out of the cabin.

Outside, I took hold of the disc like a Frisbee and pitched it into the bay. The cop shook his head. "You're making it tougher on yourself.

It'll only piss us off and Jim when we dirty everything with fingerprint powder."

"I didn't take anything."

"Charlie, what's going on here?"

I heard the killer's voice as he walked down the walkway toward his boat. By the look on his face, I could tell he was shocked to find us on his boat.

"Hey Jim, your boat was broken into by this girl, Frank Greely's daughter."

"When?"

"Ran into me going like fire about ten minutes ago."

The killer's eyes blazed at me. Then he came aboard and stood aside Charlie. "It's okay, I know her dad. I'm sure she didn't steal anything, now did you?"

His question sounded like a threat. He was vouching for me for only one reason. Now that Big Mouth Charlie revealed my presence on the *Runaway*, I had no choice but to trust him. I said a quick prayer and edged aside of the men. "No, I didn't steal anything, but look in the fish box." I looked at Charlie. "You'll find something worth your time."

Jim grabbed a thick rope with both of his hands and snapped it as if he'd like to strangle me with it. "Charlie, maybe I was too lenient. She won't learn anything if you don't lock her up."

"You can't prove I was on this boat," I said. The killer almost spoke, but I cut him off. "I destroyed the disc. It's at the bottom of the bay and the salt is degrading it." I walked over to the fish box and flipped open the cover.

"You can't do that," Jim said. He pounced on the cover and flipped it closed.

"Jim, for cryin' out loud. What's in the box?" Charlie asked.

"You can't search my boat without a warrant."

Charlie stepped back and cocked his head. They faced off. "Okay, if that's the way you want it. I'll just make sure Shannon gets home safely." Charlie stepped around Jim and headed toward the dock.

"She broke into my boat."

"Sorry, no proof, and nothing was stolen."

"You can take prints."

"And waste the department's money when nothing was stolen? Nah, don't think so."

I walked toward the dock. Charlie followed me. As I put one foot onto the dock, the other foot still firmly on the stern, I swung back and opened the fish box. Shifting, Charlie saw the body, and quickly turned, but the killer's punch landed squarely on his jaw.

I launched myself onto the dock and ran for the gate. I grabbed my phone out of my coat pocket, and dialed 911. Was the killer following me? When I looked over my shoulder, I saw that the walkway was empty. The dispatcher answered. I concealed myself behind a piling, told what had happened and the access code for the gate.

Slapping my phone shut against the instructions of the dispatcher, I stood, torn between leaving and helping the cop. When he'd come to my defense, I wondered if his earlier attitude toward me was some kind of "tough love" act. Like some of my teachers, they acted tough and threatened, but they really didn't want to get kids in trouble. Besides, after seeing the body, he had tried to protect me. He seemed more like a grandfather than a fighter, and the killer was very efficient, a fact I'd witnessed.

I turned toward the slips and snuck back to the *Runaway*. The two men were still engaged in combat. Engrossed in their fight, neither man noticed me. The killer's back was toward me. Charlie faced me, but his eyes were focused on his opponent. With his back against the cabin door, he was penned in since the killer blocked his access to the dock. When the killer punched him in the gut, he doubled over, his energy spent.

A grappling hook stood upright in a pole holder by the slip. I lifted it out, jumped on top of the fish box and hit the killer on the head with the grappling hook. He didn't drop but turned, facing me. Horrified, I froze.

Recovering from the punch, Charlie aimed a side-kick behind the killer's knees. He collapsed. Charlie pushed his face to the deck and straddled him. I jumped down, grabbed an unattached line in the port corner and threw it to Charlie, who tied the killer's wrists behind his back. The sound of a siren grew in volume as it approached the marina.

Out of breath, Charlie asked, "You called it in?"

"Yeah."

"Good girl."

An hour later, down at the station, Charlie wanted to call my house. "You're a minor. I have to inform your mother."

"No, you don't. At midnight, I turned eighteen." I pointed to the wall clock.

"Let me see your driver's license."

I retrieved it from my backpack, and Charlie confirmed my age. "Happy birthday," he said.

"Thanks."

"Shannon, we know about your mom. Urge her into treatment before it's so obvious we have to arrest her or she causes a fatal accident. She's been smart about keeping it at home, maybe not for you, but...."

Taken back by his knowledge, I asked, "How do you know?"

"Small town—I hear everything." He smiled sadly at me. "You should have told me what you saw when we met."

"I was scared." And I hadn't liked his attitude, assuming I was just like my mother, but I kept that thought to myself.

"We found Jim's jacket with the knife and gun in the trunk of his car." Charlie sat at his desk, placed his elbows on its top and said, "Hey, you did real good tonight."

"Thanks. Hey, Charlie?"

"What?"

"Do they accept eighteen-year-olds at the police academy?"

"No, you'll have to wait a year and a half."

"Guess I could take some criminal justice courses and then go to the police academy. Having a cop in the house might deter Mom."

"Just might. Wait a minute. You're an adult. You can write your own statement. Your first lesson as an adult."

"What?"

"Don't incriminate yourself," he said.

"What do you mean?"

"You figured it out."

I smiled at Charlie, picked up a pen, and said, "I'll always remember this birthday."

Charlie laughed.

ROUTINE CHANGES
BY BETSY BITNER

I should have stayed home, Julie thought as she sat wedged on the sofa between happily chatting women, a glass of Cabernet and a glossy catalog balanced on her lap. The catalog's cover matched the glossy invitation she'd received for tonight's event. Both boasted the letters "TY" in large, flowing script and both had the same tagline: "True You Cosmetics. Because BeauTY is more than skin deep."

Well, I did try to stay home, Julie reminded herself, but Donna, her best friend and hostess, rarely took no for an answer.

"It's not that you can't make it, it's that you don't want to," Donna had said when Julie called to RSVP her regrets.

"You're right, I don't want to. Sorry. I didn't mean that the way it sounded. But I'm not exactly in the market for beauty products at the moment."

"You know you don't have to buy anything. Just come and have a good time. I'm only hosting this thing as a favor to this woman I met at the gym. She just moved here and she kept asking if I would help her out. I hate these things as much as you do."

By "these things," Donna meant sales pitches to captive audiences masquerading as parties. Every home party hostess always told her guests they didn't have to buy anything, but who wouldn't feel guilty about eating her friend's food and drinking her wine without buying at least a little something? Julie had drawers full of candles, jewelry, and new-fangled kitchen gadgets to prove it.

"I don't know, Donna. I just don't feel like being social these days."

"Which is exactly why you need to get out of that house. Have a glass of wine or two with friends."

Now as she sat waiting for the presentation to begin, Julie doubted even Donna's well-stocked bar had enough wine to get her through the evening. Especially since she'd gotten a good look at the petite woman who would be pitching the True You products. Julie had seen her car parked in Donna's driveway on the way in. At least she assumed it was the salesperson's car. Donna had said she was new in town and the little red convertible with North Carolina plates screamed "clueless" about upstate New York winters.

Likewise, her appearance seemed at odds with the way most women Julie knew looked by the end of February. For one thing, her long blond hair, full of bounce and without a trace of static, indicated she was unaccustomed to wearing a hat. The rest of her outfit—pink silk blouse, short black skirt and black boots that wouldn't last ten seconds in a snow bank—was typical of someone who'd never considered the possibility of her car breaking down on a cold winter night. It was the fishnet stockings, though, peeking seductively between the hem of her skirt and the top of her boots that made Julie feel justified in her instant dislike of this woman.

Julie shivered and took another sip of wine, regretting she hadn't stayed home. Donna may have thought she was in a rut, but Julie liked the routine she'd recently taken to on Friday nights, a routine of sweatpants, the TV remote, and a pint of ice cream. Not the most exciting way to spend an evening, but one that she had found comforting for the last six weeks. She much preferred her old Friday night routine, the one she'd shared with her husband Rick for years: home-cooked, candlelight dinner for two while listening to Mahler, Donizetti, or Handel on the stereo. That routine came to an abrupt end seven Fridays ago when Rick announced he was leaving her.

Julie realized her wine glass was in need of a refill just as the blond woman began her pitch.

"Okay, ladies. Let's get started. I'm Tina Mabry and I'm a sales representative for True You Cosmetics. First of all, I want to thank Donna for hosting the party tonight. This is the first party I've done since moving here about a month and a half ago. I'm so glad we met on the treadmills at the Sweat Shop, Donna."

Julie tuned out the rest of what Tiny Tina was saying and turned her attention to the catalog, determined to make an early exit so she could go home and watch the shows she was recording. Skimming past the anti-aging products—always too expensive—Julie looked for something small like a lipstick or a travel-sized hand cream. She stopped on a product line with different packaging than the rest, but that looked somehow familiar. It was the Sea-duction line: skin care products for men and women that combined aromatherapy with marine botanicals. Julie almost choked when she saw the men's skin care products at the bottom of the page.

The white packaging with turquoise lettering looked just like the jar she had found tucked in an inside pocket of Rick's suitcase after one of his many business trips. She'd teased him when she found it, but was also flattered that he was making an effort.

"They're just some samples someone was handing out as a promotion in the hotel lobby," Rick said as he grabbed the jar of moisturizer out of her hand. It had seemed too big to be a sample and Julie noticed that he never threw it out. She assumed he was embarrassed by her discovering evidence of his vanity and eventually forgot all about it.

Now a sickening thought crossed her mind. Julie got up from the sofa and worked her way to where Donna stood in the doorway to the dining room.

"Where did Tina move from?" Julie whispered.

"I don't know. Some town in North Carolina. Near Charlotte, I think."

Oh, God, Julie thought. Rick traveled for his consulting business and one of his biggest clients was in Charlotte. Julie gripped the doorframe as if it would keep her from jumping to conclusions. Maybe they really were free samples, she told herself, trying to push out the thought that Tina's arrival in town coincided with Rick's announcement that he was moving out. Julie stared at Tina as she wrapped up her presentation. She was attractive and confident, which Rick would certainly find appealing. But the fishnet stockings seemed vaguely trashy. Julie was surprised she would be his type, but then again, Rick had been full of surprises lately.

Julie was pulled from her thoughts by the sound of her name. Looking up, she saw Tina holding a basket in one hand and a piece of paper in the other. "Julie Sullivan," Tina repeated, looking right at her. "You've won. So come on up." There was a smattering of applause as Julie did as she was told even though she didn't remember putting her name in the basket and she couldn't figure out how Tina knew her name was Julie.

Tina was babbling—something about a free facial—but Julie wasn't listening because she was focused on the display of Sea-duction for Men products on the coffee table. Finally Tina stopped talking and followed Julie's gaze.

"Oh, these are great products," Tina said, picking up one of the white and turquoise containers. "They're only available from True You consultants. And men *really* love them. Is there someone special you're buying for? Your father, or a brother?"

Julie looked at Tina and thought she detected a hint of smugness behind the smile. "No. I'm not buying anything."

"Well, take a catalog just in case. And you're still entitled to the free facial. All my contact information is right here on the back."

Tina shoved one of the slick booklets into Julie's hand. Her name and phone number were stamped at the bottom. Along with her address— which Julie realized she'd seen before.

* * * *

Julie didn't care that it was too early on a Saturday morning to be considered a respectable hour. She couldn't wait any longer so she let herself in through Donna's kitchen door and started a pot of coffee while she waited for her friend to wake up. When Donna finally shuffled into the kitchen looking like hell, Julie realized she probably didn't look much better herself. And they both had good reasons for their haggard appearances—Donna was hung-over and Julie had spent the night tossing and turning.

"It was all a set up." Julie handed Donna a cup of coffee. "Tina wanted you to host that party as a way to get to me."

"What are you talking about?"

Julie smacked the True You catalog onto the kitchen table, making Donna wince, then she jabbed her finger at Tina's contact information at the bottom of the cover. "Look where she lives."

It was the same address that had blindsided Julie when she saw it in the newspaper's Property Transactions section several weeks ago: "Richard M. Sullivan purchased property at 142 Felicity Drive, Woodmere Estates from Vincent Cardone and Premiere Homes, LLC." For some reason, she'd taken comfort in picturing Rick living in a sun-baked townhome with a parking spot for one car in front and a rusted hibachi on a cement slab in back, separated from identically outfitted cement slabs on either side by a section of stockade fencing that gave the illusion of privacy. Instead, her husband had decided to treat himself to new construction in a wooded development just past the Pine Ridge Shopping Center, where one of the area's top builders was constructing luxury homes on winding streets named after his granddaughters. And to top it off, he wasn't living there alone.

Donna was still a little fuzzy and didn't make the connection. Unlike Julie, Donna hadn't had the benefit of a sleepless night to think this through.

"Tina engineered the whole thing—the party, my winning the facial, everything. Just so she could make sure I knew who she was. She has my husband, but that's not enough for her. She has to rub my face in it, too."

It was hard to believe that Tina would go to such lengths, but how else could Julie explain winning the facial in a raffle she never entered or the slight smirk on Tina's face when she showed Julie her address. Tina must be pretty satisfied with herself to expose Rick to the financial implications his affair would have on the divorce settlement just to prove to Julie that she'd won.

The bitch.

* * * *

The following Friday, an urge for mocha almond fudge sent Julie out in the early evening. But she had to acknowledge the real reason for her errand after she'd passed the shopping center and turned onto Felicity

Drive, Woodmere Estates' main road. Searching for house numbers on mailboxes and over garages, Julie told herself she was just looking. There's no law saying you can't drive through a neighborhood on the way to get ice cream, is there?

As she drove farther, new construction gave way to still-empty lots with numbers nailed to trees. At a Dead End sign, Julie lost her nerve and pulled her car onto the nearest side street, Kristin Court, so far populated only by piles of roof trusses and front end loaders.

She made a three-point turn and was about to leave the neighborhood when she saw Rick's silver BMW pass on Felicity Drive on his way out of the development. There was just enough light left in the late February sky to make out Tina's blonde head in the passenger's seat. Julie glanced at the clock on her dashboard and figured they were going out to dinner. Apparently Rick had his own Friday night routine with Tina. Curious, Julie turned her car back onto Felicity Drive in search of number 142.

The road ended in a cul-de-sac just past Kristin Court, and Rick's house was the only one on the circle. It was dark enough that her car's headlights had come on and they swept an illuminated arc across the front of 142's two-story red brick exterior as Julie drove slowly past. She went back to Kristin Court, parked the car and returned to Rick's house on foot.

She didn't have a plan but was careful to stay on the driveway and then on the walkway leading to the backyard. The new lawn wouldn't be put in until spring and Julie didn't want to leave footprints in the mud. She tested the side door to the garage and found it was locked. Seeing a deck with a Hummer-sized stainless steel gas grill, she ran her hand under the railing.

At least some things don't change, Julie thought as she removed a key from the hide-a-key box. She and Rick kept a spare key in an identical spot at their house. My house, Julie corrected herself, as she unlocked the garage door. Tina's bimbo-mobile was parked inside, and Julie stopped short. No, she reasoned, I'm sure I saw Tina in the passenger seat of Rick's car a few minutes ago.

She took a deep breath and opened the door to the house.

Passing through the mudroom, she paused at the doorway to the kitchen and listened to make sure she was alone. The only sound was the purr of new appliances awaiting their owners' return. Lights were on in every room—another of Rick's old habits—because he hated coming home to a dark house.

I just want to look, Julie told herself, but she kept her gloves on, just in case, as she moved through the downstairs. Considering Tina's outfit, it was surprising how normal, even tasteful, the interior looked. She'd expected the decorating style to be early-harem, like a tawdry den of seduction.

Pausing outside the door to Rick's office, Julie wondered what other bombshells might be lurking in the papers on his desk. It was Tina's face, not hers, that smiled from the picture frames on his desk. Not a surprise, but it still hurt. She knew she should leave, but instead, Julie turned towards the stairs.

In the upstairs hall she stopped briefly to glance in the open bedroom doors—a guest room, Tina's office with a desk and shelves filled with True You products, and a room filled with moving boxes marked "Mabry." But it wasn't these rooms that had drawn her up the stairs. Despite the thick pile carpet, she crossed the threshold to the master bedroom on tiptoes.

The room was spacious with his and her dressers, his and her chairs in the sitting area, and his and her nightstands flanking the king size bed. There were even his and her closets. Julie opened the larger of the two, the one belonging to Tina, and stepped inside, running her hand lightly along a row of garments, which set the blouse sleeves to swinging. Julie stepped out, closed the door, and stepped into the master bathroom.

She couldn't resist touching the glossy marble sink tops, her hand stopping on the handle of a vanity drawer and opening it to find it full of True You cosmetics. Julie picked up a lipstick at random, pulled the top off and twisted the base. The lipstick appeared like a scarlet turtle poking its head from its cylindrical shell. She recapped the lipstick and checked the label on the bottom. "Temptress." Figures.

The contents of the drawer weren't exactly messy but they weren't so neat that Tina would notice right away if something were missing. Before she realized what she was doing, Julie pocketed the lipstick and closed the drawer.

Careful not to disturb anything on the way out, she returned the key to its hiding place, walked back to her car and drove away. Taking a lipstick hardly compared to taking a husband, Julie told herself, but it was exciting enough that she almost forgot to stop for ice cream on her way home.

Julie enjoyed her new Friday night routine: come home from work, eat dinner, go out to buy ice cream, and along the way stop at Rick's house to take something belonging to Tina. She told no one, not even Donna, the one friend she could tell anything. Donna couldn't possibly understand something Julie had a hard time explaining to herself. All she knew for sure was that the thrill of this routine was habit-forming.

She was careful to avoid getting caught. Careful to make sure no one was home, careful to always wear gloves even as the weather warmed with the passing weeks, and careful only to take little things she was sure

Tina wouldn't miss. Things like eye shadow, a travel-sized toothpaste, and a cheap pair of earrings. When she collected some of Tina's blond hair from her hairbrush and placed it in a sandwich bag she'd brought especially for that purpose, Julie was forced to consider whether she had an obsession.

It's not a problem if I have a plan, she told herself. The idea of using her collection to make a voodoo doll crossed her mind. Although she didn't know the first thing about voodoo, the thought of taking her frustrations out on a little Tina doll was appealing.

Now that she had a goal, Julie began to find herself smiling at work, in line at the grocery checkout, and while making dinner as she thought of all the ways to torture her Tina doll. Like sticking pins in it—that was voodoo *de rigueur*—but it was also boring. Especially when Julie could also imagine smashing it with a frying pan, or grinding the heel of her shoe into its face, or submerging it in the bathtub, or even backing over it with her car. Repeatedly.

It was the closest thing to revenge that Julie could muster and it was serious motivation to continue pilfering the floozy's things. Maybe she couldn't knock off Tina, but she could vent her wrath on a Tina knockoff. Going through some of Tina's moving boxes stacked in a spare bedroom, Julie found an old tax return. Cutting out Tina's signature and attaching it to the doll would be a nice touch, Julie thought. Then there was the photograph of Tina taken in a house that didn't look familiar. Julie wondered if Rick had taken the picture. It didn't matter—it was a good shot of Tina's face, perfect to cut out and stick on the doll for added realism.

One week she took a pillowcase—just right for the doll's body. Another time Julie found one of Tina's blouses at the bottom of the dry cleaners' bag. Judging from the amount of clothes in Tina's closet, she doubted Tina would miss it. Even if she did, odds were good the witch would blame the cleaners.

There was still one thing Julie needed to complete her tramp-in-miniature: the fishnet stockings. They represented everything about Tina that Julie hated. She'd waited to take them, believing in the virtue of delayed gratification. The time had come, however, to collect the final embodiment of trashiness for her Tina facsimile.

Knowing she'd miss the thrill of her covert missions, Julie felt a pang of regret as she parked her car on Kristin Court for the last time. She paused after letting herself in through the side door to the garage. Both cars were gone.

Maybe they were doing something different tonight, Julie thought as she let herself into the house. It didn't matter. As long as no one was home....

Wasting no time, Julie headed straight for the stairs. Once in the master bedroom she went to Tina's dresser and opened the top drawer. She knew where she'd find them—she'd scoped out their location on earlier visits. Tina's lingerie, a study in silk and lace, was neatly arranged on the left hand side of the drawer, and on the right her hosiery. And there it was, the Holy Grail of her voodoo quest: Tina's fishnet stockings. Certain her excitement could be rivaled only by Sir Galahad, she reached in and took her prize.

"Find what you're looking for?" Julie froze when she heard the voice behind her. Turning, she saw Tina standing in the doorway to the bedroom.

She couldn't run; Tina was blocking the only exit. Possible explanations for her presence ran through Julie's head.

"I was just looking around" would be negated by the fact she was holding Tina's stockings in her hand. "I'm here to water the plants" or "Rick asked me to meet him here" were both quickly discarded as ludicrous. Not that it mattered because Tina didn't seem to be expecting an explanation.

"I told Rick I had an appointment and I'd meet him at the restaurant tonight. I wanted to be able to catch you red-handed." Tina smiled as she glanced at the stockings. "Don't look so shocked, Julie. Did you think you could come here week after week and get away with it?"

Julie pressed herself against the dresser as Tina walked slowly towards her.

"Oh, that's right, I know what you've been doing. I have ever since I saw your car parked on the side road last winter. Don't worry. Rick didn't see you and I didn't tell him. I thought it would be fun to let you run with your sick little game and see how it played out. Turns out it was all pretty pathetic. Just like you. And to think Rick feels guilty for leaving you."

Tina reached into her purse and pulled out her cell phone.

"Are you going to call him?" Julie asked.

Tina held the phone in front of Julie. "I will, right after I take your picture."

In that moment Julie imagined how desperate she would look to Rick. Panicked, she reached out, grabbed a lamp from the dresser and swung with all her might. The whiplash of the lamp's cord when it was yanked from the wall mirrored the snap of Tina's neck as the lamp crashed into the side of her head. Tina's body and her cell phone flew in opposite directions but both landed on the plush bedroom carpet with the same soft thud.

* * * *

Julie stoked the fire in the backyard fire pit until it was good and hot then she went inside to gather Tina's things from their hiding places. She threw her stolen trophies into the flames, adding her own gloves for good measure, and watched the fragmented effigy burn. It was somewhat satisfying, but not as much as if she'd been able to assemble a complete likeness of Tina before the immolation. And it was missing one thing—the fishnet stockings. Those were still around Tina's neck, a tightly wrapped insurance policy in case the blow wasn't fatal.

Julie was mesmerized by the flames as the remains of Tina's belongings disintegrated to ash. The sound of her cell phone broke the trance.

"Oh my God, Julie, did you hear?" Donna rasped into the phone. "Tina's dead. Murdered. And the police are questioning Rick."

"What?" was all Julie could manage.

"Stay there. I'm coming right over." Donna clicked off before Julie could say another word. Good thing, Julie thought, let Donna think the little hitch in her voice was surprise that Tina was dead and not relief that the police were focusing on Rick.

She felt a momentary twinge of guilt for feeling relieved, remembering Tina's claim that Rick felt guilty about leaving her. Julie let the feeling pass as she poked at the fire. Rick had made his choice when he'd disrupted her routine and her life on that Friday night months ago. Now he had to deal with the consequences.

Donna arrived with a bottle of Chardonnay, which complemented nicely the bottle Julie had already opened. They sat at the fire pit late into the evening toasting their friendship, discussing the vagaries of love, and marveling at how the people you think you know best are capable of surprising acts.

It was the start of a new Friday night routine.

FISHY BUSINESS

BY JEAN HUFFMAN

Fancy Raeford Hodge stopped to smell the roses—and almost gagged in the process.

Vernon needs to empty that dumpster, she thought, waving the odor away. Or else the health department is gonna be on his backside like white on dice.

Vernon McCall's Fish Shack stood at the corner of Old Eighty-Six and Peterson Roads in Hillsborough, North Carolina, and usually had plenty of good ole' boys' trucks jammed into its dusty, graveled lot.

Today it was deserted. Why Mike wanted to meet here mid-afternoon for lunch was anyone's guess. It really didn't matter. The Shack had the best fried fish in three counties hands-down, and Fancy didn't hesitate to drive over.

She'd been coming here for over a decade and always loved catching up with Vern's daughter Piper. She'd even known wife and mother Sue McCall before her mysterious and unfortunate death.

Fancy remembered the time she found Sue stubbornly digging holes near the restaurant's front door. Sue proudly pointed out the fourteen double pink Poetic Justice bushes she'd special-ordered from an arborist in Durham and was determined to get them in the ground.

"To give the place some class," Sue said with a laugh.

"I'm not too good with roses, myself," Fancy admitted. "I don't know what it is, but mine always die."

Sue leaned in on her shovel. "The real secret is what you use to fertilize. I use the organic stuff—and best of all, it's free." She chucked her chin toward the dumpster. "I gotta tell you, there's a bunch of feral cats that get in our trash and are a real nuisance. Good thing nobody ever misses a stray cat or two."

Fancy stared back in horror. "Surely, you're not suggesting—"

Sue's grin was quick. "Just joshing you, Fancy. Scott's Rose and Flower Water-Soluble, that'll do the trick."

Fancy shook off the conversation, studiously avoiding any memory of it whenever she came to the restaurant. The roses now mushroomed out of control, reaching halfway up the casement windows, flanking the cedar-planked eating establishment with billows of pink blossoms. Fancy hurried up the steps past the buzzing bees.

Even though the Shack was 170 miles from the nearest ocean, Fancy eyed Vern's cheesy green fishnets interlaced with plastic starfish and sand dollars beside the cash register. It was his way of being beachy, she supposed.

Vern exited the kitchen. "Hey, Fancy," he said, coming around the register to kiss her on the cheek, the smell of fried goodness emanating from his t-shirt.

She smacked him back. "Mike's meeting me here for lunch."

"Have a seat. I'll send Piper for your drinks."

Two minutes later, Lieutenant Mike Hodge joined Fancy at the oilcloth-covered table, pulling out a ladderback chair across from his mother. "Whew, plenty hot today," he said, taking a handkerchief from his pocket and wiping his brow.

"I heard the meteorologist on Channel Five say according to the Farmer's Almanac this year, we were in for a hot one. The heat record's already been broken several times in the past couple of weeks."

Mike scanned the menu. "Mom, you gettin' the flounder platter?"

"Sure am. Best thing on the menu."

"It doesn't hurt that Vern gives you extra helpings of anything you want."

"A gal's got to keep up her strength somehow," she said, smoothing her clothes over her ample figure.

A young woman in her twenties, hair dyed half-purple, a couple of piercings spiking her brows, came to their table. Her face lit with a huge smile.

"Hey, Miz Fancy. Hey, Mike."

Fancy reached over for a hug. "Hey, Piper. Good to see you."

"What y'all want to drink?"

"Two teas," Fancy said.

"Be right back." Piper smiled, headed toward the kitchen.

Fancy pulled her mammoth purse close. "I swear, that Piper looks more like her mama every year, don't you think? Here, give me your hands." She gave herself and Mike a squirt of sanitizer. "How many years has it been since they found Sue McCall's body in Jordan Lake, Mike? Probably ten. Piper was such a young thing when it happened."

"Nine years ago, this August." He concentrated on the menu. "You know, we happened to pull Sue McCall's case out of the cold pile not too long ago."

"And what did you find?"

He sat back as Piper suddenly returned, setting their teas on the table. "What can I get you folks?"

"You know me, the usual," Fancy said, patting her platinum blond hair.

"Guess I'll have the flounder, too. Extra slaw, please."

Piper left. Vern stood against the doorframe, then ducked back in the kitchen.

"Well?" asked Fancy, tapping her red nails on the table. "I'm waiting."

"Everyone's alibis lined up, especially Vern's." He leaned in. "He was here at the restaurant all day and late into the evening, waiting on customers, well past Sue's estimated time of death."

"Mike, you can't be serious!" Fancy's eyes bugged. "Vern would've never killed Sue. They built this business together from the ground up. They were a team."

Mike took a long sip. "You know the first person the police investigate is always the spouse, Mom. No matter what the marriage appeared like from the *outside*."

Sad but true, thought Fancy. When her husband Rich, a cop like their son, had been alive, he'd taught her that most murderers came from within a very small circle of likely suspects, usually well known to the victim. And most often doing the gruesome deed, by a landslide, was the victim's significant other.

"Then what about motive, or means?" she asked. "Surely Vern was eliminated in those categories."

He pinched his lips. "This is all off the record, Mom, so no sharing your theories with your friends over coffee."

"I promise. It stays here."

"No clear motive was ever determined. Sue was killed from a snapped spinal cord, possibly coming from a traumatic fall. Coroner determined the fall happened several hours before her body was dumped into Jordan Lake."

"Oh, my stars. That piece of information was never made public."

"And for good reason."

"At one time, I thought the police were trying to track down a woman whom Sue had seen with. What was her name? Lorna Bates...Blakesley..."

"Lorna Bateman. A real grifter. Not much known about her other than she and Sue had become friends after meeting at the Carrboro Farmer's Market several months before. Never could pin down Lorna's whereabouts after Sue's death. Thought maybe she was the last one to see Sue alive. Thought maybe she freaked out, left Sue's car in a part of town near the Interstate, thumbed a ride, and disappeared forever into the great unknown." He stirred in another packet of sweetener, tasted his tea. "But we could never prove any of it."

Fancy drew a sharp breath. "And now something's changed to alter your perception of the case, hasn't it?"

"Let's just say we've recently acquired a couple of interesting pieces of information that should help us finish out the case, information that we've quietly been working on. Oh, here comes our food."

Balancing two white platters on his forearm, Vern walked up. Large fragrant filets, with golden battered crusts and just the right amount of crunch. A side of confetti slaw, also the best in three counties, was a beautiful creamy creation to behold. An avalanche of fresh home fries rounded out the entrees.

"Here you go, Fancy, Mike. Enjoy."

"Thanks, Vern. And shootennany—" she counted, "four filets instead of the usual three. What's the special occasion?"

"No reason. I just like my customers happy." He smiled, then left. At the register, Vern nodded to Piper who disappeared after him into the kitchen.

Mike returned to his meal. He and Fancy ate in happy silence a few moments.

Fancy dipped fish in tartar sauce. "I'm still waiting, you know. You said earlier you had new information on the case."

Piper magically appeared at her elbow, tea pitcher in hand. "Refills?"

"Yes, please," Mike said, holding up his glass. "Hey, Piper, has business been good?"

She poured. "Yeah, Daddy says he still hopes to open another place someday." She grinned widely, and the piercings drew taut. "He promised me I could try my hand running the new place when we do. Told me I could come up with the menu, the décor, the whole nine yards. It'll be my baby."

That reminded Fancy of something. "You should be just about done with that business degree from State, shouldn't you?"

"Yes, ma'am. Almost there. One more semester."

Vern joined them, evident pride in his voice. "Y'all talking about my brilliant girl here, the-graduate-to-be? Did you know she's carried a 3.9, even while working here forty hours a week?" He put his arm around her, pulled her close. "Don't know what I'd do without her. She's been my right arm."

Mike pulled off a piece of fish. "State's pretty expensive school, I hear. But I guess it'll be worth it when you two become a restaurant dynasty, right? McCall's and Daughter?"

"You betcha. That's the plan," said Vern. He noticed their emptying plates. "Hey, how's the fish? It meet your standards, Fancy?"

"Great as always, Vern."

"Glad to hear it. If I don't get to see you before you leave, hope y'all come back real soon." A phone jangled in the back. "Excuse me, I have to get that." He trotted back to the kitchen.

Piper turned to leave.

Mike spoke, halting the young woman. "You know, I saw some equipment you got out back near the dumpster. That stuff can't come cheap—there's a commercial-grade freezer sitting out there."

"Yeah, the old one broke, and we got a really good deal on a used one at Herndon's to replace it," she said, naming a restaurant supply store in Durham. "You know how it is. Stuff gets old, breaks down, you have to buy another one." She hesitated. "Can I get you guys anything else?"

Mike said, "No," and she was off, back to the kitchen.

Fancy watched this last exchange with interest. She bit into a fry. "What was that all about?"

Mike held up a finger. He punched a number on his cell, covered his mouth to speak a few short sentences, then hung up. He picked up his fork. "In the wee morning hours a couple of nights ago, a Durham county sheriff's deputy stopped the McCalls because of a missing taillight on their trailer. Vern told the officer they were hauling the big freezer in the back to their restaurant. The rest of the story was that the freezer'd come out of a deceased relative's barn in Granville County. When the officer asked why-the-Sam-Hill they were moving the thing in the middle of the night, they replied they had to get it back to the restaurant before their food supplies got spoiled."

"So. . . Piper lied to us just now."

"Yep."

"And I bet Chief Archer sent you here—"

"Yep," he said, tucking into his slaw.

"—to get some answers," she finished. Fancy swallowed hard, trying to connect the dots. "Mike, what does all this mean?"

Mike's eyes flitted toward the kitchen. "I'll explain it to you in a little while, but I need your assurance that you'll sit quietly and not try to interfere, okay, Mom? I know you have a good relationship with Piper, and she might need you a in a little bit."

She nodded, gripping her napkin tightly.

Mike finished his food, pushed his plate back, and parted the lacey curtain to watch the parking lot.

A black-and-white soon arrived, and Mike met the uniformed officers inside. The three men disappeared into the kitchen.

Fancy heard several raised voices, and the uniforms returned a minute later with Vern.

Vern exited the kitchen with his hands pulled behind, his jaw set, steely and determined. Piper cozied up behind her father, eyes red-rimmed, as if she'd been crying. Fancy could see her visibly shaking in her daddy's shadow.

"Vern," Mike said, pulling out a folded piece of paper. "We got a warrant here to seize your freezers, the one in the kitchen and the one parked out by the dumpster. We think you know something about your wife's disappearance, and we want to ask you some questions."

Piper pushed in front, eyes streaming. "It wasn't Daddy! Don't punish him."

Vern bore down on Piper, desperately locking eyes with his daughter. "That's enough, Piper. You go sit over there and stay quiet. Let these gentlemen do what they've got to do. I promise you, it's gonna be okay. Trust me."

Somehow he got through to her, and Piper plodded to a nearby table to wait, face-down, her arms wreathing her head.

Things happened in rapid succession. The two officers whisked Vern out to their patrol car to talk, while Mike exited through the kitchen to await forensics to arrive.

Fancy heard continued sobbing. She strained to hear Mike but everything out back was deathly quiet. She knew she promised to not get involved, but hadn't Mike also stated he specifically wanted her there, because she cared for Piper?

Fancy grabbed her pocketbook and scooted in next to the shaken young woman. "Honey, it's Fancy. Can I get you anything?"

Piper looked up, and the years melted away. Pigtails replaced the tufted purple hair. The make-up, the piercings—gone. Piper McCall was again a sad, small girl.

"I know what happened, you know," she said.

Alarm bells sounded in Fancy's head. "Piper, don't say anything. You have to be quiet like Vern said, you hear?"

"Fancy, I've gotta tell someone. I'm about to bust!" She sat up, her eyes wild.

Fancy pulled her close. "Shhh. Honey, we all got secrets. I think you better be thinking of your daddy right now."

Piper pushed away, a coldness settling in. "I am thinking of him. That's why I'm doing this." She turned soulful eyes upon Fancy. "I'm sick of carrying it around."

"Piper, you know they can ask me about what you say, don't you? I'll be a witness to whatever you tell me."

"I don't care, Miz Fancy. It's been so hard, trying to hide it for so long. I don't want to anymore—I'm done."

And so she began. "I knew Mama'd been seeing someone. All the whispered conversations, the outings excluding Daddy and me, the little things that didn't add up. Course, Daddy was never there to see it. He was so busy at the restaurant, he never had time for anything else. I confronted him with it once, and he was so upset with what I said, all he could do is slap me once really good, tell me I was wrong. 'Your mama would never do that to us,' he said. 'She'd never run off with another man.'"

Piper's eyes darted up. "I guess she did it because she must've been in a terribly lonely place. Now that I'm older, I can see it. At the time, I didn't—all I saw was her disloyalty, her betrayal. And you know, it hurt like the dickens."

Fancy gave her a tissue. "Oh Piper, what happened?"

"You know we live a ways off the road, with no neighbors close by. It was summer, and I was out of school. And instead of going to a friend's house like I said I was going to do, I stayed home that morning—don't remember why. I was laying on my bed upstairs when she pulled up in her new car, the one she'd bought the week before. Left the radio a-blaring. I watched her get out and noticed something had changed. I could tell by the way she was walking up the walkway. Something was definitely different."

"She came upstairs to her bedroom, pulled a suitcase from her closet. It was already packed and heavy, because she had to drag it out by the wheels. You know, Daddy never noticed that she'd already done prepared to leave us," she said dismally.

"Mama came out, and I surprised her, shocked her. I told her I knew what she was doing, and I let her have it. How could she do this to us? She had no right to go off, running around with some man, when Daddy and me needed her here.

"But she'd already made up her mind—said she was leaving that day with her new 'friend.' Told me to get out of her way, said she was getting out a loveless marriage, and that I was a silly thirteen-year-old who didn't know doodley-squat about nothing."

Fancy shuddered, reliving Sue's long-ago rosebush conversation. If Sue could abandon her own daughter without a thought or care about her well-being, she did harbor a streak of cruelty, one a mile wide.

Piper's voice snapped her back to the present. "Well, what she said stung me worse than Daddy's slap across the face, more than all the worrying I did when she was off doing God-knows-what, with-God-knows-who! For her to say that to *me*? I did *know*. And I did *hurt*. I was so mad with this anger that'd been seething inside of me, I was like a bottle of Coke that's been dropped and shook up real good."

Piper's eyes locked on the shredded tissue. "When Mama tried to push past me, I grabbed the suitcase. We jerked it back and forth. She yanked hard one last time, lost her balance. She tumbled to the bottom of the stairs and lay there in this gosh-awful position, her eyes staring up at the ceiling. I ran to her, but she wasn't breathing. I tried to get her to talk to me, to do anything at all, but of course, she couldn't."

Fancy took the young woman's hands in hers. "I'm so sorry, Piper."

Piper continued. "About that time, someone at the front door started banging for all they're worth. It was a *woman's* voice and she was saying, "Sue, Sue? Have you forgotten me, hon? Let's go! Daylight's burning! You know we got reservations in Myrtle for tonight.'

"I was still wrapping my brain around who this intruder was, when I saw a shadow move along the front of the house. I panicked and ran to the front door, locked it up tight. The shadow tried peeping in the windows, but she couldn't see anything. So she charged back to the front door, jiggling the knob, banging on it and yelling like a banshee.

"At that moment, my stupid, stubborn teenage brain came up with the only solution it could. This woman could not have my mother. She was going to have to go away, that's all, and never come back.

"That was the summer Daddy had the pool put in. It was halfway finished, and the pool company wasn't there that day. They were waiting on the fiberglass lining to lay inside that humongous hole they'd dug out back." Piper's voice became eerily calm. "I went to the backyard, hollered for the woman to come on around, that my mom had fallen into the pool and gotten hurt. So *she* came around, eyeing me, not knowing what to say. All I had to do was point to the hole.

"She went to the edge and looked in. I came up behind her, and with all the hatred I had inside of me, I swung the sharp edge of a worker's shovel against her neck, slicing her open like a bag of peas. She fell in, and I left her down there, in the dirt, to die."

Piper stopped, brushed the last of the tears. "And that's all I'm gonna say."

* * * *

"So let me get this straight. Piper McCall was responsible for the deaths of two women, her mother and her mother's lover?" Lesa Hodge asked the next night at her brother Mike's house, pausing over the salad bowl.

"Can you believe it?" Fancy heaped her own plate with greens. "She was a mere child at the time." She turned to Mike. "I certainly hope the D.A takes that information into consideration before they bring final charges against her."

Hillari Hodge shuddered and slipped her arms around her husband Mike's neck. "I'm glad my mother's got Cate tonight," she said. Fancy nodded agreement. This was not something any three-year-old should overhear.

Fancy scooped up a healthy portion of lasagna. "What I want to know is how Piper managed to cover it up so well. She was only thirteen, after all."

Mike put up his hands. "Okay, okay, I know this'll be the main topic of conversation tonight, so let me explain the facts as I know them, and then there will be far less misinformation flying about. Of course, what is said here," he said, looking at the three women, "stays here."

"Of course." Fancy made a motion of locking her lips, throwing away the key.

* * * *

After disposing of Lorna, Piper'd gone back in the house, dragged her mother's body into the laundry room lest anyone else showed up, and waited.

Vern copped to his side of the deed. He'd arrived home that night to find Piper curled up in a fetal position on the couch. When he finally got her to tell him what was wrong, she described, in broken bits, what had transpired.

Vern knew he had to make it right, for Piper's sake. If only he'd heeded his daughter's warning in the first place—

At that very late hour, Vern drove Sue's car to a deserted part of town, wiped it down, left the keys in the ignition. Even though Piper was thirteen, she already knew how to handle a vehicle, and she slowly followed behind her father in the pick-up, with a trailer hitched to it. Both of the bodies, double-wrapped in tarps, lay in the truck bed.

Vern got behind the wheel. They drove to a bridge over Jordan Lake, unwrapped Sue's body, dropped her in with a splash.

Vern knew the other body was going to be more of a problem. If Lorna was found dead in conjunction with Sue, the police would narrow the suspect field down mighty quick. No, he'd have to keep her body hidden, keep the cops guessing where the woman was, until he could come up with a more permanent solution.

Vern was always on the look-out for good used equipment, and he'd bought a freezer a couple years back that he'd stored it in his garage. The homewrecker's body could go in there, until other arrangements could be made. The freezer would be left at the old abandoned barn on third-cousin Morris's family property several miles away, padlocked and plugged in.

"But Mike," Lesa interrupted, "why would Vern chance moving the freezer back to the restaurant after all this time? Seems like he would've bought another freezer to replace the broken one, left that one right where it was."

"Oh, I think I know the answer to that," said Fancy. "Piper's just about done with four years of college. What a college education costs nowadays, they probably couldn't afford the money for another freezer right now."

"Mom, you're pretty good at this," Mike said, giving his mother a sly glance.

"Why, thank you, dear. Your daddy told me that plenty of times."

The four sat in companionable silence. "Okay," said Hillari. "I'll bite. Vern couldn't leave a body lying around for someone to find. He had to get rid of it. Whatever happened to Lorna's body?"

"Vern had moved her—little pieces at a time—to a burial site and scattered them around. Eventually she was completely gone."

"A burial site?" asked Lesa. "And where would that be?"

Mike shrugged. "Let's just say, 'A rose by any other name would not smell so sweet.'"

THE STONECUTTER

BY EDITH MAXWELL

I first saw the stonecutter working in a pool of illumination as I strolled near the cemetery on a summer evening. Sweat shone on his face as he chiseled a gravestone. Darkness surrounded him. Anyone walking nearby was lit up like on a movie set, but as soon as they passed, the black night swallowed them whole and they ceased to exist. I gazed at him for a few moments from the darkness and wondered who he was.

When I saw him enter the library a few days later, I noticed he did not look American. Portuguese maybe, or Italian. It was the style of his slacks, and leather shoes of a cut not made in this country. It was the set of his jaw, unused to English vowels. It was the open collar of his shirt, the texture of the cloth.

I was in my usual post behind the library's reference desk when he came in. He leaned forward and spoke to Jill at the main desk, and then headed into the stacks, toward where we keep books on town history. Watching him walk away, I saw an efficiency of movement, tough muscles under that European shirt, a firmness in the slacks.

Part of my job is, of course, helping people find information, so off to the history section I headed. I smoothed my hair as I went. I rounded the corner of the stacks and stopped. He sat at a table, its deep cherry hue gleaming like fine art in the morning light from the window. Several books were open in front of him, and he was copying something in a careful script on a pad of paper. His hair grew low on his forehead, and he had a full head of it combed straight back, dark and thick even though the lines on his face etched many years of living.

The air was quiet. The man stood and turned to the shelf on his left. His finger ran across the titles with the care of a connoisseur, as if he loved the sensation of the bindings more than the meanings of the words.

"May I help you?" My voice was loud in the stillness, and he turned quickly.

"Yes?" He bowed slightly and his eyebrows rose.

"I wondered if I could help you with anything." Oh. He didn't know who I was. "I'm the reference librarian."

"Ah." It was a soft, resonant voice. Our eyes linked together. He smiled at me, but his eyebrows, thick like his hair, drooped at their outside edges and his chocolate eyes did the same. "No, I have found what I need. But thank you." His accent sounded familiar, with its non-English stresses and softening of consonants.

I nodded.

"You have a fine library. A good collection"

"Thank you. May I ask what you're working on?"

He then showed me his interest: a book on genealogy, the old logs of fishing captains, a history of Gloucester. He explained that he was researching when some of his relatives had come to New England from Portugal—so I was right about that—and where they had lived in the area.

"I visited Portugal once," I said as I looked out the window. It had been my first trip alone after James left this world nine years earlier, my first excursion after the trouble with that had blown over. "Here's what I remember. I was inland in Belmonte, and the sun was intense. The hills were dry, covered with gray olive trees. Rocks pushed up out of the soil. But everyone was generous, they fed me, they wanted to practice their English."

He nodded in understanding.

"Then I went to Porto on the coast. I ate *mariscado* and drank real port wine, not the sweet stuff you find here."

"Yes, yes!" He shook his head in amazement. "I am from Porto!"

"You are?"

He nodded.

"I loved the market on the waterfront," I said.

"Yes. My grandmother sold fish there. There is nothing like it here."

"Then I went to the south. The blue and white tiles looked Arabic and the houses could have been Tunisian adobe. The beaches were empty, just beautiful. That's what I remember."

We stood there. We smiled at our separate memories, until a teenager slouched by. A tinny sound emitted from her earbuds and broke our bubble.

I cleared my throat. "How long have you been here?"

"We have been here for, let's see, ten years."

The "we" deposited a lead weight in my stomach.

"My son and his family, they are here too. But my wife is ill. She does not go out. So I work, and I do my studies here, and I play with my grandchildren."

"I see."

* * * *

Late that evening I sat on my porch with a glass of cognac. A breeze waved the scent of sweet peas past me like a letter from my childhood. Fernando Andrade was his name, he had told me, and then had asked me to join him in a coffee next door. When I told him mine was Eleanor, he called me Eleanora, in a musical five syllables, and I felt foreign and special. We talked over our coffees in the café for as long as I thought I could stretch my break. When he said he wanted to take me to eat *mariscado* in a Portuguese restaurant he knew in the next town, I didn't ask why he didn't have to be at home for dinner. We arranged to meet the following day.

After work the next afternoon, I changed my shoes and crossed over to the park, picking up the pace until I was at my power-walk speed. The air amid the greenery was mild. It smelled of summer: a strong, sweet flower, a distant sprinkler, the earth's scent rising. I thought more about Fernando. I suddenly wanted to escape this life I had enclosed myself in: comfortable and unspeakably routine.

At home, I showered and then did not dress in my usual tailored clothes. As a sea breeze danced with the curtains, I put on a long maroon skirt and matching silk blouse. My hand was steady as I applied cologne to the backs of my ears, my wrists, my temples, and I could hear Mother saying, "Always put scent where you have a pulse." I added a dab between my breasts for good measure, shaking my head at my foolishness. I pulled on tall leather boots from Lisbon, as old and comfortable as gloves and, parading in front of the mirror in my own private fashion show, I felt twenty-two, but my reflection showed a woman with silver hair on the path to old age.

"Well, you don't look half bad, really," I told my image, surprised at this feeling of anticipation. It had been a long time.

I was waiting on the porch when Fernando drove up in an older model Volvo, pristinely clean and maintained. He met me at the passenger door. When he turned to look at me, I saw raw red lines on one cheek.

"What happened?" I said, alarmed. They looked like scratches from something very sharp.

"Eleanora, it is my wife. She is schizophrenic, and became upset when I said I was leaving." The pain was in his eyes again. "It is hard for her to stay on her medications. They are hard on her. She paces and sees demons. Sometimes she calls me the devil."

"Oh. I didn't know." The delicious excitement I had felt about the outing agitated with fear of this new information.

He caught my eyes with his. "Don't worry, she is with my daughter-in-law."

I watched him and waited. I kept my hand at my side, and prevented it from stroking his other cheek.

He took a breath and let it out. "This has happened before, and it will happen again. Now, if you will come with me, it is time for dinner."

At Casa do Mar, we ate small, pungent olives the color of night. We drank Dão wine. We feasted on *mariscado*'s succulent seafood, the tender squid in *lulas guisadas*, and paper-thin potato slices fried to a crisp. We didn't only eat. He spoke to me of his years cutting stone, about his love for the permanence of gravestones. He said he would search for a pattern in the granite to match the deceased's personality.

I told him about not being able to have babies, how I couldn't bear to be around young children for many years. How, when I finally volunteered to help with the Girl Scouts in our town, I delighted in their energy and fresh approach to life.

We didn't talk about his wife or James, about the near future or the current war. We rode the wave of the present as if the walls of the restaurant were the edges of the world and our only cares were here in front of us.

We ate slowly. We sipped our wine and asked for more. Finally the waiter cleared our plates. Fernando had joked with him in Portuguese throughout the evening, and now asked the waiter to bring something, but I didn't understand what.

Two tiny cups of espresso appeared in front of us, and two small glasses of a clear liquid.

"*Bica e bagaço!*" He pronounced this with great satisfaction. "This is the finest coffee and our national liquor, *bagaceiro*. We finish all good meals this way."

He took a sip of the coffee and lifted his glass to me. "Here's to you, Eleanora."

"And to you."

A lilting Fado played in the background as the waiter set tables for the next day. We were the last diners to leave. Fernando pulled out my chair for me, and then offered me his arm. He smelled of smoke and wine and an old-world cologne, and the cloth of his shirt was smooth against muscle. Then, halfway to the door, his arms took mine and we were dancing. Slowly we moved to the melancholy Lusian folk song. I stood almost as tall as he, and when my cheek touched the wounds on his, he pulled me closer, and I felt like I'd been there all along.

* * * *

We began to see each other as often as we could. He cooked *mariscado* for me in my kitchen while I weeded my herb garden. He told me stories of his grandsons and I made him laugh with tales of my scouts. Once he told me that the only food his wife would eat now was Portuguese kale stew, which no one else in the family liked. We worked on his genealogy together and visited the former house of his great uncle down on the point. We drove north where we didn't know anyone and walked on a beach arm in arm. We spent long hours in my bedroom, enjoying each other's bodies and tracing the lines of our lives. We went dancing, although we drove into the city to do so.

"Are you happy, Eleanora?" he asked me one day as we sat in the garden at dusk. Iced tea cooled our hands. A gentle wind off the Atlantic swept the mosquitoes away.

I nodded. I didn't tell him that at night, alone, I dreamed of freedom with him, of a future without his wife.

I asked him the same question.

"I am happy with you, my friend," he said, clinking his glass with mine, but the pain never really left his eyes.

I saw them in late August near the medical building. She was gaunt and pale, with white streaks piercing her dark hair. A lit cigarette shook in her hand. Fernando looked grim. He held her elbow like he was trying to persuade her to go somewhere she didn't want to go.

When I asked once why he didn't place her in an institution where professionals could look after her, he told me, "It is my duty to care for her. I am her husband, after all."

I looked sharply at him. "What about your duty to love? To me?"

He just shook his head and kissed my hand.

* * * *

On the last day of September, right before a fierce thunderstorm, he brought me an armful of red carnations. I watched him at my kitchen sink. In the darkening afternoon, he clipped the ends of the stems under running water and arranged each flower with care in a heavy glass vase. His stonecutter's hands were as gentle with the blooms as they were when they touched me.

"I didn't know men like you existed," I said, addressing the compact strength of Fernando's back.

He turned to me. "I am just me, not 'men like me'," he said. A tropical rain blew in and, as the gale beat the windows, we talked into the night. Our conversations sometimes now tasted bittersweet. We wove a cocoon of our passion and caring. We dared not look outside it.

* * * *

One day in late October Fernando did not show up for a date to go bicycling in the state park. He was always prompt, and called from his cell when he was to be late. I waited for an hour, and then went alone. I rode slowly on the path through brilliant leaves and the detritus of summer:

sagging vines, ferns chilled into brittle tan ghosts, the treacherous red beauty of poison ivy. The light was slanting low as I rode home.

I couldn't call him. I felt physically sick from worry and uncertainty. Had something happened to him? Had he fallen out of love with me? Was he just exhausted from leading a double life? I was as miserable as a teenager in my fretting, and as mad as one, too.

Walking home from work two days later I felt a hand on my shoulder as I passed the coffee shop.

"Elly."

"Fernando!" I looked at him like he had been missing for a year. I couldn't soak up enough of his skin, his thick hair, his sad eyes. "Where have you..."

He took my arm and said, "May I walk you home?"

I looked at him and nodded. As we walked, he was silent and gazed ahead of us, not at me. My heart began to feel a comradeship with the end of the season and the cold breath of winter.

We sat in the swing on my porch side by side until he finally spoke.

"I have decided to take your advice, Eleanora, and place my wife where she is safe."

I felt the warmth from his arm against mine. We could finally make a life together, this man and I.

"I'm so glad, Fernando," I said, reaching for his hand.

"Don't be." He shook his head. "I have found a residence for her. It is two days driving from here, and I will be living there with her." His voice was of a gentle steel, but the edges of his mouth quavered. "We leave on *Dia dos Mortos.* On Saturday."

"Why so far away?" I shivered. Sunlight, sparse in its autumn feebleness, lit up the blood-red blossoms of a chrysanthemum on the porch, but it didn't warm me. "Why now?"

"I am sorry, Eleanora." He put his arm around me and I leaned into his scent and his strength. I was sad to the bone and furious at once.

"Fernan," I said after a long silence, turning my face to his. My heart raced. "You can't leave me! I won't let you."

He stroked my cheek once, slowly, softly, then put his hand down. "I cannot help my life. I cannot abandon my obligations."

I thought frantically. "Come by tomorrow. Please? Just one last time? I have the day off. We could..."

He put up a hand to stop me. "I will come in the afternoon. But only for a moment."

I stared as he walked away.

* * * *

That night I couldn't sleep. I tangled in my sheets, searching my crazed thoughts for some solution, some way to keep him with me. I wanted to cast my net over him and draw him toward me through the water of our lives, like an enchanted Azorean fisherwoman. Today was Wednesday. I couldn't bear the thought that I would never see him again after tomorrow. I climbed out of bed and paced my house. My skin burned as if I were ill. I opened a window, but the north air chilled me and I slammed it shut. A full moon lit my garden, shimmering on the purple monkshood flowers and the dark red asters.

My heart rate slowed as I gazed outside. Maybe I could sleep now.

* * * *

Ghouls in spiderwebs leered at me as I walked into the Cape Ann Market when it opened at eight the next morning. I'd forgotten about Halloween. I tossed several bags of candy into my basket before picking up kale, onions, garlic, cilantro, and chicken stock. By ten o'clock my kitchen smelled like it was dinnertime, the air fragrant with sautéed alliums and greens. I went outside, pulled on gardening gloves, and filled a wheelbarrow with weeds and dead plants. I clipped a handful of leaves in the hardy section of my herb garden and added them to the stew.

The temperature dipped low with the sun as I sat on the porch swing in my parka that afternoon. The trick-or-treaters would need to wear PJs under their princess dresses and zombie costumes tonight. My eyes followed Fernando as he walked toward me, his head down.

We sat in silence. Fernando covered my hand with his. I looked into his sad eyes and squeezed.

"Here." I stood and extended the handles of a small bag to him. "I made her some kale stew."

Fernando grasped the bag. He rose, then embraced me. He made his way slowly down the steps.

"*Até logo,*" I called after him. I'll see you soon.

He glanced back, shaking his head.

* * * *

I walked slowly through the cemetery late Saturday morning. Families sat in the cold on picnic cloths. A slender woman in black laid a mass of flowers on a grave then raised a glass of red wine to the headstone. Children played hide and seek. The sad All Soul's Day festivities seemed to include almost the entire Portuguese community.

When I arrived home, I turned on the local news. Fernando's picture flashed. My hand covered my mouth of its own accord. My ears throbbed. My feet felt numb. I leaned toward the screen.

"Local authorities are investigating the suspicious death of area man, Fernando Andrade." The young newscaster looked into the camera and shook his head, eyebrows knit in TV sincerity. "We talked to his son, George." The image switched to a tall man with Fernando's hair and sad eyes. "We can't think who would want to hurt him. My father was a good man, a husband, a father, a grandfather. He was about to move with my mother, who's mentally ill, to a residence where she could receive the care she needs." The camera switched back to the newsman. "Police are looking into the origins of a soup that was apparently a gift to the family, and say they have identified a person of interest."

The thin wail of a siren grew louder. I left the television and walked out back to sit by the stone Buddha that watched over my garden. I felt my cell phone in my pocket. The phone Fernando had called me on. My heart was an icy stone that chilled me from the inside out. He said he didn't eat kale stew. As sirens grew near, I wondered what kind of granite would suit the personality of Fernando Andrade.

ABOUT THE AUTHORS

Gloria Alden's short story "Cheating on Your Husband Can Get You Killed" won the Love is Murder contest and was in *Crimespree Magazine*. Her short story "The Professor's Books" appeared in the *Fish Tales* anthology. Her first book, *The Blue Rose* will be published this year. Website: www.gloriaalden.com   Blog: www.writerswhokill.blogspot.com

Mysti Berry has won awards for her fiction, screenplays, and technical writing. She earned an MFA from University of San Francisco and a Linguistics degree from UCSC. Mysti lives in San Francisco with her husband and is hard at work on her first crime novel.

Betsy Bitner hopes to write a full-length mystery some day. Unfortunately, she's a slow runner, a slow reader and often slow on the uptake, so it's no surprise that she's also a slow writer. But she is a humor columnist and blogger. You can find her at www.betsybitner.comand www.lostintheadirondacks.com.

Warren Bull, a multiple award-winning author, was nominated for a 2012 Derringer award. He has more than forty short stories published. His novels *Abraham Lincoln for the Defense, Heartland, Murder in the Moonlight* available at http://www.warrenbull.com/kindle_editions.html and a short story collection, *Murder Manhattan Style* available at http://www.warrenbull.com/

Michelle Markey Butler holds a doctorate in English Literature specializing in direct address in medieval drama. She is the author of several academic articles as well as short stories, and is working on a handful of novels. After twenty-some years in Pittsburgh, she recently moved to Maryland, to which, curiously enough, her ancestors were transported from Ireland in 1688.

Kara Cerise has five saltwater fish aquariums in her home. Strange and scary events occur in them, mostly at night. She worked in advertising near a Southern California beach and now lives in the shark infested waters of Washington, D.C., where unusual things happen, both day and night.

E. B. Davis's short stories have appeared online and in print. *Chesapeake Crimes: This Job is Murder* included "Lucky in Death." The *He Had It Coming* anthology contained "The Acidic Solution," and "No

Hair Day" was chosen for *A Shaker Of Margaritas: Bad-Hair Day*. She blogs at http://writerswhokill.blogspot.com.

Kate Fellowes' working life has revolved around words—editor of the student newspaper, reporter for the local press, cataloger in her hometown library. She's the author of five novels and numerous short stories and essays. Married, she and her husband share their home with a variety of companion animals.

Kaye George is a twice-Agatha-nominated novelist and short story writer. She belongs to Sisters in Crime and Guppies. Her stories have been published separately and in several anthologies. She reviews for *Suspense Magazine* and blogs for a group blog and a solo one. She and her husband live near Waco, Texas. Visit http://kayegeorge.com/ for more details.

Beth Hinshaw is a graphic designer, writer, slave to her brother's sweetpotato dog chew company. She lives in the gorgeous Pacific Northwest with her husband of thirty *odd* years, daughter, two Brittanys. This is the first story she had the guts to submit. She is allergic to fish, mushrooms, and soft cheeses.

Jean Huffman is a busy pastor's wife, mom, and aspiring novelist from Durham, North Carolina. She also writes Christian women's fiction under the pen name of Sislyn Stewart. You can catch more of her work at www.sislynstewart.com.

Teresa Inge grew up in North Carolina reading Nancy Drew mysteries. Since then, she's worked as an administrative assistant and has published articles about existing trends in the administration profession. Combining her love of reading mysteries and working as an assistant led to writing short fiction stories and a novel.

KB Inglee is an interpreter at two Mid-Atlantic living history museums where she grinds cornmeal at a waterpowered mill and tends a flock of heritage sheep. She blogs every other Tuesday at Writers Who Kill and every Monday at Goodreads, where she talks about writing and history.

Edith Maxwell writes the Local Foods Mysteries. *A Tine to Live, A Tine to Die* introduces organic farmer Cam Flaherty (Kensington Publishing, June 2013). *Speaking of Murder* (Barking Rain Press, September 2012, under pseudonym Tace Baker) features Quaker linguistics professor Lauren Rousseau. Edith, a technical writer, lives north of Boston.

Gigi Pandian writes the Jaya Jones Treasure Hunt Mystery Series. The first book in the series, *Artifact*, was awarded a Malice Domestic Grant and named a "Best of 2012" debut mystery by *Suspense Magazine*. Gigi is a writer, graphic designer, and photographer in the San Francisco Bay Area. Find her online at www.gigipandian.com.

Katharine A. Russell is a former bioscience executive who divides her time between Palm Desert, California, and Baltimore, Maryland. Her novels include *A Pointed Death* (the first in the Pointer Mystery Series), *Deed So*, and *Buddy's Tail*. Her first short story collection, *Ghostly Tidewater Trilogy,* was released this year.

Harriette Sackler serves as Grants Chair of the Malice Domestic Board of Directors. She is a past Agatha Award nominee for Best Short Story for "Mother Love," which appeared in *Chesapeake Crimes II.* "The Factory," homage to turn of the twentieth century immigrant life, appears in *Chesapeake Crimes—This Job is Murder.*

H. S. Stavropoulos was born and raised in a small Greek Village in the middle of Oakland, California, and writes about being born in America of Greek immigrant parents and living between those two worlds. A frequent visitor to Greece and having hundreds of relatives there, H. S. Stavropoulos writes about life in Greece, Greek food (of course!!), the wealth of Greek culture, mythology and traditions, and the complex and wonderful Greek people.

Steve Shrott's mystery fiction has appeared in many online and print publications as well as various anthologies, including *The Gift of Murder*. He has crafted comedy material for well-known performers and written a "how to" book on humor. Some of his jokes are in The Smithsonian Institute.

Judith Klerman Smith has published nonfiction articles and fiction short stories. Her first published mystery, "Trickery," praised by Carolyn Hart as "superbly plotted," appeared in the anthology *Murder X 13*. Smith's stories also have appeared in *Futures* and *Mouth Full of Bullets* magazines. She is currently working on a cozy mystery novel.

Elaine Will Sparber is a freelance writer and editor from Long Island, New York. A co-author of a travel book and ghostwriter of two health books, she is currently working on a mystery novel featuring the same amateur sleuth as her short story. Visit her website at www. elainewillsparber.com.

Julie Tollefson grew up in the sand hills of southwest Kansas, far from any large bodies of water. Now, she lives and writes in the opposite corner of the state, where she and her family often enjoy peaceful evenings at a nearby lake. Visit her website at http://julietollefson.com.

Diane Vallere is a fashion industry veteran-turned-mystery writer, which means she can turn you into a character and make it look like you don't know how to accessorize. She launched her own detective agency at age ten and has maintained a passion for shoes, clues, and clothes ever since. Find her at www.dianevallere.com.

ABOUT THE EDITOR

Ramona DeFelice Long is an author, independent editor, and writing instructor. She has edited and co-edited several story collections, including *Fish Tales*, the first Guppy anthology. As an author, Ramona's fiction and non-fiction have appeared in literary, regional and juvenile publications. She's received grants and fellowships from the Mid-Atlantic Arts Foundation, the Virginia Center for the Creative Arts, the Delaware Division of the Arts, the Pennsylvania State Arts Council and the Society of Children's Book Writers and Illustrators. A native of Louisiana now living in Delaware, Ramona was been recognized by the DDOA in 2009 as an Established Artist in Fiction and in 2013 in Creative Nonfiction. She is active in the Delaware Valley arts scene, and her literary blog may be found at www.ramonadef.wordpress.com.

Made in the USA
Charleston, SC
22 April 2013